HOPELESS

JUDGEMENT OF THE SIX

Book 1

MELISSA HAAG

HOPE(LESS)

Freedom is so close Gabby can taste it. After years of meeting single werewolves and successfully dodging the mating bullet, she's on her way to her last Introduction to say "No, thanks" one final time. As a human, she has no plans to attach herself to a werewolf. But, she didn't count on meeting Clay.

With a single look, Gabby knows Clay is the one. And, unfortunately, he knows it too. The silent, ruggedly-handsome werewolf is determined to win his mate by any means necessary. Gabby does what any sane girl would do and runs. Not only does Clay follow, but something truly dangerous does as well.

Now, hunted for the secrets she's spent her whole life protecting, Gabby must turn to the one man she didn't want for the help she needs. Time is running out to discover who or what wants her, and Gabby's just starting to realize there's more at stake than the heart and freedom of one human girl.

CHAPTER ONE

I KNEW THE LOCATIONS OF THE PEOPLE AROUND ME AS IF MY HEAD came equipped with a giant fish finder. When I focused, a vast darkness opened in my mind. Instead of blips on a radar, tiny sparks of light shimmered, matching the location of people in the area immediately around me. The colors of the lights, always a yellow center and dark-green halo, never varied. Except for me. My spark had a vibrant orange halo, making me unique and alone. Always alone...

I STOOD at the entrance of the park while the bus pulled away with a screech of hydraulics. Dusk had already settled, casting shadows. Before walking my usual path through the park, I opened my senses to make sure it was as deserted as it seemed.

Though no sparks decorated the darkness in the area around me, I kept my senses open. The void was endless, but my sight did have a maximum distance. So I monitored the area around me as I walked the path and started thinking of the homework I still needed to do.

Distracted, I didn't at first notice the pale blue light with a bright green halo lingering near the pond. There had never been a color variation before. My steps slowed. Perhaps this new color meant I could see something other than humans, maybe animals. As interesting as that would be, the idea of my sight suddenly changing worried me. What if it wasn't an animal? What if it was someone like me? I could keep walking, and whatever the spark was would never know I saw it. But, I was too curious and hungry for answers to walk away. I stepped off the path to investigate.

The lawn muffled the sound of my approach. Near the edge of the pond, I spotted a shadow moving. It was much too large for an animal. I moved closer. The shadow continued to move, and in an instant, I identified the shape. A man. I froze in shock. He stood close to the water's edge.

His presence didn't freak me out as much as the lack of the normal yellow-green life-spark. In its place shimmered the oddly tinted spark. I'd actually found someone like me–a person who had a uniquely colored life-spark. Excitement built even as caution reined me in. What could this odd coloring mean? I'd never run into any variations before. Stay or run? Investigating a color I thought could be an animal was one thing, but approaching a strange man in a dark park? Not the best idea...yet my curiosity won.

As I edged closer to the grove of trees, I recognized the older man. I'd bumped into him, literally, a few days ago at the hospital. The man, who had kind brown eyes, a friendly smile, and grey hair, had apologized for bumping into me and continued on his way. That's why I remembered him.

Typically, men didn't just continue on their way after seeing me because, along with the ability to see those life-sparks, I also had a certain pull. Just on men. From adolescent to grandparent, I unwillingly drew them to me. The degree in which I affected them varied. Some just studied me like a puzzle that needed solving, but forgot about me as soon as I disappeared from sight. For others, I became an obsession.

I crept forward as I watched the man sit and remove his shoes and socks. But, I stopped when he began unbuttoning his shirt. What was he doing stripping down in the park? Given his apparent age, perhaps he suffered from some type of dementia. Maybe he thought it a good place to take a swim.

When he stepped behind the trees for a moment and reemerged completely naked, I began to think he might have more serious issues than dementia.

Still debating whether I should call out to him, I gasped when his silhouette collapsed. I automatically moved forward, thinking he had fallen. My feet covered some of the distance between us before I saw he had dropped into a low crouch with his fingers touching the ground. I skidded to a stop so abruptly the grass tore up beneath my feet.

His skin rippled like sand in a current. Immobilized, I watched his body contort and fold in on itself in some places while it stretched in others. What would make him move like that? Was he sick? Something contagious? I couldn't make myself move away. If he was hurt or sick, he needed help.

Then the sounds started. His knuckles cracked and popped, and his thumbs shrank from the rest of his fingers. I took a step back and then another. Other joints began popping in earnest. It sounded painful. Through it all, he remained silent. My pulse pounded, and I eased another step back.

His skull grew larger, longer than it was high, and his nose and mouth extended with it. I forgot to keep moving. His ears shifted higher. A grey down emerged from his exposed skin, and grew into thick fur. He shook it out when his slow transformation from human to large canine completed.

My mind screamed *werewolf* even as it denied the possibility. Werewolves were legend, myth.

His head swung in my direction. His eyes glowed eerily from the distant lights. My paralyzing shock left me, and I ran. The park entrance beckoned in the distance, but I knew I would never make it. Thanks to my second sight, I saw him rapidly closing in on me.

Rather than being attacked from behind, I spun to confront the big, grey beast bearing down on me. One well-placed kick to its throat, that's all I needed to get in before it mauled me to death. Yeah, I was going to die. I braced myself.

As soon as I turned, the beast slowed to a trot. Within ten feet, it slowed to a walk. My breath still tore through my throat in ragged, terrified gasps.

A yard away, it sat on its haunches. I stared at the creature, poised to run again. Intelligent blue eyes watched me. For several long moments, neither of us moved, and a debate raged within me. What did it want? Should I run, or should I wait to find out?

Holding its gaze, I slid a foot back. It stood. I froze, heart hammering.

The creature began to circle me. I pivoted, following its progress. Finally, we stopped when it had positioned itself between me and the north side of the park—the way home. Then it began to stalk forward, backing me toward the pond. My breathing spiked again. I didn't want to go back to the darker area of the park. Yet, I moved backward fearing what would happen if I didn't.

Just as I considered making another run for it, the creature sat down. What was he waiting for? Suddenly, it yipped. The sound scared the breath right out of me. As if that breath had been the signal he'd waited for, he trotted around me to his pile of clothes. There he morphed back to the man he'd been before; the transformation took less than two heartbeats.

Without perversion, I watched him dress, still too stunned and afraid to look away. I thought about running, but couldn't ignore the fact that he and I shared a connection. Unique life-sparks. I feared what that meant for me.

While buttoning his shirt slowly, he looked up and met my wide gaze. I tried to calm down. Was he like a real canine? If he smelled my fear, would he attack? I'd been afraid since he'd changed into his fur, and he hadn't attacked me then, so I supposed he wouldn't now either.

My rational thoughts fled when he paced toward me with his hands in the pockets of his khakis. I tensed to bolt.

He removed one hand from a pocket and held it up, palm out, signaling I should wait. Right...

"My name is Samuel Riedel, but calling me Sam suits me just fine. I'm sorry for the scare, but showing you was the only way for you to believe."

Believe I'm crazy? Done. I took a few steadying breaths before talking.

"Why did you show me? What do you want?" I fought hard to keep my breathing under control. My mind continued to race.

Sam smiled, turned, and walked toward a bench near the edge of the water. He sat and motioned for me to join him. A small noise of disbelief escaped me. He'd just changed into a dog large enough to pass for a pony. I stayed in the not yet dark shadows of the evergreens.

"You're different, but not as different as I am," he said, keeping himself turned so he could watch me.

He knew something about me? I fidgeted with the strap of my dark brown messenger bag. He could have the answers I needed to explain why I saw the lights in my head or why men acted so differently around me. The temptation of learning something, anything, rooted me. Yet there was also the possibility that he knew nothing of my gifts, that what he knew was something completely different from what I already knew.

"What do you mean I'm different?" I decided I had to be sure we were talking about the same thing before I could reveal anything more.

"You smell different. You're not exactly human, but you're not a werewolf either."

Having him say "werewolf" aloud made everything I'd just witnessed surreal. How could werewolves be possible? How could I be possible? At least, I now knew I wasn't a werewolf like him.

I still stood exactly where I'd been, yet I felt like the entire world had just changed while the crickets continued their night song.

"For clarification...no, I don't need a full moon. No, I don't eat raw meat, although I do enjoy medium-rare steak on occasion. And, no, silver bullets won't kill me any better than regular ones will." Sam chuckled while he moved over on the bench, making plenty of room, and patted the empty space invitingly. "You, dear, are not a werewolf," he repeated.

I blinked at the absurdity of his invitation to sit with him.

"What do you want from me?" I asked, not bothering to

acknowledge his invitation. I still didn't understand why he'd shown me at all.

"You may not be a werewolf, but you are still special. How old are you?"

At five feet five inches, with a slight build and few curves to speak of, I looked young. The freckles sprinkling my nose didn't help me look any older either.

"Sixteen," I answered absently. "How exactly am I special?" I shifted my bag to the other shoulder.

"I was drawn to you. You have a certain scent that calls to my kind. I couldn't name the smell for you other than to say it's interesting, unlike anything else you've ever smelled."

"Is that why guys don't leave me alone?" What if I'd been born with more pheromones than the average person? I'd learned about them in biology. Pheromones attracted the opposite sex. It would explain the pull I had on men and why it'd grown stronger as I'd matured.

I couldn't pin it on anything about me physically. I had straight, shoulder length ash blonde hair, a medium complexion, and hazel eyes like a million other girls. My nose fit my face well enough, neither too wide nor too long, and my mouth wasn't so generous it'd give a guy dirty thoughts. No, it had nothing to do with my looks. Something else pulled them, and I wanted to understand what. Having extra pheromones didn't explain the lights though.

"What do you mean? What guys?" He sat forward too quickly for my comfort.

I flinched back a step and eyed him warily. When he moved like that, he looked a lot younger than his grey hair and weathered skin indicated. So, although he kept his tone light, I remained cautious.

"Guys under sixty and boys over ten."

"Well, you're young and pretty, so I'm sure it's not unusual for men to be attracted to you, dear." He settled back with a laugh.

He'd said it easily and without inflection as if he'd made an observation and stated a fact, reaffirming the pull I had on men didn't seem to affect him. Did that mean he didn't know about my gift and might not understand? Part of me deflated a little. Should I try to explain it? If I smelled different to his kind, it might still relate to my gifts. Confiding in him might be worth the risk. Besides, he could hardly run around telling people that I had special abilities when he'd just turned into a wolf in front of me.

I took a step closer, partially forgetting caution.

"No, it's more than that... A boy in school, extremely shy, picked on by jocks to the point of physical cruelty, nudged past those same jocks to wait by my locker to ask me on a date. A man shopping with two kids stopped me in the grocery store to ask if I'd consider dating an older man once I turned eighteen. The eighteen bit he threw in after my foster mom gasped in shock." I inched closer, becoming more animated as I spoke, trying to make him understand. "When I turned him down, he went back by his kids, red-faced and told them that he'd just been asking for grandpa who wanted to date again. I knew that wasn't true." I paused a moment then added, "Those are just examples of what happens to me every day."

Sam studied me for a moment.

"What's your name, dear?"

"Gabrielle Winters. I prefer Gabby."

"Well, Gabby, I don't know why men act the way they do around you, but I'd like to help you figure it out. Few people would believe what I've shown you tonight, and I ask that you not try talking anyone into believing. I revealed myself to you because you're special and worth the risk."

He stood and approached me. With the pond reflecting dimly behind him and the warm breeze ruffling our hair, I knew that memories of this night would stay with me for a long time.

"There is so much about werewolves that you need to know. The first is that I'm not the only one."

My heart sank. I didn't like the sound of that.

"I'd like to meet your foster parents, and I'd like to get to know you better. I want to be there for you if you ever need anything." He stuffed his hands into his pockets and rocked back on the heels of his brown-laced shoes while I considered his words.

"You said that I smelled good to your kind. Does that mean I'm going to be run down by other werewolves?" The prospect scared me, but I managed to keep any tremor from my voice.

"It's unlikely, but precisely why I would like to be involved in your life. I can help guide your introduction to our world, so it's not as scary as tonight."

He waited quietly while I thought it over. I watched him closely. I liked that he maintained eye contact. It was a refreshing change since the majority of conversations with men occurred while they tried to discover, visually, what about me attracted them.

He offered me an opportunity. With his help, maybe I could find out the reason behind my abilities. And given his condition, I felt certain he'd be able to keep my secret if I decided to tell him about the lights. Could I trust him? Not blindly, but I could start small.

"I'm willing to get to know you better, but I'm not ready for you to meet my foster parents." I wasn't sure if I ever would be.

I wanted to protect Tim and Barb Newton from what could be a monster. They were the first set of foster parents I actually liked. But, if I wasn't willing to bring him home, then just where would we get to know each other better? Dark nights in the park were out, and I had more brains than to suggest his place. He still scared me. Did I think he was going to hurt me? No...he had plenty of time to try to hurt me tonight and hadn't, but I barely knew the man so anything was possible. Safety in numbers. Somewhere public. Then, I remembered he already knew I volunteered at the hospital thanks to our run in.

"Let's meet Wednesday nights at the hospital café. Around six?"

"That sounds good. I look forward to seeing you next week and am truly sorry for scaring you tonight." He held out his hand for a handshake.

I looked at him closely and ignored his hand. Instead, I decided to go for blunt. "You're not going to turn creepy uncle on me, are you, Sam?" I honestly didn't expect him to admit it if he did have that planned. I just wanted to see his reaction to the question.

He barked out a laugh and dropped his hand back to his side. When he saw I remained serious, he sobered.

"I suppose that's a fair question, given what you've just told me. With me, you're safe. Honey, I'm older than I look. Heck, I'm probably old enough to be your great grandfather." He looked at me for a moment. I mean really looked at me, studying my face as if he could read all my secrets there.

"When I look at you, I see a young girl I want to help. I see a grandchild I could have had if only I'd met my one and only. And I see hope."

Fair enough. I'd wait until next week to pass any further judgments.

"All right, then. I've got to get home. See you next week."

He nodded his goodbye.

Reluctantly, I turned my back on him. Fear skittered along my spine as I walked away. My feet whispered through the grass until I reached the paved walk. When I looked back, he no longer stood by the pond, but I monitored his progress with my other sight as he left the park.

My already complicated life had just gotten more so. I took a huge risk meeting with a complete stranger, but how could I refuse? Learning about him and his kind might give me more insight, if not actual answers about my abilities–abilities that had caused me so much grief over the years. I really wanted an explanation.

When I got home, it was later than I thought. Barb and Tim waited for me in the kitchen. They fed me dinner and sat with me at the table while I explained what kept me. I didn't mention a werewolf, just an old friend of my grandfather's I'd bumped into.

I mentioned my plans to meet up with him at the hospital the next week to talk some more. Barb looked at Tim with worry a moment before Tim asked when they'd get to meet him. I asked for their patience and said I wanted to get to know Sam—again—first.

THREE WEEKS LATER, I exited the sliding glass hospital doors with Sam. We both eyed the dark clouds. The imminent downpour had cleared the usually bustling sidewalks, but the charged air filled me with anticipation.

I turned to Sam. "What do you think? Still want to go? We will probably get wet."

Sam, dressed in his unusually trendy attire for an old guy, continued to study the sky as we walked toward the bus stop.

He had been kind and informative during the first two meetings, telling me as much as he could in such a public place about his "relatives" in the hour I allotted for our meetings. Wary of outsiders, many of his kind chose to live in a closed community across the Canadian border. It had plenty of land, and the rural population of the surrounding area allowed them more space to roam freely. It also had a few old buildings that, up until twenty years ago, had been more for show than living.

After the marriage of their leader, things changed. The leader's new wife helped the community see they'd slipped too far from society and that their only chance to survive was to adapt.

A few people agreed and left to help reintegrate. A few more stayed in the buildings and started making small improvements. However, several of the structures needed larger-scale remodeling and, collectively, Sam's "relatives" just didn't have the money for it. Although remote, a few of the community's members ventured out to find work in nearby towns and supplemented the income needed to support their not yet fully self-sufficient way of life.

Gradually, those who'd denied the need for change started seeing the reality of what they'd become...a dying species...and more of the men not yet married went out looking for work. When the leader's sons were old enough, they too left.

Sam had been sent even further from the community to get the lay of the land in a more urban setting. Trying to blend, he'd decided he needed to dress more like the people of the area. At that point in his narrative, I'd wondered what he'd been wearing. Furs? When he'd gone shopping, he'd asked a sales clerk's advice regarding what to buy. The sales clerk had been about my age, which explained Sam's trendy choice of clothes.

It amazed me how much I'd learned about the man walking next to me. The compassion for his people's plight impressed upon me his selflessness, and watching him interact with other people around us, showed he had a sense of humor. Those defining characteristics had decided it for me—it was time to introduce him to Tim and Barb.

We'd reached the bus stop without a drop of rain.

"A little rain never hurt anyone," he said answering my earlier question.

Another thing I liked about Sam. He sensed when I was lost in my own thoughts and let me be.

"Okay, I'll text Barb and let her know you'll be coming over. They've been asking about you every week." He looked at me questioningly.

"I mentioned you that first night we met in the park. They wanted to know why I was late. I said I ran into an old acquaintance, a friend of my grandfather's."

A city bus drew to a halt in front of the sheltered bus stop. Sam and I waited for the other passengers to board. He surprised me by pulling out his own city bus pass to pay. The familiar driver looked at me curiously when I took my normal place behind him and slid over on the worn grey vinyl seat to make room for Sam.

Sam and I didn't talk much on the bus ride. Instead, I watched out the window, waiting expectantly for the rain.

At our stop, Sam stood and exited. He didn't offer me his hand. After only knowing me a short while, he knew I didn't like to be touched. It wasn't that I didn't like being touched. I didn't like growing attached. When you touched people, you developed attachments. Then, when they left, it made it harder to say goodbye.

He waited for me to hop down from the last step then fell in beside me as we made our way down the paved park path. Although we still had an hour of daylight left, the dark storm clouds writhing in the sky above cast the city into an early dusk. Ever since Sam had revealed himself to me, tension drove me to walk quickly through the park. Particularly in the dark. I liked having someone to walk home with me, even if that someone had started the whole thing. In Sam's company, I didn't worry as much.

"You're certain I won't disrupt things at home just popping in like this?"

"I don't think you can disrupt it any more than it's been," I said. "Barb, my foster mom is pregnant, which really is a good thing. Barb and Tim have been trying to get pregnant for years. Thinking they'd never have kids of their own, they decided to foster."

We were halfway across the park. Sam slowed to give me more time to talk. I hadn't mentioned any of this to him before. The swings in the abandoned playground to our right started to sway in the increasing winds, their older chains squeaking slightly with each forward swing.

"They own a cute little two bedroom house. If she carries the baby to term, there won't be enough room, you know?" I kept my eyes focused on the path, not wanting to see his expression. "Because she hasn't yet passed her first term, they haven't notified my social worker."

I had no regret. I really did feel happy for Barb and Tim, and I'd moved around enough in foster care to know the drill. Plus, I counted down the days...months...until I turned eighteen, legally free from anyone's guardianship.

Sam remained silent beside me.

Leaving the park, we turned right on the sidewalk. The phone in my bag buzzed, and I quickly searched for it. The rain still held back, but the sky overhead rumbled ominously. I checked the message and smiled at Sam.

"Barb said she's very excited to meet you, and since you and I just ate, they'll have cake and coffee ready."

Sam nodded. A fat raindrop splattered on the sidewalk in front of us and without a word, we both started walking faster. When we turned the last suburban corner, I pointed out the Newton's house to him, not pausing the brisk pace we'd set.

Barb and Tim both waited for us on the front stoop. Tim had his arm wrapped around Barb's shoulders as he peeked around the awning to look up at the clouds. When Barb nudged him to point us out, he looked our way and waved.

They greeted Sam enthusiastically and invited him in. I could see Barb sizing him up and finding him acceptable. In a rare twist, Tim did most of the talking that night and asked Sam about himself. When Sam said he originally hailed from Canada and managed the family business investments, I figured he stuck as close to the truth as possible. They did ask him about my grandpa, and he wove a beautiful tale about them growing up together. Since I never talked about my grandfather, the Newtons didn't know any differently. The skill with which Sam lied made me a little uncomfortable. If he could lie that easily to them, how easily could he lie to me?

The rain stopped before he finished his second cup of coffee. Sam stood and smiled at Barb.

"The cake and coffee were wonderful. Thank you for letting me drop in like this." He extended a hand to Tim. "I won't overstay my welcome or the coffee."

Tim clasped Sam's hand with a warm smile as the adults all laughed.

"It was a pleasure to meet both of you."

"We appreciated you stopping in," Barb said, already collecting the cups to bring to the sink. "When Gabby said she ran into you, we were both very curious."

"I can imagine. Now that I found her, I don't want to lose track of her. If it's all right, I'd like to stop by now and again to check in on her."

"We insist you do." Tim patted Sam's back in a manly display of affection as they walked to the front door. I quickly helped Barb put the dishes in the sink so she could follow them. Barb was a little compulsive and couldn't walk away from a dirty kitchen.

"What about dinner next Wednesday?" Barb asked, raising her voice from the kitchen as she washed and dried her hands at the sink. She hurried to the front door where Sam bent to put on his shoes.

"That sounds like a good idea." Sam finished tying his shoes and turned to me. "Is that okay, Gabby?"

Leaning against the arch dividing the living room and the kitchen, I watched the adults interact. In a way, it reminded me of the animal channel. I struggled not to crack a smile at the thought since Sam really did have one foot in the animal world.

"After I finish volunteering at the hospital, it should work for me."

Satisfied they would see each other soon, the adults said their goodbyes and Sam left. Not bad for a first meeting.

Each time I met with Sam, I learned more about his world. Nothing that I could apply to myself, yet. I still had hope though.

SAM VISITED PERIODICALLY over the next two months, and life continued as normal for a while. Barb started to show, and the normally reserved Tim couldn't stop talking about it. My time with the Newtons ticked away like the seconds of a clock.

On one of our scheduled Wednesday nights, I opened the door for Sam as soon as he knocked. He didn't show any surprise when I swung the door open after just one knock, but then I didn't expect him to.

Despite meeting at my home where we couldn't speak freely, I'd managed to learn a little more about him and his kind. For example, he had exceptional hearing. He knew when I got nervous or upset by the change in my pulse. He could hear whispered conversations taking place in other rooms as long as the door remained partially open. He could even hear whispers through thin walls. In addition to keen hearing, he also had better eyesight. In the dark, his pupils expanded to a freakish dimension, allowing in as much light as possible and enabling him to see when a normal person couldn't. This explained the way his eyes reflected.

"Hi, Sam." I stopped him from taking off his shoes. "We're eating on the patio since it's nice out." He wiped his feet extra well on the rug before following me through the house to the back patio.

The solid concrete slab patio took up a fourth of their backyard space. The patio wasn't that big, the yard was just that small. But surrounded with a classic wooden privacy fence, it would make a perfect play area.

We walked onto the patio, and Tim looked up from the grill to our left and nodded a greeting. Smoke drifted lazily upward as he flipped a burger.

"Sam, thanks for coming."

Barb stopped setting the table and moved to greet Sam with a hug. Sam gave one back with a smile. She long ago stopped trying to hug me.

Tim brought the burgers from the grill, and we all sat to eat while Tim and Sam dominated the conversation with fishing stories.

When Sam asked if I'd ever been fishing, I nearly choked on my bite of burger. "No," I said definitively.

He put on a mock shocked face. "How can a girl your age never have been fishing?"

"Many have tried, and all have failed, Sam," I said slightly amused. "I'm not an outdoorsy type."

His next comment wiped the smile from Barb's face.

"You should come with me for the weekend. I'll take you to the cabin your grandpa and I went to before you were even born. It has indoor plumbing now, so I bet you could talk a friend into coming with."

I glanced at all the faces at the table. Sam still smiled, Barb focused on me with an alarmed expression, and Tim glanced between me, Barb, and Sam. I took another bite of burger to stall.

In private, Sam had asked about my plans for the future. Barb's baby bump was hard to miss now. He had mentioned he had a spare room at his place if I ever needed it. He'd also mentioned he would like to take me on a trip to meet others of his kind. I felt fairly certain that's what he meant now. Having him ask tonight without any warning took me off guard. I could have done some prep work, like dropping hints that I had an interest in spending more time with him or something. But it did make sense that he asked now. Why try to delay the inevitable? The doctors saw no reason Barb's pregnancy wouldn't go full term this time. School would let out soon, and I had no summer job.

Setting down my fork, I picked up my glass and took a long drink of water. They all waited. I decided to save the adults the long dance around a subject none of them wanted to face full on. I turned toward Barb and Tim.

"I've spent a lot of time getting to know Sam over the last two months and told him about the baby on the way." I looked at Barb, meeting her beautiful dark brown eyes. "We all know that I won't be able to stay once the baby's here." Barb started to tear up and speak but I stopped her with a raised hand. "I also know that you want me to stay. I don't doubt that for a minute. You've both been so great to me, and I thank you."

I turned to Sam. "You said that you live in a three bedroom house and that I was welcome to visit anytime. What about visiting until I graduate?" I didn't want to go back into foster care.

Sam continued to smile at me and nodded.

Barb started to sniffle, and Tim reached over the table to pat her hand.

CHAPTER TWO

Friday night, Barb and Tim dropped me off at Sam's. Though it was only for a weekend, they knew what it would mean if everything went well. So I willfully squashed my discomfort and endured Barb's hug. Tim, thankfully, settled on a nod and a wave as I climbed into Sam's truck.

I used the eight-hour drive to ask Sam direct questions about werewolf life, and tried to soak up everything he said. I stopped talking when we turned off the blacktopped road onto a deeply rutted dirt lane I doubted saw much use. For a mile, I braced myself against the rough ride. Finally, we emerged from the tree-lined path into a wide clearing.

A large two-story log cabin style structure dominated the space, its wings branching out to connect to outlying buildings. Sam parked on the combination of old gravel, stubborn grass, and plain dirt in front of the buildings.

The werewolf community reminded me of an old wilderness resort, one closed for a few years. If not for the lights pouring from several of the windows, I would have locked the truck door instead of getting out.

I shouldered my bag and trailed Sam onto the covered porch. Sam pulled the solid wood door open without knocking. Inside, an eclectic array of rugs along the perimeter of the large main entry accommodated numerous sets of shoes. Hooks on the walls held a bounty of coats, jackets, and overalls.

"We don't have to worry about stealing here," Sam said when he caught me looking at the mass of shoes. "And it keeps the rest of the place cleaner if we leave our outside things here." He started taking off his shoes, and I bent to remove mine.

"You would not believe how messy this place was thirty years ago," a voice called from the hall.

I looked up from untying my shoes. A tall woman with blonde hair and a gentle smile walked into the entry. I estimated her to be in her late twenties.

"Hello, Gabby," she said coming to stand next to me. "I'm Charlene. Sam's told me about you. I'm so thrilled to meet another person like me." She held out her hand in greeting as I stepped out of my shoes.

Excitement coursed through me. Finally! Sam had mentioned Charlene, another human among the werewolves, during one of our many talks. The possibility that I wasn't as alone as I thought obliterated any hesitation I might have had, and I reached out and clasped her hand.

Charlene's grip was firm and sure, but I barely noticed it. The darkness of my other sight had burst open and the brilliance of the sparks surprised me; their normal soft glow amplified so much that the blinding light obscured their gentle colors. I let go of her hand while maintaining my focus. The lights dimmed considerably so I could again discern their soft colors.

Sam's spark glowed blue with a green halo and hers, while

still containing the yellow center like any human, had a red halo. I'd considered the possibility that my orange halo was because I couldn't see myself correctly using my other sight. But seeing Charlene's assured me our uniqueness was real.

Beyond our sparks, I noticed other blue-green lights. Not in the immediate area, but spread throughout my area of awareness. The coloring of those lights matched Sam's. Werewolves then were blue-green, I thought. Color by species made sense, but Charlene and I didn't match. Why?

"Like me?" Her words suddenly penetrated my study of the sparks. Could she see lights too?

"So far, we are the only two humans who seem to be compatible with werewolves," she said, still smiling in welcome.

My hope sank. So we were human and...wait, what?

"Compatible?" I looked at Sam in confusion. I knew that I smelled differently to werewolves, but he hadn't mentioned anything about compatibility. Charlene answered before he could.

"Yes, werewolves choose their Mate—husband or wife— instinctually. They have no history of ever before selecting from humans for their Mates, but here we are. Whatever it takes to become a Mate, we apparently have it, too."

My mouth popped open in shock as I understood. I turned on Sam.

"You brought me here to hook up with a werewolf?"

"No, Gabby. I apologize for upsetting you," Charlene said from behind me. I turned to look at her. "Yes, we're different in that a werewolf might choose us, but that doesn't mean that they must choose us or that we have to choose them. At your age, there will be no hooking up."

She looped her arm through mine and gave me a motherly pat. As soon as she touched me, all the sparks around us brightened again. I didn't even need to focus. The lights just flared and continued to glow brightly without effort. Weird.

She led me toward the hall from which she'd entered. After a few steps, she stumbled and pulled her arm from mine. With relief, the lights in my mind extinguished, and I concentrated on her words.

"I asked Sam to bring you so you and I can talk. As I said, there is no one else like us that we've found. I came here when I was younger than you—long story—and met Thomas, the pack's leader. It was a very hard adjustment with a huge learning curve on both our sides. I don't want you to have to face any of that on your own. We'll introduce you slowly to this new world you're now a part of. If you have any questions, don't be afraid to ask them."

She led us down a second hallway and stopped in front of a closed door. When she opened it, I saw it led into a very small apartment.

"This is still a work in progress. Let me know if you need anything," she said, looking at Sam. He nodded.

I took a moment to take in my surroundings as Charlene walked away. The small, main room had only a few mismatched pieces of furniture. The bedroom, which I suspected had once been a walk-in closet, barely held a twin-sized bed, nightstand, and lamp. Sam insisted I take that room as he set his bag on the foldout couch. I didn't complain. I figured sleeping in a half-sized bed ranked higher than Sam's sleeper sofa.

A tiny bathroom right off the main living area completed the suite. The apartment definitely qualified as rustic, but I didn't mind.

S AM WOKE me after a few hours of sleep.

Despite Charlene's assurances that my stay didn't include finding a boyfriend, I still felt leery over Sam not telling me about the compatibility thing. I'd thought I could trust him, and his omission stung a little.

I wanted to excuse it—maybe it'd slipped his mind—but it'd taken eight hours to get here. Granted, most of that time we'd talked about the progress the community had made and the customs, like pack hunts, that they no longer followed. Still, he could have mentioned that doozy. *By the way, Gabby, werewolves will want you as their Mate.* I paused then shook my head at the thought. Yeah, I would have reached for the door handle and tried to jump from the moving truck. Maybe, he'd made an okay call. Only time would tell.

I got out of bed and dressed. Sam already had his bed made when I opened my door.

We left the apartment and he led me to a large room, which he referred to as the commons, to get a bite to eat. The space served as a cafeteria and an entertainment area with sitting arrangements scattered around the room. It even had a pool table set in the back corner.

Charlene saw us and came over to our table. Two young men followed in her wake. She introduced them as Paul and Henry. She thought I might like the opportunity to talk to people my own age. She even suggested we go into the woods so they could show me more about the werewolf way of life.

Sam heard my panicked heartbeat, and before I could refuse, he suggested we use the lounge in the commons to get to know each other, instead.

Paul and Henry didn't treat me the same as human boys did. As curious about me as I was them, they asked a myriad of questions.

"What's school like?" Paul, the boy with dark hair and a carefree smile, asked while sitting on a padded dish-chair close to me.

"You don't go to school?" I couldn't believe it.

"Nah," said Henry, a short stocky kid with bright blue eyes. "We're home schooled here. It's way quicker to graduate since we can study at an accelerated pace because we don't have to break for holidays or anything."

"That actually sounds pretty great...what school should be, minus the no breaks part." I cringed inwardly at the thought of school year round then answered his original question. "The majority of the teachers spend their time hating their jobs and finding ways to be as disagreeable as possible while the students look at it as a popularity contest and spend more time worrying about who's dating who than studying," I explained.

"Date?" Paul glanced at Henry, who wore an equally puzzled expression. "I heard Charlene talking about that once. Sounds weird."

"Really? You guys don't date?" I didn't ask what they did to get to know a girl instead of dating.

"No, we get invited to Introductions," Paul said as if reading my mind.

"What's that?" Sam hadn't mentioned anything like that to me, and I wondered if I should add it to his list of omissions.

"When a female comes of age, she's brought to the

Introduction room where she can meet werewolves she has never met before. The Elders are there to make sure the girl is safe and to give the guys a few minutes to talk to her. You know, to really get her scent. When there's a connection, a guy just knows and Claims her. If not, the next group comes in for their chance."

I started to sweat as I sat there. First, what did he mean by Claim? Second, they kept a girl in a room while guys came in to look her over and smell her? I reached for my water that sat on the coffee table in the center of our sitting arrangement. My hands shook a little, and I tried really hard to calm down and not let my imagination run away.

"Hey, Gabby, you okay? Did Paul say something wrong? Charlene said we could ask any questions we wanted..."

They had no idea how foreign what they'd just said sounded to me.

"Hey, Gabby, you don't have to worry about Introductions if that's what's scaring you." Paul looked at me with concern. "For you and Charlene, the attraction works different. She explained it to us when she said that you were coming. You guys have a level of appeal, or chemistry, with just about all werewolves." He is not helping, I thought while he continued. "Because the level of attraction to you varies, it wouldn't be safe to put you in an Introduction room."

"Yeah," Henry agreed and, with a spark of excitement in his eyes, leaned forward in his chair. "That's when the mating duels happen. It's rare with a werewolf couple, but when Charlene was first brought here, I heard the guys went crazy because they didn't know what was happening. They fought over who had the strongest tie to her. But you don't have to worry about that with us. Paul and I think you're okay, and you smell good and everything, but we knew when we met you that you're not right for either of us. That's why Charlene left you alone with us."

My stomach churned. Werewolves were going to start fighting each other for me? No thanks. They both smiled at me encouragingly. They probably thought their explanations helpful, but the information they threw at me stunned me.

"What did you mean by 'Claim'?" My voice came out light and airy with anxiety, but I needed to know.

"It's when we bite our Mate. The bite draws blood but doesn't hurt," Paul explained reassuringly.

"What?" I nearly shouted. My freak-o-meter bypassed meltdown. My head spun dizzily, and no doubt, all the color had drained from my face.

"Oh, not for you, Gabby," Paul said, quickly leaning forward. He made shushing motions with his hands. "We can't Claim humans like that. When your Mate finds you, it's up to you to Claim him."

So, I would need to bite someone? Not going to happen. It was easier to calm down now that I knew I had control. I didn't want to be "the right one" for anyone at this point in my life. I hoped that the rest of the werewolves, like these two, would correctly use their keen sense of smell to determine my unsuitability.

I heard the main door swing open and saw Sam walk in with an older woman and another older man. Sam nodded to me and then moved with his group to another area of the room. They sat down and started talking. Paul and Henry shifted their attention to the new people, listening. I couldn't hear the conversation but had no doubt they could. Just as I knew Sam would hear if I asked either Paul or Henry to tell me what the group said. I decided to change the subject.

"What about sports? I noticed there are no TVs. Do you guys play or go watch any sports?"

"Nah, we don't get good reception out here, and the television tends to hurt our ears, but we do like to play football. There aren't enough of us for a team, though."

The door behind us opened again, and I watched two younger men, about our age, enter. They glanced our way but headed toward the group with Sam. I turned around and took another drink of water while thinking about this Mate business. According to these two, I needed to watch for a werewolf who acted as most human men would toward me, intense and weird.

Sam startled me out of my thoughts when he spoke next to me.

"Gabby, I'd like you to meet Eric and Derrick. They are the twin sons of a couple who lives here. They're home from college and have to leave again tomorrow."

I smiled and said hello. They both nodded to me but didn't speak. Awkward.

Uncomfortable, I looked back at Sam, who nodded at the two. They turned and left. If they represented the normal reaction to me, I needed to watch out for someone even more intense and weird. Maybe I just needed a plan to avoid them all.

Sam waited until they'd walked out of the room to explain.

"I want you to get to know the people who live here. In summer, we'll spend a lot of our weekends here." He looked at Paul and Henry. "You two keep an eye on her. I'm counting on you to help explain our ways."

Sam walked back to the group, and I looked from Paul to Henry with an arched eyebrow. Was it just me or did that feel weird? I wanted to ask but remained quiet. There were still too many ears to overhear. They seemed to understand my unspoken question and both shrugged in return.

Sam interrupted our conversation twice more, each time bringing someone to introduce to me. My mind caught on the word "introduce."

Paul and Henry's assurance that I would never face the Introduction room clicked everything into place. Sam had started slowly introducing me to the eligible male population of this little community right here, right now—in this room. After the third set left, I caught Sam's eye.

"Sam, would you mind showing me around outside for a bit?" I stood and made my way to the main door, not waiting to see if Sam followed. After three months, I'd felt sure enough of Sam that I'd risked a trip to an unknown destination with him, alone. I'd been willing to explain away the little doozy he didn't mention on the way here; but now, his actions and omissions devastated my confidence in him.

Already familiar with the layout of the Compound, I didn't hesitate to walk out the front door and stride purposefully toward the dirt lane. Sam didn't take long to catch up to me. If I told him I wanted to go back to the Newton's now, would he take me? If he did, then what? I couldn't stay there forever.

"Sam," I said when we walked side by side. "I don't want to be on the streets, but that's where I'll go if you think you can pull this crap if I move in with you." I didn't look at him; I was too angry. And scared. "I understand the condition of living at your place is that we come up here. But my condition is that you have to be completely honest about our purpose in coming up here. Each time," I stressed. "I don't know if I can trust you."

"I'm sorry, Gabby. You can trust me. I have your best interests in mind. This is another one of those things that is easier to believe when you experience it firsthand." He kept pace next to me as I led us further from the Compound.

"No, Sam. You need to lay it out for me straight."

He stayed quiet for a few minutes, and I wasn't sure he had anything to say until he actually spoke.

"Well, I heard what Paul and Henry told you. That part's right. We do Introductions for our females in a controlled environment to keep them safe until they find their Mate.

"We learned from Charlene's time here that you'd need to be handled differently. I told you that werewolves would find your scent interesting. Since we're branching out into more urban areas, it would only be a matter of time before you attracted attention. So, we wanted to control your Introduction. A formal Introduction without mass challenges was out of the question.

"This is the compromise; they come into the commons, say 'hello' to you, then talk to the Elders. Because the level of attraction varies, we interview them. They must formally request permission from me to come see you again if they think of you as more than just interesting. They are not allowed to approach you while you are on your own. If they were to approach me for a second meeting, I would speak with you first before approving or denying their request."

The light filtering through the canopy cast the road into dusky shadow. I stopped walking and turned to Sam.

"What you're saying is, eventually werewolves would find me; but, if I stay with you, you'd be my buffer?" He nodded. I studied him. "And I'd only have to say hi to these guys. It'd be up to me if I wanted to spend any additional time with them?" He nodded again.

I liked Paul and Henry. They oozed useful information and didn't react to me at all. The others I'd already met hadn't seemed too interested, either.

When Paul and Henry had mentioned mating duels, I imagined drowning in a writhing mass of hostile bodies, all in various stages of transformation. I still dreamt about Sam shifting. The dreams and my fueled imagination bothered me. But since arriving, everyone had remained in human form and nothing freaky had happened. The general population of werewolves couldn't be all bad. I just didn't like the way I had to meet them. Yet, now that the werewolves knew I existed, trying to live on my own didn't sound like a good idea. I'd be better off with Sam. He'd keep the others away.

"Fine, let's go back."

Paul and Henry were playing cards while they ate their way through a stack of sandwiches set out on the coffee table. They waved me over, and I gladly joined their game and grabbed a sandwich for myself.

Several more werewolves came in throughout the day. Sam led each one to me. Most left after a polite nod of hello. A few asked for a second meeting. Each time, Sam would look at me and, at the shake of my head, reject the request. It relieved me to see him keep his word and restored some of my shaken confidence in him.

We packed up and left Sunday morning. I mostly paid attention to the scenery since I'd missed the majority of it on the way there. While I watched the trees flash by, I thought about the weekend. None of the guys I'd met seemed too upset over any type of rejection. For as much emphasis as they'd put on my smelling good to just about all werewolves, their laid-back attitude didn't make much sense to me.

"Why did the guys seem okay with their second request being rejected?"

"Although you smelled good to them, they knew it wasn't just right. When it is, they won't give up, which is why staying with me is so important. We have laws that control certain aspects of the social side of the pack. One is that unMated human females, like you, cannot be approached without the approval of the nearest Elder."

"Then, why can't you just tell them all 'no' for me in advance, so we don't have to mess with this whole Introduction thing?"

"Because I have to give them the chance to see for themselves that it's not right. Was it that bad? Meeting people? No one treated you the way some human men have treated you."

I couldn't disagree. "How often is this going to happen?"

"Once a month."

I sat up straighter. "No way." I shook my head for emphasis. It was a cool enough place, but sixteen hours of driving in a single weekend every month would get boring. "Once every two months."

"Every five weeks, with flexibility to switch weeks if needed," he said.

"Seven weeks."

"Six," he said with a sideways glance at me.

"Fine, every six weeks," I compromised. Then I threw in another condition. "Until I graduate. Then, I'm going to college and won't be obligated to take time out of studying for dating —or whatever you want to call this—if I don't want to."

"Deal," he agreed.

I stared at him. He'd agreed too easily. Was that a hint of a smile on his mouth? Why did I feel like I just got the raw end of the deal? I'd have to play my cards carefully so I didn't find myself hitched in some weird backwoods werewolf custom.

CHAPTER THREE

Sam sat at the worn, oak table in the middle of the sunlit kitchen. He scowled at its dull surface, and when I walked into the room, he transferred the glum look to me. I shook my head at him and went to make his morning coffee.

Sam and mornings didn't mesh well. I'd realized that as soon as I'd moved in. How a werewolf, usually graceful and strong, could stumble and mumble until he had his caffeine still confused me. With his werewolf metabolism, I doubted it really did anything for him. Regardless, I still took pity on him and tried to wake up first to start a pot—even though it wasn't my drink of preference in the morning.

Today, however, his familiar morning scowl didn't solely relate to his need for coffee. After two years of almost monthly visits to the Canadian werewolf community, this weekend would be my last, and he didn't like it. Happily, I hadn't met a single werewolf who had any type of pull on me.

The way I figured it, I'd fulfilled my end of our deal. Though school had scheduled graduation for Sunday, I'd opted not to attend. I had no desire to put this visit off for another week. The faculty could mail my diploma. After this weekend, I planned to work as much as possible to save up what I could before going off to college.

I measured out the coffee grounds and reflected back on my time with Sam. I'd kept him company, and his mere presence had kept me safe while he'd provided me with the information I needed about the werewolves and the pack community. Although Sam had shared so much of the werewolves' life and culture, I acknowledged I still didn't know everything. It didn't matter, though. I'd learned enough...and not just about werewolves.

Sam was a great role model for responsibility and planning. It's what he did for the pack. Because of him, I already worked as much as I could after school. But, it wasn't just his example that pushed me to become so dedicated to work and financial responsibility. Shortly after I moved in with Sam, I'd discovered that work commitments ensured he couldn't talk me into going to the Compound more than we'd bargained. He knew I'd need the means to get an education and support myself and never tried to talk me out of working. So, I worked and I tried to bank enough money to hold me over while I went to school.

As an Elder of the pack, Sam was extremely down to earth and wise. He carefully thought through all decisions with a deliberate calm that I admired. He didn't think of himself when making any decision, only of the pack. Their welfare ruled his life. Thankfully, even though he hadn't managed to tie me to anyone, he considered me part of the pack. That meant when I talked, he listened with his full attention, which I really did like.

Coffee brewing, I leaned against the counter and openly smirked at Sam.

"Come on, don't be pouty about this. We made a deal, and I stuck to it. I've met more man-dogs than I can remember. Some, even twice." My made-up term seemed to amuse him.

I pushed away from the counter and walked behind his chair. Resting my forearms on his shoulders, I rolled them outward and pressed down with my full weight. The tension slowly left his shoulders, and I rested my chin on his head. Yeah, I was that short compared to him.

"Tell me you're going to be okay without me here." I couldn't remember my real grandpa, but over the last two years, Sam had filled that role well, despite our rough start. I knew he had managed his own coffee in the morning for years before I'd moved in with him, but I still wondered what he'd do without me here to keep him company.

He sighed gustily and reached back to pat my cheek, the extent of affection I allowed with him. It had been a gradual progress to work up to it. He knew most physical contact made me uncomfortable. He understood it and never seemed offended by it. I'd held myself away from people for so long, I wasn't sure I'd ever be completely comfortable with casually touching anyone.

"You know I will," he said sounding tired. "I don't understand why you won't go to the community college here. Out of state is so expensive."

"No, it won't be," I said, pulling away from him. "I have scholarships and aid because of being a foster." I made my way to the coffee. A warm breeze brushed past the kitchen curtains to swirl around the room. As I poured him a cup, I continued defending my choice.

"Besides, you know very well why I'm going out of state." It was an old argument. My place in pack society, forever the bachelorette, bothered me. I wanted out. No other female went through such a long Introduction period. Over the last two years, I'd become the one all the guys wanted to meet and hoped to Claim by the end of the weekend. Though they treated me with kind hopefulness, my attitude toward finding a Mate hadn't changed. I didn't want one. Besides, two years of being the family disappointment was enough.

"I want my own life before someone else tries to take it over. Sam, I've always had to follow other people's rules. I want to live by my own rules for a while."

Sam harrumphed. "What rules have I ever enforced on you?"

I gave him a steady look as I handed him the steaming cup.

"Besides insisting on the Introductions..." He dropped his gaze to the proffered cup and accepted it with a lack of enthusiasm. Not meeting my eyes, he blew on the brew and turned the cup in a circle on the table before he began to sip it slowly.

Suspicious, I continued to study his face as I waited for him to look up again. He seemed unexpectedly guilty for such an innocent remark.

Though I chafed at his rules, they were simple enough. Go to the Introductions. Spend the weekends getting to know the pack and the pack laws. Never stay out past dark without a way to get home, which meant a ride from Sam since owning my own car made him uncomfortable. How could he not see he completely controlled my life with those rules?

Though I understood the reason for the restriction, it didn't make them more palatable. The very real draw men felt when near me had only grown stronger as I'd matured. It made time alone risky. Sam had insisted I take self-defense classes. Those had been great until the instructor suggested one on one training sessions a bit too loudly in class. Before I bailed on the course, I'd learned enough to keep men at bay...but not werewolves. Despite knowing I had no protection against them other than Sam, I still wanted to try it out on my own. Sam's rules were simple, however, they weren't mine.

"It won't be safe," Sam said, interrupting my thoughts. He looked up from his half-empty cup. "You know it won't be safe."

"Sam, I'll get a dog." I could see by his expression that he was gearing up for another round in an old debate. Why couldn't he understand that I'd rather get a dog than be Mated to a werewolf? I hurried around him for the bathroom down the hall.

"I better go shower. We don't want to keep the wolves waiting." I spun into the bathroom and shut the door with a snick to stop any further objections.

JUST BEFORE DINNERTIME, I pushed open the door of Sam's old pickup and, ignoring its groan of protest, climbed out. My feet crunched on the gravel parking area. Not much had changed. Though, still rundown and in need of repairs, to me the familiar buildings exuded welcome. With a twinge, I realized I'd probably miss these frequent visits. I pushed the door closed, reached around to the bed of the truck, and grabbed my canvas bag.

"There a pack meeting tonight?" I asked Sam, looking at the other vehicles.

I couldn't remember ever seeing so many cars before. Yet,

for the number parked in the yard, the Compound was unusually quiet. Typically, before a meeting, groups of people stood outside to talk and renew acquaintances. I glanced at the buildings again. Though quiet outside, thin lines of light escaped from behind thick curtains in many of the windows on the main house. Definitely, a full house tonight. But why stay inside?

Sam just grunted in response to my question, shouldered his own bag, and headed toward the main building.

I studied Sam's back. He certainly seemed rushed. He'd even sped so we arrived in just over seven hours. We'd only stopped once for a five minute, gas-up, eat, and pee break. I hadn't questioned why, but it was unusual.

He'd stayed abnormally silent and pensive the entire trip, too. I didn't mind the quiet, but he generally updated me on current pack activity during the drive. Bored, I'd alternated between listening to my mp3 player and watching the country pass in silence.

I turned a slow circle, studying the area while I breathed deeply, and began to focus. In two years, the area of my sight had expanded so I could see much further in the vast darkness of my mind. It didn't exhaust me as quickly as it used to.

I closed my eyes and continued to turn a slow circle. At the Compound, focusing was harder. Typically, for humans, some sparks came in strong and glowed bright like a newly replaced light bulb while others were weak, more like a lightning bug's glow. I didn't know why; it just was. The lights of the werewolves were different. Their sparks tended to flash in and out of focus regardless of how bright or dim I perceived them. I considered the flashing a false perception. Instead, I believed I was watching the amazing speed at which they moved—there one second, gone the next, then back again. Since I hadn't yet shared my ability with Sam, I couldn't confirm my suspicion.

In the darkness behind my closed eyes, I saw the usual flashes of light, but they jumped around in a pattern that made me dizzy. I could see flashes in the Compound and many more in the surrounding woods and beyond.

I stopped turning before I made myself lightheaded. When I opened my eyes, I faced the woods to the right of the Compound just inside the gate. I felt watched. Not moving, I listened. Nothing but silence and my own breathing. I mentally shrugged and turned away from the trees to walk toward the main building. If any werewolves lingered out there, they would show themselves, or not, depending on their nature and if we'd already been introduced.

Several men exited through the main entrance as I stepped onto the porch. Two gave me kind, but dispassionate—perhaps even indifferent—nods of greeting. Mated. The other two watched me alertly and nodded politely. UnMated. I nodded a greeting in return and walked past them, safe with the Mated males nearby. Pack law: Protect unMated females from unMated males. Another pack law: Don't place yourself in a situation where you'll be alone with an unMated male or it could be seen as acceptance of his suit.

Inside, further down the long hall that branched from the main entry, more men headed my way. I kicked off my shoes, nodded, and walked past them. Again, a Mated male amidst the unMated.

"You're early."

I smiled at Charlene, who walked briskly toward me.

"He drove fast. Are Paul and Henry around?"

"I haven't seen them, but I'm sure they're around

somewhere. I'll see you at breakfast." Charlene didn't slow. She had a pile of clothes in her arms.

She seemed more hurried than normal. As a Mate to the leader, she tended to be busy, but she usually always made time to talk to me.

With a tingle of apprehension, I hurried toward our assigned apartment. The same one we'd first stayed in, but with big improvements. The once sparsely furnished apartment now made a cozy weekend getaway. A plush rug protected the refinished hardwood floors. Pictures decorated the walls and various knickknacks adorned the room, just a few of Charlene's efforts to make it homier for those staying here. It also now had a small kitchen, which included a sink, dishes, and mini fridge. It still lacked appliances for cooking since we all took meals with the rest of the pack in the commons. The kitchenettes in the apartments were there for private convenience. Sam and I never used ours, but we weren't the only ones who stayed here. Though we had priority on the apartment, I knew visiting Mated werewolves used it on our off weekends.

Sam had already thrown his bag on the foldout couch in the living room when I walked through the apartment door. I walked past him, tossed my bag on my own bed, and returned to the living room to watch him and to try to puzzle out his mood. The last few informal Introductions had been less than typical with an unusually high number of unMated males coming to the Compound from greater distances. I figured this one would be no different. Maybe he was worried about the number attending.

"So, when do we get started?" I paced around the room to stretch my legs after the long drive.

"Soon as you're ready, I guess." Sam riffled through his bag, looking for something.

"How many this weekend?"

He didn't look at me. In fact, he seemed to be making an effort not to look at me and had been making that effort since breakfast. My stomach wanted to do a flip, but I firmly smashed down my emotions. I needed to figure out what was going on before I reacted in any way. Emotions around werewolves gave you away. They could smell some and hear others.

"I'm not sure. All of the Elders put a call out since it's your last one. Ready?" He straightened, with pencil and paper in his hand, and still did not meet my gaze. He kept himself busy by tucking the pencil into the spiral of the notebook as he moved toward the door.

"Yep." I fell into step behind him. "So, what does that mean?"

"That there are more ears than usual." He opened the door for me.

A werewolf fun fact to keep in mind at all times: They have excellent hearing. I didn't say anything more. Sam typically stayed very open with me, but something definitely felt different about tonight. I followed him down the hall. Our footfalls echoed softly on the hardwood floor.

Despite my effort not to react in any way to the oddities I kept noticing, a tension built inside of me. Not about the Introductions. I'd grown used to those. They could throw as many unMated at me as they wanted. I knew it wouldn't work.

In the past two years, not once had I felt any physical interest in any werewolf. There'd been some nice ones I'd enjoyed talking to, but nothing more. No spark that Sam had insisted I would feel. He'd stressed that whatever I felt, the male would feel infinitely stronger, a compulsion that they wouldn't be able to deny.

No, the tension wasn't about meeting more werewolves. It was Sam. The tension continued to grow as I puzzled over whatever Sam hid, whatever made him act so nervous and guilty at the same time.

When we didn't turn to go to the commons, but instead, went down the hall I knew housed the infamous Introduction room, his odd behavior suddenly made sense. They planned to go old school for my last Introduction. Since Sam had stressed a formal Introduction could be dangerous to me, his nervousness and guilt were understandable. But I didn't understand why they thought a formal Introduction necessary. Did they really think the results would be different?

"Sam...you should have told me first."

He said nothing as he stopped and opened the door at the end of the hall. He motioned me inside. Resigned, I entered.

The windowless room had the same comfortable log cabin design as the rest of the Compound. However, near the center of the room, ten worn X's taped to the floor formed a gentle arch. A few feet away, a solid line ran from one side of the room to the other, separating the front and back halves of the room. On my half of the room, folding chairs waited along the wall, a place for Elders to wait and observe. Having Elders present meant disputes were resolved quickly and without bloodshed. It also meant better protection for the female. Each side of the room had a door.

According to tradition, five men would enter from the opposite door, which led outside, and remain in the room for five minutes. The Elders present would watch my reaction to these men and their reactions to me. Five minutes gave enough time for me to introduce myself to each of them. It seemed pointless to me, though. Through their own admission, true Mates would know within a minute of meeting each other.

All ten marks came into play during Introductions for older, unMated were-females. Once Introductions started, unMated males traveled from distant states until the Elder network announced a Claim.

The males competed aggressively for a Mate since fewer females were available to men. Sam had told me, statistically, the birth rate was about three to one. Some thought it nature's way to keep the werewolf population low. Other's disagreed. They argued that it didn't make sense when human females appeared to be evolving to fill in the need.

I understood the seriousness of this Introduction and stood near the door I'd entered. If trouble broke out, I would step through the sturdy, thick door, lock it behind me, and run like hell. The locked door wouldn't slow a determined werewolf. Without an Elder standing between an oncoming werewolf and me, I wouldn't stand a chance. Still, locking it would make me feel better once I stood on the other side. Declared a safety zone, I was supposed to remain in the hall beyond to wait until the Elders calmed whatever disruption might occur.

Although the setting had changed, the rules hadn't. They couldn't force a Mate on me. It was up to Nature. One more weekend to play it cool, then...done.

The Elders began to enter behind me. During the informal Introductions in the commons, two or three Elders always remained nearby. If informal Introductions called for at least two Elders, I knew to expect more for a formal Introduction. Definitely three. Maybe four.

Sam already sat on a folding chair to my left. Gradually, four more filed in; four men, including Sam, and one woman. The number surprised me, but I didn't mind the extra eyes. I'd met Nana Wini two years ago while still learning about Introductions. A kind and patient teacher, she'd explained so much to me. Having her here comforted me, and I looked forward to talking to her afterward.

Once the last Elder sat, the outer door opened and ten men stalked in. Ten? I successfully kept my feelings from my face, but I knew they would smell my confusion. Ten explained the extra Elders. Werewolves in their fur were all powerful and vicious, Elders more so because of their position in the pack.

In addition to the increased number of Elders, the ages of the werewolves who stood on the X's ranged from young to old without restriction. Screw Nature. No way would I be even remotely interested in someone old enough to be my father. Especially when I had no clue who my father might be.

Wanting to get the Introduction over with, I stepped forward so the toes of my socks rested just behind my safety line and met the eyes of the first man. I nodded a greeting, turned with military precision, and paced to the next taped X to meet the second man's eyes. I slowly walked down the line and met the eyes of each man I passed. At the last man, I turned around to face all of them.

"Thank you for coming."

They all stepped back from the tape and turned to leave.

I stayed on my side of the tape and watched their retreating forms. The door on their side of the room opened so they could file out. It felt weird not learning their names as I usually did in an informal Introduction. But I knew this was typical of a formal Introduction. Any man interested in me would remain on his taped mark while allowing the others to step back to leave. This would give Sam a moment to note the interested party. Anyone on Sam's list would have an opportunity for a second Introduction where I would actually converse with him. The second round had more danger.

Movement in the recently vacated doorway broke my chain of thought. The doorway had barely cleared before the next set of ten entered. Was it always this rushed?

Breaking protocol, I glanced at Sam. He watched the men, still not looking at me. Without frowning at him like I really wanted to, I turned back to focus on the men who now stood on their marks. In this group, all of them were over forty. I repeated the same process from the first group, acknowledging each of them as I walked past. One appeared to have the start of a black eye.

I thanked them for meeting me and watched one remain on his mark while the rest marched out. The remaining man waited for Sam to make a note then nodded at me before he turned to leave.

Again, ten more filed in as soon as the room emptied. This felt wrong. Too rushed. They weren't even waiting the full five minutes once the men stood on their marks.

Instead of moving forward toward my line, I put my hands behind my back and kept my eyes on the ground. The rules said that the Elders would not interfere unless they perceived danger. They would not speak unless it was imperative to my wellbeing. It ensured no outside influence to any decision I might make regarding my choice of Mate. That rule made it impossible to ask Sam for an explanation and actually get an answer.

Why did they change to a formal Introduction now? Why

on the last visit? What were they trying to accomplish? The unMated males entered ten at a time and faster than the normal five minutes.

I looked at the line on the floor. The crisp tape looked new even though I'd heard from Henry and Paul, still my best sources of information, that it hadn't been replaced in years. It looked new because it had never been walked on, never crossed. You leave by the door you enter. That's the rule.

I looked up. Rules are meant to be broken. Answers waited beyond the opposite door.

Stepping to the line, I met each of the unMated males' eyes. While doing so, I noted dried blood under one man's nose.

"It's nice to meet you," I said and waited, saying no more. They all stepped back to leave, and the door swung open.

"A moment, please." As one, they stopped before any of them reached the door, and turned to look back at me. I could feel the Elders watching me but didn't look at them.

I broke protocol, crossed the line, and walked toward the door. Since none of the men acknowledged any interest in me, I hoped I'd be safe enough.

"Gabby, wait," Sam called.

Hearing him stand and follow me caused my stomach to dip. My steps slowed for a heartbeat. Stepping through the door could compromise my wellbeing...but staying inside wouldn't get me answers. The door beckoned. I stepped through onto a packed dirt path and looked around.

The light that spilled from the door illuminated a small area. The trees that crowded the building left only a small gap of about twenty feet between the treeline and the roofline, which cast the area in an early dusk. In the cleared space near the back door, twenty men waited quietly. I frowned, puzzled.

Something still felt off. I'd expected to see many more given the rushed Introductions.

Closing my eyes, I breathed deeply and focused. Tiny sparks flashed around me in the darkness. Sam, I saw, stood to my right. His spark glowed steadily, not blinking at all. The group of twenty was different.

Some of the werewolves' lights blinked like strobes. Some faster, some slower. Some so slow, I at first thought they might have left. As I studied them, it began to make sense. I wasn't seeing werewolves quickly running all over the place, rather an arrhythmic indication of a werewolf's location. I focused beyond the twenty. Lights too numerous to count stood out in the darkness. It would take hours to meet them all.

Had all the prior Introductions been a farce, a game to keep me from running until Sam could arrange the real thing? How strongly were the Elders determined to see me Mated? Would they let me leave unMated? Had my thoughts of college been a dream? I struggled with my growing frustration and panic. No. Not a dream. I wouldn't give up.

I opened my eyes already knowing that the group of twenty had doubled. I studied their faces and noted more bruising and blood. Some men dressed in jeans and shirts while others wore clothes too filthy from fighting to identify. Seeing the filth and blood, I understood why they wanted to rush the Introductions. Too many werewolves had arrived for this; and the Mating challenges the Elders feared, had begun.

I didn't say anything. I couldn't. Anger churned in my stomach at Sam for not telling me. I felt tricked and yet sad for the men waiting.

"Sam," I said, turning my gaze on him. There was nothing playful in my look. I wanted to tell him that I would never forgive him for this but knew the werewolves listening would take my words as a rejection. It would take away what little hope they had facing these numbers. Instead, I let my look convey everything I felt.

He lowered his gaze and broke eye contact, something he never did first. Good. He knew.

I turned away and studied the growing crowd. I'd lived among them enough to know not to show intimidation. They respected strength. With their hearing, I didn't need to raise my voice. Even those still hidden within the trees would hear me.

"No more fighting. There's no need to wait and fight for your place in tonight's Introduction. I will meet you all. Start a line here, and I'll walk it. If I am not right for you, there is no need for you to remain after I've passed you. You may leave and know that I am honored by your presence here tonight."

CHAPTER FOUR

MEN SILENTLY STEPPED FROM THE TREES AND MOVED TO CREATE A line as I'd asked. They continued to emerge from the woods even as the line extended around the corner. Because of that, new rows started behind the first line. The shuffling continued until roughly five hundred gathered. So many men focused on me, all at the same time, made my stomach churn. If they were human...I suppressed a shudder at the thought.

Ignoring the vast number, I moved toward the first man, nodded stoically, then turned to start the slow walk down the line. The Elders kept pace with me. I didn't bother pausing to meet anyone's eyes. Only my scent mattered.

As I'd asked, those without a strong interest stepped out of the line and walked back into the woods. It allowed those behind them to move forward and take their place. When I reached the end, I turned around to walk it again. I paced the line several times in silence so all would get their fair chance. As the number remaining decreased, my mood lightened. Sam made note of names as needed. Soon only a handful of men remained.

While my future loomed brighter, theirs dimmed. I nodded solemnly to those remaining and watched them melt back into the trees. I truly felt for them, but I'd experienced no attraction to any of them—no pull that Sam and the other Elders and werewolves had assured me I would feel when—not if—I met the one. A triumphant smile wanted to break free, but I contained it, not wanting to offend anyone. Finally, my duty was complete. I breathed deeply of freedom, ready to go back to my room.

Behind me, the Elders moved, reminding me of their presence. My mood shifted. The anger and betrayal from their lack of warning resurfaced. With a stiff back and tight mouth, I made my way toward the door and the waiting Elders. I didn't meet any of their eyes.

Sam had hours during the drive to say something but hadn't, and now all of his secrecy had been for nothing. I hadn't found a Mate. Did he realize the pointlessness of his gesture? I seriously doubted telling me in advance would have changed the outcome other than to make me nervous during the drive up. That, however, would mean I shouldn't be mad at him so I quickly disregarded the thought. Honesty was honesty. He should have told me.

Walking the dirt path, which I realized I'd tread over several times in my socks, I saw a peculiar shadow on the ground melding with the shadow of the still open door.

I looked up at the space behind the door and saw the flash of eyes just before a man stepped into view. I froze. My stomach dropped, and my heart did a strange little flip. Before I could take my next breath, a shiver ran up my spine and gooseflesh rose on my arms. My anger spiked, uncontrolled.

"You have got to be kidding," I whispered to myself without thinking. I'd been so close to escaping.

His filthy long, dark hair trailed in front of his eyes and shadowed his face into obscurity. An old, dull-green army jacket, just as filthy as his hair, hung from his frame while his bare feet shone pale against the black sweats he wore. I couldn't tell his age, the color of his hair, or the color of his eyes—because of the tangle of hair—but I could see the glint of them as he moved away from the door.

He stalked toward me. I remained frozen and tried to deny the significance of the encounter as my stomach continued to do crazy little flips. Just before he reached me, he turned away and walked around the corner of the building, heading not into the woods as the rest had, but to the front of the building.

I stared after him, momentarily confused. He'd recognized me. Just as I had him. Why had he turned away? Did it matter? Move! Escape before he changed his mind!

Finally, my feet obeyed, and I lurched toward the door.

"Sam, I've more than fulfilled any obligation I had to you or the pack. I'd like to leave tonight." The Elders stepped aside before I bowled them over.

I rushed past them, through the Introduction room and into the interior hall. There I paused to pull off my dirt-caked socks. Charlene would have me cleaning floors if I walked through the halls in my filthy socks.

Maneuvering through the fortuitously quiet and empty halls, I struggled to control my emotions. Over the years, I'd learned control, knowing those around me would be able to smell things like fear, anger, lust, or even sadness. But tonight all that control evaporated. Anger and fear swamped me.

Anger at Sam for arranging the whole damn thing, and fear that the Elders knew what had just happened.

I'd been so close to freedom. Sam had set me up, stacking the odds against me with the sheer number of werewolves in attendance. Why would it have to be the very last one I saw that sent a bolt of lightning right into my stomach? Was it too much to ask for just one break in my life?

Self-pity began to flood me, but then a spark of hope surfaced. Could it be possible that no one noticed? Maybe they had attributed my reaction to the way he looked. I turned a corner, almost to our rooms. If I didn't acknowledge him in front of others, then it didn't count...right?

Once in the apartment, I headed straight to my room and grabbed my bag from the bed. Thankfully, I hadn't unpacked.

Moving quickly, I went to Sam's bed and zipped his bag closed just as he walked through the door. His slightly mussed, grey hair gave away his agitation. Good. He deserved a little bit of it to match my own.

He met my gaze. I resented that he did so now, after the Introduction was complete, and he'd gotten his way.

"Now, Gabby," he started in his soothing tone.

"Stop." I held up a hand to forestall anything else he had to say and to keep my temper in check. He might not know he'd gotten his way. Even if he did know, he didn't deserve the pithy remarks running through my head. He deserved my respect for all he'd done for me in the past and for everything from which he'd shielded me. Still, I wasn't going to listen to any more tonight. Amazingly, he didn't try to continue.

"Are you driving me or not?" I asked as I picked up his bag.

He held out his hand. I surrendered the bag and wondered what I'd do once we got home. I still had a whole summer ahead of me. A summer filled with two jobs and roommate interviews. Would Sam still let me leave like I'd planned?

I followed him out the door and closed it softly behind me. I knew I couldn't escape this place permanently because of my tie to these people, but I hoped not to see it again for a long while.

Sam's easy stride annoyed me within two steps. Was he stalling? I took matters in my own hands and strode past him to get to the entrance.

The longer we stayed, the more likely I'd run into that guy again. According to the information I'd gleaned over the years, he shouldn't have turned away in the first place. Maybe he hadn't been attracted to me.

In the entry, I stuck bare feet into my sneakers, which felt wrong, but I didn't want to waste time to stop and put on socks. A part of the heel folded under and wedged itself behind my foot. I was taking too long. Scalp prickling with tension, I struggled to pull the crimped back out. Why had I crammed my foot into the stupid thing? I took my shoe off, fixed it, and slipped it back on as my gaze darted around the room searching for any sign of *him*.

Sam had continued his leisurely pace and just stepped into the entry as I tugged on the door.

Nerves strung tight, I almost screamed at the sight of someone standing there illuminated by the yard light. Instead, I only stopped abruptly. Not someone. Many someone's crowded the porch. A whole group of werewolves. For that split second, when I'd opened the door, I thought that man had returned for me.

The men fortunately didn't notice my near heart attack or me. They were too busy watching something in the parking lot.

Standing shoulder to shoulder, they blocked my view. I didn't really care what had them so engrossed; I wanted to go home.

I heard Sam behind me, muttered a quick "excuse me," and moved around the small group. It took me less than a second to spot the object of their attention. Once I did, I couldn't look away.

Sam's truck had exploded. Ok, maybe not literally, but that's what it looked like at first glance. The detached hood leaned against the right front fender. Dark shapes littered the ground directly in front of the truck. My mouth popped open when I realized I was looking at scattered pieces of the truck's guts. Little pieces, big pieces, some covered in sludge. Deep inside, I groaned a desperate denial. Not Sam's truck. I needed it.

A clanking sound drew my attention from the carnage to the form bent over the front grill. He did this, the last man I'd met. He studied the gaping hole that had once lovingly cradled an engine—one with enough life to drive me home.

"Gabby, honey," Sam said from behind me, causing me to jump. "I don't think he wants you to go just yet."

My heart sank. Not only did the man's actions scream loud and clear "she's mine" but Sam's calm statement confirmed my worst fear. The Elders had noticed. My stomach clenched with dread for a moment, and I wrestled with my emotions. No, it didn't matter who noticed. I wasn't giving up or giving in. I'd told Sam I'd come to the Introductions. I had never agreed to follow their customs.

"There's more than one vehicle here," I said.

"If we go inside to ask anyone else, we'll come back to more vehicular murder."

I turned to look at Sam. He watched the man and his truck. He was right. I couldn't ask anyone else to deal with this guy's obvious mental disorder. As soon as that thought entered my mind, I felt a little guilty. I usually didn't judge people. I preferred to avoid them altogether. But this guy made himself hard to ignore.

"Fine." I shouldered my bag, turned, and walked toward the main gate, pretending I didn't hear Sam's warning.

"You won't get far," he said softly behind me.

The yard light's glow didn't extend under the branches canopied over the Compound's dirt road. Crickets sang and night creatures distantly rustled in the undergrowth. With a hint of anxiety, I marched toward the distinct boundary between light and dark. The dark didn't concern me as much as the things hiding within it. But my fear of that grimy man overshadowed any concern I had about crossing over that boundary. Darkness blanketed me. I slowed while my eyes adjusted.

I used my other sight to watch for signs of pursuit. None of the sparks from the yard moved to follow me.

My fear kept me walking for miles. No werewolves ever entered within the perimeter of my sight though I thought I spotted a bear. Maybe a werewolf escort wouldn't have been so bad.

Hours later, tired beyond imagining and satisfied that Sam's dire predictions had turned out to be false, I spotted a motel ahead. The empty parking lot screamed vacancy better than the creepy, flickering red sign mounted in the office's window. My feet and legs hurt too much to ignore the opportunity to rest. Sighing, I pushed open the office door and rented a room for the night using the emergency cash I always carried. My plan remained simple enough. In the morning, I would find the nearest bus station and buy a ticket home or as close to home as possible.

Key in hand, I walked to my door and let myself in. A damp, musty smell engulfed me. I stretched out a hand and patted the wall until I found the switch. I grimaced at the room. It didn't inspire any thoughts of recently washed sheets. I kicked off my shoes and set them near the door. About an hour into the walk, I'd stopped to put on socks, and as I padded across the dirty carpet toward the bathroom, I was thankful for their protection.

The shower curtain looked brand new, but the tub and floor hadn't seen a scrub brush in a long time. I used the toilet but didn't look at it closely before or after. Sometimes ignorance was bliss.

The water dripping from the faucet had stained the porcelain brown. So I let it run while I dug through my bag. My stomach rumbled, and I regretted not grabbing some food before leaving. Ignoring my protesting stomach, I scrubbed my teeth. When the water ran clear, I spit and rinsed, smelling the water too late. Rotten eggs. Instead of wishing for food, I wished I'd just left the toothpaste in my mouth.

I wanted to go home where a clean bed waited, where inadvertently swallowing water from the bathroom sink wouldn't put me in the hospital, where I could pretend this weekend never happened.

Purposely not thinking of anything but the present, I left the bathroom light on and moved to the main room. I set my bag on a chair, turned off the light, collapsed fully dressed on the bed, and pleaded with the universe that nothing gross contaminated the coverlet.

The drama of my day had taken its toll. My eyelids refused

to stay open. Grossed out and hungry, my last thoughts were of the creepy guy at the front desk and chaining the motel door.

I STRETCHED, only half awake, and fell off the bed. For a queen-size bed, I must have rolled around on it a lot to work myself so close to the edge. Laughing at myself in the darkness, I pulled myself back up on the mattress and winced at the soreness in my legs. I paused. Darkness? My stomach flipped in fear as I remembered the light I'd left on in the bathroom.

I blindly stretched out my arm. There should have been a wall near this side of the bed. The door to my room swung open. Light flooded in, blinding me.

A shadow moved to block the light, and I suffered a moment of disoriented panic. Was it the man from the front desk? By my third squinted blink, I saw Sam standing silhouetted by light. Behind him, I spotted his foldout bed.

"You okay?" he asked.

"What am I doing here?" I turned and looked at my familiar room at the Compound.

"Dunno," he mumbled. "He brought you back before dawn. Didn't say a word, just knocked on the door carrying you. I let him in. He set you on your bed then left." Sam's hair stuck up in places, and he absently scratched the hair on his chest, wobbling a bit as he stood in his flannel house pants. He needed his coffee.

I looked down at myself. Dirt stained my clothes as if he'd dragged me all the way back here from the motel...by my feet...through mud. I reached up to comb my fingers through my hair, and a leaf fluttered to the floor. I stared at it in disbelief and let my hands drop back to my sides. He'd left me looking like a wreck. What was going on with this guy?

"What happened after I left? Did he follow me?" I watched Sam closely. If he didn't respond with complete honesty, I wouldn't be responsible for what I said next.

"Not right away. When you started walking, he looked up from the truck and watched down the road for a while. Long after you passed from sight anyway. Then, he just took to the woods, leaving my truck in a heap."

Apparently, he wouldn't let me go easily. Not that walking half the night had been easy. It also meant he'd left after I'd walked far enough that I could no longer see his spark. He'd probably tracked me by scent, keeping his distance. Clever. But why?

I needed to talk to him and figure out what he wanted. There were probably new rules—his rules—that I needed to learn, too. My impotent frustration grew. Better to get it done now so I could figure out a way out of this mess.

"Where is he?"

"Gabby. Before you do anything else, I'd like two minutes of your time. You need to hear what I have to say."

My anger at Sam still lay in a dark, dormant pool inside me. I didn't want to listen to anything he had to say. Some of my anger and frustration collapsed in on itself as I acknowledged the truth. Sam's dishonesty bothered me, but my brush with freedom, to have it so close and then ripped away in the last few seconds, hurt more. Besides, if I didn't hear him out, I'd wonder what he had wanted to tell me. Defeated, I agreed.

"Fine, but please hurry."

Sam turned and walked back to his bed. I followed.

"His name is Clay," Sam said, sitting on the lumpy mattress.

"Clayton Michael Lawe." He looked up at me as I moved closer and eyed me from head to toe.

In the brighter light of the living area, I really did look like I'd been dragged, or at least rolled, in mud. How had I slept through someone carrying me for miles?

"He's twenty-five and completely alone. His mother died when he was young. An accident. Shot by a hunter while she was in her fur. His dad took him to the woods."

That meant he'd been raised more wolf than boy. Sam had explained much of the recent pack history to me when we'd first started coming to the Compound. They'd only maintained enough of the original buildings to keep up appearances and used the 360 acres that came with it to live as wolves. Charlene's arrival had brought about huge changes, mostly in the social aspect of the pack. Afterward, most pack members started acclimating to their skin. Only a few of the old school werewolves still preferred their fur.

"His father died a few years back," Sam continued, pulling me from my own thoughts. "Clay's been on his own ever since, still choosing to live in his fur more than his skin. He's quiet and has never been trouble. He comes when an Elder calls for him but still claims no pack as his own. So, by pack law, he's considered Forlorn."

Forlorn. I closed my eyes tiredly and recalled my werewolf history.

Prior to Charlene, the decimated numbers had only supported one main pack in Canada and a few packs overseas. Over the last two decades, the Canadian pack had grown enough to consider splitting their numbers.

Because of the dangers of discovery, joining a pack ensured an individual's safety and continuity for the pack. Some, like

Clay, stubbornly remained reclusive. The majority of those who stayed solitary did so because they disagreed with the changes Charlene had helped to establish. Many felt the superiority of the pack entitled them to an elitist isolation from humanity and the world.

By staying on his own, Clay had effectively stated his opinion on the pack's reentry into human society. However, Sam's comment about never being trouble meant Clay had not yet actually sided with the other opinionated Forlorn.

Yet Forlorn, not having a link to a pack, still had the link to the Elders. A link all werewolves shared. Elders acted as the lawmakers and enforcers for all werewolves while the pack leader enforced the rules for the pack, settling disputes. Elders and pack leaders worked hand in hand to keep the pack healthy and growing. Though a pack leader did not control any Forlorn, the base society rules laid down by the Elders still bound them.

According to Sam, a werewolf could not break their society laws. Once an Elder declared a law, it became an ingrained piece of the werewolf. Sam had compared it to a hypnotist. The werewolves heard the law, could contemplate it, have opinions about it, but followed the law regardless of their thoughts and feelings. Most laws made sense and werewolves didn't try to fight them, but even when a werewolf disagreed with a law, there was no choice other than to obey it.

At least, no one had proven otherwise. However, I'd overheard Sam speaking with another Elder about several instances where a Forlorn had ignored certain aspects of their laws, which made the relationship between the pack and Forlorn even more strained.

Sam sighed and rubbed a hand over his face.

"He was here last night to help keep the peace. He didn't come to be Introduced to you."

At least that explained his presence by the door and not in the line with the rest of them. My conspiracy theory that Sam had set me up shriveled.

"There are two things I can promise you. Though he is technically Forlorn, he's always followed pack rules. He has no issue with humans. With him, you are safe. His control over the change is unusually strong."

When over stimulated, the change could burst upon a werewolf with less than adequate control. Sam had drilled that into me when I first started hanging out with Paul and Henry unsupervised. He didn't want me to freak out if one of them went wolf on me for no reason. He'd stressed that whether in their fur or in their skin, they had the same intelligence and instinct. The change was just a defense mechanism because in their fur, they had teeth and claws to fight. So, what he meant was Clay had control, and he kept his emotions in check.

"And he won't give up," Sam added.

Clay hadn't been looking for a Mate like most werewolves did once they reached puberty. Did that give me any advantage? I doubted it. Sam had repeatedly stressed that instinct ruled this business. And fighting instinct proved extremely difficult for werewolves. So Sam's final warning was a given. Once they scented their Mate, they couldn't turn back. I sighed. Why couldn't werewolves get strategically-timed head colds like the rest of us?

"All right, where is he?"

"I think he's still tinkering with my truck. Try there."

Sam slid back under his covers, and I turned off the lights for him before walking out the door. My sock-covered feet, the only thing on me that didn't seem too dirty, muffled the sound of my passing. By the front door, I found my mud-caked shoes and put them on. They hadn't been that dirty when I'd taken them off at the motel. I couldn't believe he'd put them back on me before abducting me. Had I really been that tired? Maybe there'd been something wrong with that water. But why were my shoes caked with mud if he'd carried me?

CHAPTER FIVE

When I stepped out the door, the sun, already high in the cloudless sky, shone brightly. Moving off the porch, I closed my eyes for a moment and tilted my head back to soak in the warmth. The sound of a ratchet drew me back to my purpose.

I found Clay right where Sam had said, his torso bent over the grill of the pickup. He looked closely at the engine. Purposefully relaxing my shoulders, I started toward the truck. The yard was empty compared to yesterday. It left Clay more room to spread out the pieces he continued to remove.

Slowing my approach, I studied him a bit. The mid-day sun didn't make him look any better than he had in last night's shadows. He still wore that heavy jacket, despite the warm day, and some type of very dirty, baggy cargo pants. His bare feet looked surprisingly clean after walking miles last night, then carrying or dragging me back.

I looked at his feet again, then down at my shoes. No way! How were his feet cleaner than my shoes? He couldn't have worn my shoes; his feet were bigger than mine. Didn't Sam just tell me he had complete control over his change? Couldn't he have partially shifted his feet? Maybe. It still didn't explain how I slept through being carried.

He continued his examination of the truck. I knew he could hear me coming, but I waited to speak until I stood next to the detached hood.

"We weren't officially introduced last night. My name's Gabby. Gabrielle May Winters." I tucked my hands in my back pockets and hoped I wouldn't have to shake his hand or anything.

He straightened, turned toward me, and gave me his undivided attention. I didn't think it possible, but he was even dirtier than I'd first believed. Long hair hung in clotted strands obscuring his eyes while his unkempt facial hair covered the rest of his face. I kept my thoughts about his hygiene to myself.

At no less than six feet to my five-five, he intimidated me, and I fought not to show it. His continued silence didn't help matters. It puzzled me until I remembered Sam's comments about his upbringing. Maybe he didn't even have the social skills to return a greeting.

There had to be a way out of this. Please let there be a way out of this.

"Sam said that your name is Clay." I waited for some type of acknowledgement, but didn't get one. He just continued to look at me. At least, I assumed I had his attention. I couldn't really see his eyes to know for sure.

"Listen, Clay, I know you think I'm the one for you..."

I decided to change my approach. Choosing my words carefully, I started again.

"I don't have a sense of smell to depend on, like you do. Although the Elders say to trust the instinct of werewolves, I don't trust blindly."

He didn't move. How was I supposed to know if he understood what I was saying? We stood maybe five feet apart with the front quarter panel of the truck separating us. I couldn't read his expression or anything in his body language to hint at what he might be thinking. I decided just to say what I wanted.

"I really want to go home. If I asked to borrow someone else's car, would it live?"

He turned away and continued with his examination of the truck, his body language, finally, easy to translate.

"Ok. I'll take that as a no," I mumbled more to myself than him.

He surprised me by turning back toward me again. I struggled to decipher his mood from his face. His ridiculously long and shaggy facial hair obliterated any trace of a smile or frown.

"Clay, I'm not trying to be rude here, but I'm struggling to figure us out. What's the plan?"

No visible response.

"Am I just supposed to stay here until you decide I'm not really your Mate?" I hated saying that word.

Again, nothing.

"Would it help speed things along if we spent a little time together?"

This time a shrug. One-way conversations rarely worked well when trying to get to know someone.

"Do you talk?"

And again, I lost his attention to the truck engine.

"Ok. No talking. Got it."

Did being raised in his fur mean he'd turned feral? The thought of spending time with a Tarzan mentality werewolf worried me. Who knew what he might do? Only Sam's assurance of my safety eased my fear before it could fully take hold. No, he couldn't be feral. He appeared to understand everything I said. For whatever reason, it seemed that Clay had no intention to speak to me.

I sighed, pulled my hands from my back pockets, and leaned against the truck. Chin in hands, I watched him check the different fluids.

"You seemed to like the idea of spending time to get to know each other," I said. He turned toward me again. "But what's the point in spending time together if you don't want to talk to me? Isn't the point to get to know one another?"

And he turned back to the truck. Good to know the windshield washer fluid was getting low.

Frustrated, I wanted to kick a truck tire but figured I'd just hurt my toe. Instead, I walked back to the main entrance. The one-sided conversation hadn't given me any useful information. Why keep me here if he didn't want to talk to me? And he obviously wanted me here. First, he'd killed Sam's truck. Then, he'd brought me back to the Compound in the middle of the night after letting me walk for hours. That reminded me...I needed a shower badly.

Inside, the hallways remained empty. I let myself into the quiet apartment. Sam no longer curled under his covers. His bed was made. He'd probably left in search of coffee.

I grabbed some clean clothes, headed to the bathroom, and cringed at the sight of myself in the mirror. He wouldn't speak and dragged me through mud and leaves. How exactly was that a good start to a relationship? I spent longer under the hot spray than I would have liked as I tried to work the leaf debris from my hair. Too late, I concluded brushing the leaves out first would have been better.

Someday, I'd have to get the full story about how I got so dirty. But how could I? He wouldn't speak to me. He seemed willing to listen though...until I said something he didn't like. When I talked about talking, he stopped listening. Did that mean he wanted me to do all the conversing? It made sense that he wouldn't really want to reveal anything about himself given what Sam had mentioned about his childhood. I could empathize. There wasn't much I wanted to share with a stranger about my childhood either.

I tugged on the last of my clean clothes, a pair of cotton shorts (I'd been counting on a lounge day) and a tank top. Having planned a three-day weekend, I hadn't packed much. I balled up the dirty clothes, tossed them into a plastic bag, and set it by the bedroom door. Hopefully, Sam's washing machine could take the abuse.

I sat on the edge of my bed and, swinging my bare feet over the carpet, thought over my options. Stay and accept my fate or find a way back home to continue with the plans I'd made for my own future? Sure, I could stay and make an effort to understand and learn more about Clay. But I'd already made my plans. How fair was it to expect me to change them? If Clay truly lived in the wild, it wasn't as if he had any plans. Maybe he didn't even understand the concept of planning. Could I possibly talk Clay into letting me go? He didn't seem too fond of me.

Absently, I started to towel dry my hair. When I had hinted we might not be Mates, he hadn't turned away. Did that mean he had doubts too? If he did, maybe I had a chance.

Determined, I tossed the towel aside and stood. Due to the

pull I had on human men, I'd honed my skills of reason and avoidance. If reasoning didn't work, I avoided them. This would be no different. Piece of cake.

I gave myself a pep talk as I hurried through the halls. A few of the men I passed gave me curious glances. I remained focused on finding Clay, while thinking of, and rejecting, the possible reasons for his doubt.

The main door swung open with a nudge. I hopped off the porch into the sun and winced when my bare feet met with the sharp gravel. Too absorbed in my purpose, I hadn't thought of shoes. Resolute, I tiptoed across the parking area as quickly as possible.

Clay still tinkered with the truck. However, when he heard me, he turned to watch my approach. Other than a few quick glances at him to ensure he didn't leave, I focused on placing my feet in the smoother areas where tire treads had cleared the stone and left sand behind. My ill-timed, stiff steps made a prancing dance. I hoped no one had a video camera.

As I neared, he took a shop rag from his pocket and set it on the ground near the truck. I paused mid-prance and looked down at the soiled rag. I'd just showered. What was with getting me dirty? Not a fair thought. My soles were probably already filthy. The insistent bite of the gravel decided it. I stepped onto the rag, wiping my feet on the grease and carbon stained surface to dislodge the piercing shards still stuck to them. The relief made it worthwhile.

"Thanks," I said looking up at him.

Since he'd set the rag directly in front of the truck, I stood closer to him than I would have liked. I could see brown eyes staring at me from behind the stringy hair. He studied me intently, and I felt that strange pull in my stomach again. It reminded me of my problem. We had an obvious connection; one I didn't want and one he might not want. Maybe, instead of trying to figure out why he might doubt our connection, I needed to explain why I didn't want it in terms he could relate too as a Forlorn werewolf.

Taking a breath, I plunged into a lie. I knew I played with fire. Living with Sam had taught me werewolves could sense a lie through increased heart rate, smell of fear, or anxiety. But, the simple beauty of the situation—the dash across the gravel, which had elevated my pulse—made the lie hard to detect.

"Sam just told me that you're to be confined to a room for the remainder of the day. With me. They want to see how we react to each other so they can determine if you really do have a Claim to me."

A low growl rumbled from him before I finished speaking.

"What? You don't want to spend time with me?"

He stopped his growling and looked down at my feet on the rag. I glanced at them too and noted what the gravel hadn't done, the rag had. They were filthy again. If Charlene found me walking though the hallways with feet this dirty, she'd give me an earful.

I looked back up at him. "You do want to spend time with me, don't you?"

He shrugged, still looking down. Not staring at my feet, then, but thinking. I continued to press my point before he caught on.

"So, it's not me. Don't you like being indoors?" He shrugged again, this time looking up at me. "Ok. If it's not me, and not being indoors, then what?" I let the question hang briefly before I said what I already knew. Ultimately, Forlorn didn't join packs because...

"You don't want to be told when or how to spend time with me. You don't want someone telling you what to do. Is that right?"

He didn't look away. Didn't move at all.

"Yeah, me either."

I watched him closely, waiting for some sign he understood I'd lied to him. His motionlessness felt like a standoff and temporarily shriveled my hope. Maybe there was no reasoning with Clay. No, I just chose the wrong tract.

Ignoring the pain, I stepped off the rag and bent down to pick it up. I shook it out and handed it back to him.

"I'm sorry I lied to you, Clay. I thought maybe if you knew how it felt to have your choices taken from you, you'd understand why I want to leave. It's nothing personal."

He took the rag from me and turned back to the truck. Someone had brought him more tools, and he was in the process of taking something off what I assumed was the engine. He picked up a ratchet and started to loosen a bolt.

His inattention didn't deter me. I had to keep trying.

"Your instincts say I'm the one. I don't have those instincts. Instead, I just keep thinking how I don't even know you. And the little bit Sam's told me...that you spend most of your time in your fur, doesn't help me understand how there can be an us. I have no fur. I can't just run off into the woods with you." The clicking of the ratchet began to slow. He listened.

"I've enrolled in college—one I chose—despite Sam's opposition. Do you know why I picked it? Because it was far enough away that I knew it'd be harder for people to tell me what to do. Major decisions, up until this point, have been made by others based on what they thought would be best for me. Sure, they ask me what I think and try to consider it, but not always. How do you think Sam got me to Introductions for the past two years? It wasn't by asking me each time if I felt like going."

The ratcheting stopped, but he remained facing the engine.

"I don't mean to sound heartless. I've been through enough Introductions to know what they mean to your kind. I'm not trying to throw your traditions back in your face. I'm just asking for some compromise. Don't ask me to forget the one thing I've chosen on my own."

My pleading didn't appear to sway him any further so I switched tactics and offered him a little hope.

"If you're serious about me, then come to the city with me and learn while I learn. We can get to know each other. I need that in order to even consider there being an us." He still didn't move. Frustration crept into my words. "I know I'm asking a lot. You'd need to start talking, stop growling, and bathe. No offense meant, but you look like a crazy man the way you are."

He moved slightly as if I'd poked him in the ribs. So he did understand how bad he looked. Inside, I jumped up and down on the balls of my feet, clapping my hands excitedly. I leaned against the truck to take some weight off my bare feet and pressed my case further.

"I know it wouldn't be easy on you. You'll be surrounded by people. It'll probably be uncomfortable after you've been on your own for so long. But we'd be able to spend time together, to get to know each other—the normal, human way—and see how things go. We'd both be giving a little, then. Well, you'd be giving a little more, but...will you think about it?" I didn't wait for his reaction. I turned and walked back to the Compound. It had to work. Please let it work.

I spent about five minutes trying to wipe my feet clean on

one of the entry rugs before I gave up and walked back to my room. My speech continued to run through my head. Either it would work or not. We both knew I couldn't live in the woods. He would need to rejoin society. He'd see I wasn't worth the effort.

With a mental sigh, I pushed it from my thoughts and focused on the present. I planned to lounge in the apartment and finish the novel I'd started over a month ago. My stomach rumbled loudly. And eat.

THE NEXT MORNING I woke early. I'd grown so bored reading the day before that I'd gone to bed by eight. So it was no surprise when I opened my eyes and saw my phone flashed five a.m. Sam would kill me if I woke him up. I only hesitated a moment before I threw back the covers and got out of bed. In the pitch-dark room, I managed to pull my zipper hoodie on over my tank top, tiptoe to my door, and open it without a sound.

I only managed three steps into the living room when the light near the sofa clicked on, blinding me for a moment.

"Doesn't anyone sleep around here?"

"Sorry. I should know better than to try not to wake you." His hearing made him a very light sleeper.

"What are you doing up already?" He sat up and ran his hands through his hair as if trying to wake himself up more.

I doubted it would work and didn't think he would appreciate an offer to make him coffee given the time. He'd rather just go back to bed.

"I was going to check on the truck. He had it mostly taken

apart yesterday afternoon. I wanted to see if he'd started putting it back together."

"What did you say to him yesterday?" Sam surprised me by getting out of bed and stripping the sheets. We always changed the bedding just before we left so it was ready in case anyone else ever used the rooms. But it was five a.m....

"What do you mean?" I took a few steps backward to lean against my door and watched his progress. He almost tripped over his bag while pulling off the fitted sheet.

"Do you want me to start some coffee?" It wasn't normal for werewolves to be anything less than agile. Coffee couldn't be good for him.

"No, I'm fine," he said, answering my last question first. "I mean, he asked for the keys to the truck last night and brought them back earlier this morning. Truck's fixed. I checked myself. So, I'm wondering what you said to him."

My mouth popped open. I couldn't believe he'd actually listened to me. A silly smile tugged at my mouth. Did this really mean he'd let me go? My barely formed smile faded. Or would I just wake up back in this apartment tomorrow morning if I tried to leave?

Sam continued to remake the bed with the clean sheets from the hidden compartment in the matching sofa ottoman.

There had to be a catch. Sam had told me a tied pair didn't part until completing the Claim. When Clay had scented me, and I'd recognized him openly, the Elders saw us as a pair. They, in turn, announced it to everyone over their mental link. Every werewolf, whether in a pack or Forlorn, recognized our tie. If my words truly changed Clay's mind, great—but Sam's question caused me to begin to doubt that possibility, and I struggled to come up with what I'd overlooked.

"The truth," I said answering Sam's question. "Let's say he is my Mate. He's an uneducated man from the backwoods. How are we going to live? I can't turn on the fur like you guys can and live as a wolf like he's done for most of his life. Where does that leave us? I just pointed out that I had to go to school to get the education I needed to land a good job to support myself because he can't."

Sam had stopped remaking the bed and looked at me in disbelief.

"Well, I said it nicer than that."

He gave me a disappointed look.

"You don't know anything about him, Gabby. He may have lived most of his life in his fur, but it doesn't mean he isn't intelligent or that he's more wolf than man. You may have caused yourself more trouble than you intended."

I shifted against the door. "Hold on, I didn't say either of those things to him." Granted, I did tell him he needed to bathe. "And what do you mean 'more trouble'?"

"He said that you suggested he live with you so you could get to know each other better."

I froze in disbelief. That is not what I said.

"Wait. Did he actually talk to you?"

"Well, I had to put on my fur to understand him since he was in his, but yes."

Sam's kind communicated in several ways when in their fur —typically, through body language or howls. Claimed and Mated pairs shared a special bond using an intuitive, mental link. Once establishing a Claim, the pair could sense strong emotions as well as each other's location. Mated pairs had the same ability to communicate with each other as the Elders had with everyone in the pack.

I closed my eyes and thought back to my exact wording.

"I didn't say we should live together, but that he should come back with me to get an education." Fine, I hadn't worded it well, but how did he get "hey, we should live together" out of that?

"Like I said, you've got trouble." He gave me another disappointed look, folded the bed back into the sofa, then picked up his bag from the floor. He strode to the bathroom and closed the door on any further conversation.

Crap. I needed to talk to Clay again and find out what he intended. I'd been counting on his feral upbringing and his need for freedom to cause him to reject my suggestion—a suggestion that hadn't included him living with me. I'd meant he should find a place nearby so we could go through the motions of human dating, which was the extent of my willingness to compromise. I hadn't thought he'd take any of it seriously but that, instead, he would just let me go.

I left the apartment and stole through the deserted hallways. At the main door, I paused to put on shoes then stepped out into the pre-dawn darkness. The yard light cast shadows near the vehicles. I stood on the porch for a moment but heard nothing.

Cautiously walking across the empty expanse, I found the repaired truck, but no Clay. My stomach knotted as I studied the truck. Sam's words about Clay's intelligence haunted me. A man raised in the wild knew how to dismantle and reassemble an engine. I'd underestimated him. No matter which way I looked at it, it all pointed back to the fact I didn't know enough about Clay to try to guess what he'd do next.

Back in the apartment, Sam waited, ready to leave. I didn't

bother with a shower but remade the bed and grabbed my own bag.

We made it back to the truck without any sign of Clay. Sensing my mood, Sam didn't say anything to me as I climbed in, and we started the long drive home.

It was several hours into the ride when I finally stopped looking behind us or stretching my second sight to search for werewolves. There'd been no sign of Clay following us, but there'd been no sign of Clay following me the night before last, either.

CHAPTER SIX

I was on edge the first week back, unsure if, or when, Clay would show up.

Desperate for distraction, I plunged into my two part-time jobs and worked as much as possible. I woke up early each morning, showered, ate breakfast, and packed a lunch, all long before Sam got out of bed. And because I still cared, I started his coffee before I walked out the door. In the evenings, a dark house greeted me when I returned home, worn out from the long day. Usually, Sam had something set aside for my dinner. I'd eat, go to bed, then start the cycle again the next morning.

I could have asked Sam if he knew what Clay planned, but he hadn't mentioned Clay since we'd left the Compound. I feared, if I brought it up, he would think I missed Clay or something. Since I didn't want Sam sending out a call that might cause Clay to show up when he otherwise wouldn't, I kept quiet. Worry ate at me; but, as time passed, and my hectic schedule successfully prevented thoughts of Clay, I started to feel safe again.

Three weeks before the start of school, I found the perfect

roommate, Rachel. I'd been watching the papers near school when I came across her ad for a roommate. We hit it off the first time we spoke on the phone. She attended the same school in which I'd enrolled and was going into her third year in the nursing program. She rented a two-bedroom house. Her roommate from the prior year had moved out after graduation. Rachel had tried living on her own over the summer, but the bills grew too expensive and the house too quiet.

After our call, I did some research and found the house wasn't in the best part of town, but I couldn't find anything closer that I could still afford. Plus, the unoccupied bedroom she offered came furnished with a bed and a dresser; I didn't own the bed I slept on now and didn't feel right taking it with me when I left. So, I called Rachel back and let her know I wanted the room.

Sunday, a week before school started, I once again packed my possessions, an old familiar routine I'd forgotten while living with Sam. Sam pretended not to care I was leaving, but I knew he did. I'd only stepped out of my room for a minute to grab my shampoo and brush from the bathroom, and when I walked back into the room, I caught him slipping some money into the emergency cash I kept hidden in a half-full tampon box in my dresser. He pretended to check the dresser as if ensuring I hadn't forgotten anything. I went along with it.

Packing didn't take long. Everything I owned fit into several messenger bags and an old suitcase I'd gotten at a secondhand store. By lunch, we had what I needed loaded into the back of Sam's truck. A passerby wouldn't have noticed the small pile.

After one last look around the house to make sure I had everything, we climbed into the truck and started the journey. Sam looked slightly depressed as he drove. Excitement filled me, but I fought hard to keep it from showing. I didn't think my joy would give him any comfort.

"You'll call me if you have any trouble?" Sam asked, yet again.

"Yes, Sam. But I'm over four hours from you. I'll need to face things on my own."

"Not on your own. Elder Joshua has moved nearby. I'll be able to contact him if you have a need."

Sam had mentioned Elder Joshua to me a few days after I'd found Rachel. I knew Elder Joshua's recent move was for me but didn't make any complaint. As long as he stayed away until I needed something, we'd get along just fine.

When we arrived, Rachel sat waiting on the front step of the small ranch house. She'd described herself on the phone as just over average height with brown hair and eyes. She'd left out everything else. Her deep, brown hair hung silky-straight, and the beautifully bronzed tone of her skin had me wondering if she had any African-American heritage. Her perfectly arched brows didn't appear tweezed or penciled, and they highlighted her darkly lashed eyes.

At about five-foot ten inches, she surpassed average height. Long, lean legs extended from her cutoffs, and her V-neck top showed sufficient cleavage to know she didn't need to stuff her bra, either. Overall, she was gorgeous enough to make a straight girl wonder if she should switch teams, and that worried the hell out of me. Oh, not that I'd switch teams. As annoying and obsessive as men were, I still preferred them. No, her attitude the first time a man overlooked her and focused on me, worried me. Let's face it. Pretty girls can be very mean.

I drew my brief gaze from her as she stood to watch Sam do

a Y-turn to back into the driveway. Using the side mirror of the truck, I studied the house.

A cracked and uneven sidewalk led to the front steps. Faded yellow aluminum siding and brown trim gave the small house a slightly run down look. Rachel had mentioned room dimensions to me to prepare me. After living at Sam's place, this house did appear small from the outside. Only two windows adorned the front of the house. There was a large picture window, which probably meant a living room, and, on the side of the house close to the driveway, a much smaller window. With the shade half-drawn, I assumed it belonged to a bedroom. How many houses had just two windows on their front? At least, they looked new, as did the roof.

As Sam backed into the driveway, I smiled and waved to Rachel. She walked toward the truck while Sam parked.

"Hi! Gabby, right?" Rachel said with an excited smile.

"Yes." I opened my door and stepped out of the truck. She caught me off guard by pulling me into an embrace. With my arms pinned to my sides, I fought the urge to pull back. "I hope you're Rachel." With that, she let me escape from her exuberant hug.

"I'm so glad to see you look so normal," she said looking even happier than she had a moment ago. "I was worried I'd end up with someone weird when I put that ad in the paper." Ah, that explained the happiness. Too bad, she had no idea how "weird" I was.

Sam came around from his side of the truck.

"Rachel, this is my grandpa, Sam."

"Hi, Sam!"

He quickly extended his hand for a friendly handshake, and I hid my smile. He'd noticed her boisterous hug.

Rachel clasped his hand. "Would you like to come in and see the place before we carry everything in?" She darted a puzzled look at the back of the truck.

I smiled. "We'll be able to carry it in and take a tour at the same time. I don't have much."

We grabbed my bags and walked around to the front of the house. The door opened to a tiny entry, with the vacant bedroom immediately to the right, a small hall closet straight ahead, and the living room to the left.

We all stepped into my room to set down my things. I'd been correct about the window being a bedroom window.

As Rachel had promised, my room came furnished with a full-sized bed. I had just enough space around it to walk. Accustomed to a twin, it seemed overly large. Thankfully, I had the correct bedding for it. A gift from Sam. The closet was a small rectangle, but more than enough space for what I owned. The only other piece of furniture—a small, battered wood dresser—leaned against the interior wall. Nothing decorated the walls, which Rachel said she'd done on purpose, so I could add my own flair to the room.

Rachel gave us the grand tour of the five-room house. The living room was long, but not very deep, and occupied the rest of the front of the house. Rachel had it tastefully decorated. Two sets of curtains hung in the picture window. The soft cream-colored ones faced the road, while the inside set matched the color of the worn, brown leather couch centered in front of the window. Square, wooden end tables held cream-colored lamps with matching shades and crowded each end of the couch.

A chair, set at a sharp angle against the interior wall, used the remaining space in the living room. The TV wall she'd painted a medium brown while the standard off-white covered the rest of the walls, which included my bedroom and the entry. A large, dark-brown rug, a shade close to the color of the couch and the curtains, covered all but a small swath of the living room's beige carpet. Overall, the room looked comfortable.

Through the living room's arched doorway, on the same wall as the TV, a small hallway connected the living room, her bedroom, a tiny linen closet, the kitchen, the bathroom, and the door to the basement.

Rachel turned left and briefly showed her room, the larger of the two bedrooms. Then she turned us and opened the door between the living room arch and the bathroom. She flicked on the basement light and told me we had our own washer and dryer and plenty of room for storage.

She gave the bathroom, opposite her room, a quick wave. "It's small, but it could be worse."

I noted that, although the bathroom measured half the size of the one at Sam's place, it didn't feel cramped. The pedestal sink, tub, and toilet abutted the wall shared with my bedroom. White tile covered the walls to about midway, except for the shower area where the tiles ran from tub to ceiling. Dark-blue paint coated the walls and offset the overabundance of white. She'd also defused the white of the plastic shower curtain by layering a dark-blue, cloth shower curtain over it and used a cute, white flower clip to swag it to the side. Everything looked neat and clean.

Finally, she led us to the kitchen. An addition there extended the room five feet into the backyard and brought it from worthless to functional. Just inside the kitchen arch, to the right, a table for four sat against the interior wall. Along the wall that faced the driveway, a wall-to-wall counter supported the sink and provided four cupboards. Two separate wall cupboards hung on either side of the sink, allowing light through the kitchen's only window. The refrigerator stood to the left of the arched kitchen entry, along with four more cupboards top and bottom. Standing free, the stove occupied the unclaimed space on the exterior wall. Just enough room separated the cabinetry from the stove to allow the bottom cabinet door to swing open. A garbage can hid between the stove and the door that led to the wooden deck and backyard.

Overall, the exterior condition of the house didn't match the inside. The exposed carpet in the living room looked worn but relatively stain-free. The walls and ceiling could use a fresh coat of paint, but with the string of switching roommates over the last five years, the landlord probably hadn't had a chance.

Rachel concluded the tour on the back deck.

"We'll take turns mowing the lawn and shoveling the snow, and since it's only a one-car garage, we'll switch parking, too. But we'll work that out when it starts snowing."

I nodded in agreement as I looked at our small backyard. A new looking barn-red wooden fence separated our yard from the neighbor's behind us while evergreen hedges barred the rest of the yard from the neighbor's on each side. With the deck and garage, there really wasn't a lot of grass to mow in back, but the front yard made up for it a bit. It reminded me of the Newton's place, and I suffered an uncomfortable moment of longing before I strangled the feeling.

During the tour, Sam had remained quiet as he followed us and scrutinized the house. Outside, he stood beside me, studying the backyard as well.

"Well, Gabby, looks like you'll be comfortable here. I'd better start heading back. You need anything, let me know." He patted my cheek and stepped off the deck, neither of us comfortable with drawn out goodbyes.

I watched him climb into his truck and waved when he looked back. Again, my emotions ran amuck for a few moments as he pulled away, nostalgia robbing me of my moment. I'd been so ready to leave and start out on my own I'd not inspected my feelings for Sam too closely. Now I knew. I'd miss him. A lot.

Rachel seemed to understand my mood as we went back into the house.

"You have a nice grandpa," she said, sitting on my bed as I unpacked.

I agreed and tried to shake the unhappiness that lingered. Less than five hours ago, I had looked forward to making my own rules. Here, in this house, I had the freedom I'd wanted. No more obligatory weekends in Canada. No meeting men I didn't want to meet. My internal pep talk began to work, and I started to unpack with more enthusiasm.

Rachel took a few of the wire hangers from the closet and helped hang the t-shirts I'd crammed into a bag.

"Please tell me there is more in these bags than t-shirts," she said. "I don't mind them—they're comfy—but where's the clothes for going out?"

"Um, I really don't own any." Watching her while I said it, I didn't miss the shocked expression that briefly flitted over her features. I looked over my small pile of clothes, most of them already on hangers thanks to her help. They lacked diversity. I'd never noticed before.

She changed the subject. "Got your bathing suit handy? With the backyard surrounded, the deck is perfect for working on a tan. Join me when you're done." Without waiting for my answer, she popped up from the bed and left the room.

Bathing suit? I didn't even own one. I finished unpacking and heard the back door a few minutes later.

Tucking my suitcase under the bed, I covered the mattress with the sheets from Sam. Instead of feeling sad, a new feeling bloomed. Resolve. I needed this, living here with Rachel, someone my own age. Well, close to it. And female. Normal things like lying out in the sun had escaped me over the years. She'd help me catch up. That she didn't seem adversely affected by me, gave me hope. Granted, she hadn't yet faced rejection from a man because of me. Maybe we could work on becoming friends first. Who knew, it could help prevent the ugly hostility I'd grown accustomed to. I liked the idea of having a real friend. Sure, I had Paul and Henry, but I wanted a friend of the same gender.

I changed into the shortest shorts I owned and a strapless top that Barb had given me for my eighteenth birthday. I'd kept in touch with my foster parents because of their insistence. Even though they had a beautiful little girl of their own, they still thought of me, especially on my birthday. Feeling light at heart, I headed out to the deck.

Rachel turned her sunglassed-gaze my way when I closed the screen door.

"Where's your suit?" she asked curiously.

"I don't own one," I admitted, lying on my stomach on the cartoon beach towel she'd laid out for me. "Didn't want to embarrass my grandpa. He's a little old school." Honestly, I kept my wardrobe modest because it was safe...and I hadn't wanted him to suggest I bring a swimsuit with me to Canada.

"Really? You don't own one?" She propped herself up on

her elbows and glanced at me over the top of her sunglasses. A wide smile spread over her lips. "Wanna go shopping? I'll use any excuse to go."

I hesitated. If I declined, we'd be starting out on a poor note. If I said yes, we'd most likely have an issue with guys somewhere along the way. But if I didn't say yes, how could I hope to win her over as a friend? Any normal girl probably wouldn't even stop to think about this. I really wanted to try for normal.

"Sure, let me go change," I agreed.

"Yay!" She jumped up, grabbed both towels, and danced into the house behind me.

Since she had the car, she drove us to an outlet mall that she promised was the best and cheapest place to shop. Stunning in a tank top, short shorts, and cute little sandals with a heel, she outshined my drab, worn t-shirt, jeans, and sneakers. Still, I twisted my fingers in my lap and tried to quell my worry.

"While we're here, we should look for some clubbing clothes for you." She pulled into an open space and parked the car. "And don't be afraid to tell me if I'm being too pushy. I love shopping, but have too many clothes already. By shopping for someone else, I get my fix without adding to the mayhem in my closet."

"No, you're not being pushy. I could use a swimsuit and a few new tops. But, I have to be honest...I'm not really into the party scene. Guys act too weird around me, and it makes me uncomfortable."

"Weird how?" she asked as she reached for the door.

"Wait."

She paused, turning to look at me.

I'd rather tell her where no one else would overhear. I took a deep breath. Normal. I needed to sound normal.

"Every friendship I've ever had was ruined by competition over a guy. Only problem was, I was never competing. I wasn't interested in the guy my friend was. But the guy was interested in me."

Behind her sunglasses, her eyes searched my face. I struggled not to squirm or look away. Anxiety bloomed. I should have kept my mouth shut.

Her lips curved into an amused smile, and she laughed.

"You're a serious one. I can see that already. Don't worry, Gabby. If a guy doesn't trip over himself to get to me, I'm not interested. I don't want to waste my time chasing what doesn't want to be caught." She opened the door to the sunbaked parking lot, and I followed.

We'd just crossed the black expanse, stepping onto the sidewalk in front of the stores, when Rachel nudged me.

"Check out this hottie."

The man she'd spotted exited the same door we headed for. As I expected, he first looked at Rachel then at me. I looked down and kept my eyes on the sidewalk as we strolled past him.

Rachel obviously didn't know about the "wait for the door to close" rule because she started laughing before I'd even made it over the threshold.

"He kept his eyes on you the entire time. I can't wait to see what happens the first time we go out."

I wanted to groan.

The clerk at the register glanced at us just then because of Rachel's laughter. His double take at me caused her to start laughing even harder. I pulled her toward the back of the store before he decided he wanted to talk to us. Her carefree attitude about my effect on men did bring a smile to my face. Maybe things would work out.

After helping me pick out a swimsuit, a rather daring bikini that she insisted would not cause her the least bit of animosity no matter what attention it brought me, she talked me into a few more stores.

In three hours, I'd purchased two "clubbing" tops and a black mini skirt. I probably wouldn't wear any of it. Sexy was a dangerous look for me. Heck, mildly attractive was even dangerous. But I liked spending the time with her. My careful spending slowed the process down a bit, but she didn't seem to mind.

Back at the house, the pleasantly warm breeze and inviting deck beckoned us, and we decided to catch the dying rays before calling it a night. Really, I just wanted to try on my bikini.

I shook my head at the sound of the back door opening and closing five minutes after being home. How she managed to change so fast amazed me. My new clothes hung in my closet, except for the bikini. Since I was pale from spending most of my summer working, Rachel had insisted I purchase a bright pink number with vibrant yellow straps. She said it would give me a little more color. Normally, I'd be reluctant to wear anything that called attention to me, but Rachel had been adamant that people our age didn't wear one pieces with built in skirts, the style I'd deemed safer. The top with its strings and triangle coverage concerned me, but I'd given in because of the boy-shorts style bottom. When she'd held up a different option with even less material, I'd quickly judged the pink and yellow suit the better option.

I pulled the tags off the bikini and slipped it on. Then, I twisted and turned in front of the mirror in my bedroom, worrying. The string top covered me decently. The boy-shorts bottoms hugged my backside. However, a lot of skin reflected back at me. I did like the suit...I just needed to get used to it.

Grabbing the sunglasses I'd bought, I left my room. When I reached the kitchen, I heard Rachel's crooning voice outside. I stopped. Was someone here? Did I want to go out there in this?

I looked down at myself. Hiding myself because of the pull hadn't made me self-conscious...more like extremely cautious. Men reacted less if I kept to myself, which included staying modestly covered. What would happen in a bikini? Better to find out now, at home, if I could wear it in front of someone else than to go to a beach with it. I straightened my shoulders and walked out onto the deck.

"Gabby, look," Rachel squealed as I pushed open the screen door. "A dog!"

On the deck, Rachel reclined on her side, stretched out on a beach towel. Between her towel and the one she'd set out for me, lay a monster of a dog, relaxing in the sun. I stopped and stared. What was that thing? Although the size of a mastiff, it looked nothing like one. At least seven feet from nose to tail, the dog's shaggy brown coat gave it a wild look. Rachel didn't seem to mind, though. She continued to pet its head affectionately.

It turned its head, which moved it out of Rachel's reach. Its soft brown eyes met mine.

Rachel shifted to a sitting position to reach its head again.

"It just walked up the porch steps and lay right down. I nearly peed myself. Have you ever seen a dog this big before? What kind do you think it is?" She continued to pet it lovingly.

I remained glued in place, my stomach sinking. Any lingering homesickness died as my suspicion grew. What are the odds that an extremely large, random dog just appeared at my door scant hours after Sam dropped me off? Improbable odds. When I'd said I would get a dog, I'd meant it as a joke. I couldn't afford a dog.

"And you're not going to believe what its tag says," Rachel said, not seeming to care that I hadn't answered her questions. "'If found, please provide a good home.' Isn't that funny?" She ruffled his neck fur, which made his hidden tags jingle. The dog continued to watch me and ignore Rachel's ministrations.

"Yeah. Funny," I mumbled. The size of the dog would ensure men didn't bother me. But a dog half its size would do the same. Why get one so big? Its size compared to Sam in his fur. Did Sam think some of his kind might bother me? If so, I didn't see how a plain old dog would help. My eyes widened as my own idiocy dawned on me. Not a plain dog.

I needed to call Sam, find out what he'd been thinking, and then give him an earful for sending someone to the house to keep an eye on me. I was about to turn and go back into the house when Rachel said something that made my stomach drop to my toes.

"His tag also says his name is Clay. What do you think? Should we keep him?"

CHAPTER SEVEN

I turned to look at Rachel, eyes wide with shock.

"What?" I glanced down at *him*.

He continued to watch me, his eyes not wavering from mine. He'd left me alone the whole summer. I had thought he'd truly let me go, despite Sam's ominous warning, and had forgotten about him.

"Aw, you aren't allergic are you?" Rachel said with a small pout. "The lease says a single pet is allowed as long as it's licensed."

I doubted the lease had taken into consideration that Rachel would fall in love with a freakishly large monster bearing similarities to a dog.

"No, I'm not allergic," I said distractedly. He had all summer to make his move. Why now? And why when I wore a bikini for the first time ever? A bikini did not say "stay away." I considered grabbing the towel and wrapping myself in it, but discarded the idea after I thought about how it would look to Rachel. Instead, I continued to stare at the frustrating dog until he huffed out a breath, turned away from me, and laid his head on his paws.

Clay had finally shown up and, apparently, he still didn't want to talk.

"Good. He's so cute!" Rachel reached over to scratch his ears, and he closed his eyes.

"I'm going back in," I said as I turned toward the door. Clay sprang to his feet before I reached it and crowded behind me. I looked down at him then back at Rachel, who watched us with an enormous grin.

"Looks like another guy who can't take his eyes off you. Living with you is going to be a riot." She laughed and picked up the towels. "Let's all go in. The neighbor's tree is going to shade the deck soon anyway."

Having little choice, I opened the door for Clay. His fur brushed my bare thighs as he moved past me into the house. His head came to about my sternum. He really was huge...a huge problem.

Sam had warned me Clay had taken my speech as an invitation to live together. At least, Clay had shown up in his fur. However, any relief I might have felt went unnoticed as I contemplated how he'd found me in a completely different state. If Sam told him, I'd have to kill Sam. Since I didn't have the stomach for outright murder, I'd break his coffee maker.

I took a deep breath to clear my hectic thoughts and followed Clay and Rachel inside. She patted him again, and I knew I wouldn't be able to tell him to leave. Especially with Rachel around as a witness. It'd make me look like a complete psycho if I started to speak to the dog, not only as if I knew him, but also as if I was giving a breakup speech. I didn't really have much of a choice...for now.

"We can keep him. But he's going to shed everywhere," I predicted then walked away.

Wisely, Clay stayed in the kitchen with Rachel. She continued to talk to him. She told him how cute he was and asked him if he wanted anything to drink. I heard dishes clank as I closed my door.

Even knowing Clay could probably hear me, I grabbed my cell phone and called Sam. Sam answered before it rang on my end; he knew I wouldn't call so soon for just any reason.

"Gabby, what's wrong?"

"Clay is here. In fur," I said as quietly as possible.

After a brief pause, Sam chuckled. "What did you expect, Hun? He scented you as his Mate. He's probably been following you since. Only, when you were with me, he trusted me to protect you and kept his distance. Moving away...well, you might have forced his hand a bit. Then again, I think he had planned on joining you from the start."

"Right..." I heard a creak of leather and knew Sam had sat in his office chair to get comfortable for a long conversation.

"Listen, this isn't so bad. With him there, you won't need to worry as much about other men, right?"

"Yeah, but what about him?" I went to my dresser to look for clothes.

"I told you...he has control. You won't have to worry about him becoming aggressive with you."

Before I could say anything, Rachel's muted voice called from the kitchen.

"Hey, Gabby?"

"I gotta go. Just wanted to tell you he was here. I'll call if anything stranger pops up." I didn't wait for his goodbye. I closed the phone, tucked it into one of my messenger bags on my dresser, and hurried to change. After putting on lounge pants and a tank top, I headed toward the kitchen.

"What's up?"

"Do you think I can feed him leftover steak?" she said sounding a bit muffled.

Bent at the waist, Rachel riffled through the fridge. Clay sat off to the side with a perfect view of her string bikinied backside, only he wasn't looking. He faced the arched door, watching for me. Should I be happy that he'd ignored the perfect view or annoyed? Instead of thinking about it, I answered Rachel.

"I'm pretty sure people-food is bad for dogs." Yes, I knew it wasn't nice, but if he wanted to play the dog, I'd play along. "We can pick up some dog food for him in the morning. He'll be fine overnight."

I sat at the kitchen table, pulled my legs up, held my knees, and watched Rachel straighten from the fridge and let the door close. She turned to look at Clay with concern, but Clay ignored her and continued to watch me.

My stomach growled.

"But dinner does sound good," I said to Rachel, ignoring Clay. "I should have thought of groceries while we were shopping."

"No problem. I forgot to tell you during the grand tour that there's a cupboard over there that you can stock and call your own. The top shelf in the fridge is mine. But don't worry about it for tonight. I was lazy yesterday and ordered take-out pizza. There's still plenty if you don't mind leftovers."

"Leftovers are fine with me." My stomach rumbled in agreement.

"We've got cheap plastic plates in the cupboard to the left of the sink—inherited from a prior roommate. Grab two, will you?" she said as she re-opened the fridge.

I unfolded myself from the chair and grabbed the plates while Rachel pulled the pizza from the fridge. Clay lay down where he sat and put his massive head on his paws. I could see his eyes move to follow my progress.

Rachel chatted about our neighbors and the university while we warmed the pizza in the microwave. She was easy to be around and fun to listen to.

"What kind of movies do you like?" she asked changing topics abruptly once both plates held several steaming slices.

I had to think about it for a moment. "Action-comedy, I guess. I don't watch movies often."

She handed me a plate. "Let's eat this in the living room and watch a movie."

Clay stood and walked toward the living room before either of us moved. When he passed through the arch, he only had two inches of clearance on each side. I wondered if his fur made up his bulk. Not that it mattered. Our tiny house didn't suit a dog his size.

Rachel laughed as she watched him. "I think he's going to fit right in."

She had no idea how much he didn't fit in. I turned off the light in the kitchen and followed them into the living room. Clay settled on the floor and stretched out in front of the couch, which forced us to step over him. Rachel sat on one side of the couch, and I took the other.

The movie Rachel selected not only held my interest, but it seemed to hold Clay's as well. I ate two of the three pieces of pizza Rachel had put on my plate and set the remaining piece aside. During a quiet moment, Clay stood, stretched, and turned to study my pizza. Rachel noticed.

"Just one bite?" Rachel begged.

"If he's never eaten it before, he might throw up. Are you willing to clean it up? I'm not." I wasn't about to make living with us easy for him.

She pouted prettily, not really upset. Her easygoing personality allowed me to speak without having to censure my words too much. A few minutes later, I saw her break off small pieces and set them on the edge of her plate. Clay innocently turned around and snatched the pieces.

"Fine," I said when the movie ended. "Give him the steak."

Rachel cheered, hopped off the couch, and called to Clay as she went to the kitchen. He looked at me dolefully and followed her.

"Your choice, bud. Not mine," I whispered knowing he'd hear me over Rachel's puttering as she heated the steak for him.

I grabbed my plate and cup and made my way to the kitchen to quickly wash and dry them.

"Thanks for the shopping and movie, Rachel. And the leftovers. You've made this feel like home in less than a day." I quirked a half-smile at her. "But I'm beat and going to bed. See you in the morning."

Before I left the kitchen, I looked back to make sure Clay didn't follow. He sat near Rachel, watching me. Hastily looking away, I escaped to my room. The last thing I needed was for him to think that backward glance had been an invitation to join me.

Odd as it sounded, having Clay in the house made it easier for me to fall asleep. Although still a stranger to me, I knew his world and his rules. He'd keep me safe. Yet, regardless of Sam's assurance that I needn't worry about him, he remained a concern.

THE NEXT MORNING I woke feeling great. Sleeping on a full-size bed definitely beat sleeping on a twin. I didn't think I would ever be able to go back. The new comforter had done a better job keeping in the heat than my old one. My feet were nice and toasty.

I stretched my legs from their curled position and hit something warm and solid through the covers. No...he wouldn't. I sat up and glared at Clay, who was already awake and contentedly stretched out at the end of my bed. His eyes met mine.

"No," I whispered. "No dogs allowed on my bed."

He snorted out a sigh and laid his head down, closing his eyes.

"Seriously, Clay. Don't you think this is just a little inappropriate?"

He didn't move.

"Fine." I used my feet to try to push him off the bed, but he didn't budge. Leaning back, I braced my hands on the wall and pushed harder, straining to move his stubborn, irritating fur from my new comforter.

He still didn't move but did open one eye to look at me.

I gave up and glared back. "If you shed all over my comforter, I'm locking my door at night." I tossed back the covers and got out of bed. "With an eyehook," I added for good measure.

He wisely didn't follow me as I made my way to the bathroom. Rachel already moved around in the kitchen.

"Are you a coffee drinker?" she called to me.

With a mouthful of toothpaste, I had to spit before I could answer.

"No. More of a milk or orange juice person." I finished up in the bathroom, joined her in the kitchen, and noticed her scrubs.

"Going to work?" I asked as I sat on a kitchen chair and pulled my feet up from the cool floor.

"Yep. Sorry to leave you on your own so soon. I'll be back around five. If you need anything, just call my cell. If I don't answer, leave a message, and I'll get back to you." She filled a travel mug with the coffee she had made and rinsed out the pot. "Oh, when I went to bed, Clay whined at your door, so I let him in. Hope that was okay..."

"Yeah, that's fine." What else was I supposed to say without sounding weird or bitchy? Inspiration to pay him back for his sneaky method struck.

"Have you thought of taking him to a vet?"

Rachel paused mid-rinse. "I hadn't, but you're right. He should probably go if we're going to have him in the house with us. I'll call around and make an appointment. I need to check into licensing him, too. Ugh. Shots are probably going to cost a fortune." She looked at me pleadingly.

Darn idea to get back at him would cost me money. "Yeah, I'll go in halves." I got up and started back toward my room.

"Great. Talk to you tonight," she called as she went out the back door.

Clay still sprawled on my bed. He took up the full width with his back paws folded in toward his stomach so they wouldn't fall off. I stood in the doorway and studied him while he, in turn, watched me. We were finally alone, and I was determined to set some rules.

"First, I'd like to clarify that this does not qualify as getting to know each other. Second, you smell like wet dog. If you want to continue to sleep in my room, on my bed, you'll let Rachel give you a bath when she gets home." He snorted at that but didn't get off the bed. "Third, once I'm awake, you get out. I know what you are, and I am not changing in front of you."

He outright harrumphed at that one, and I swore I saw a canine smile. But, he did hop down from the bed. He left the room with quiet dignity.

I closed the door behind him, remade the bed—thankfully, he didn't appear to shed—and grabbed some clothes. I had two goals for the day. First, I needed to figure out how long it would take me to walk to the campus from here. Then, I needed to learn the bus schedule for the days I ran late or the weather prevented walking. If worst came to worst, I'd buy a beater car to drive.

Opening the door, I was startled to see Clay sitting there patiently waiting for me.

"What are you doing?" I asked when he didn't move. Of course, he didn't answer.

I eyed him warily and walked past him. In the kitchen, I grabbed the house key from the counter then moved to the back door. Clay's nails clicked on the floor as he followed me.

"I'm going for a walk, and you're staying here," I said when he made to follow me outside.

Clay growled slightly in response.

His deep growl gave me pause. He sounded scary.

"Please don't do that. Unless you really *are* trying to scare me."

His fur continued to bristle, but his growl stopped. Our relationship wouldn't go anywhere if he thought he could bully and maneuver me to his way of thinking.

"And don't crab at me. I'm not the unlicensed dog without a leash. Do you want me to talk Rachel into buying a pink collar for you?"

He coughed out a strangled bark then turned and walked back to the living room.

"See you later," I said, feeling a little smug.

The walk to campus took about forty minutes. I didn't mind the time, but the distance and the number of catcalls I'd received made walking impractical and unsafe. After checking the bus schedule and stops, I knew I'd need to buy a car. A necessity that would put a significant dent in my savings.

On the way home, I stopped at a small grocery store to pick up some essentials. Browsing, I found a new bar of soap, an extra toothbrush, dog food, and groceries for the week.

Loaded down with the bags, it seemed to take forever to reach the house. When I finally got there, my arms ached. I would need to remember to bring one of my messenger bags if I ever walked there again. It made carrying things so much easier. I made my way to the back of the house and saw Clay sunning on the deck.

"Nice to know you can let yourself out," I said as I walked past him. I nudged open the door and kicked it closed behind me. With a sigh, I put the bags on the table and began to unpack.

After a sharp bark from outside, I grudgingly turned to let Clay in.

"What? Can't let yourself back in?" He didn't respond,

except to sit by the sink. I went back to the table and reached into one of the bags.

"Look what I got you." I pulled out a small bag of dog food.

Clay growled again, but it lacked any menace.

"You want to look like a normal dog don't you? Well... as normal as a dog your size can look, anyway." I set the bag on the floor next to the bowl of water Rachel had set out for him and continued to unpack, saving the soap and toothbrush for last.

"These are for you. You have two choices. You can use them when Rachel's gone, or you can wait until she's back, and I'm sure she'd be happy to help you."

He studied me for a moment then walked out of the kitchen, turning toward the bathroom. I followed a few steps behind.

A startled yelp escaped me when I rounded the corner and caught sight of a naked backside. Without much thought, I tossed the soap and toothbrush in and slammed the door shut.

"You could have waited until I put the stuff in there," I said through the door as my heart thundered in my ears. I took a steadying breath and heard the water turn on, the clink of his dog tag hitting the sink, then the shower curtain move.

Who would have thought he would even know how to use a shower? I hadn't. On the way home, I'd started to think of all the different things I would need to explain, like making sure to position the curtain inside the tub. Standing outside the door, still reeling from the view I'd gotten, I realized I might see the same thing again if I didn't get him a towel.

I'd packed two bath towels. Purchased from a discount store, they both sported gaudy floral designs. I grabbed one and waited outside the door again until I heard him splashing in the shower. Then, I knocked.

"I have a towel for you," I said through the door. "If you're still in the shower, I can open the door and toss it on the toilet seat. Okay?" I didn't hear anything. No surprise. "Okay, I'm coming in." I waited a moment for any indication that I shouldn't enter.

When the water continued to run, I cautiously opened the door. As soon as I saw a clear path to the toilet seat, I tossed the towel. Standing just inside the bathroom with my hand wrapped around the door handle for a quick exit, I paused. His new toothbrush rested on the sink.

"My toothpaste is the one marked with the pink nail polish on the cap. I'll let you use it as long as you promise not to squeeze the tube from the middle."

His answer took the form of an accurately aimed splash of water over the top of the shower curtain. I barely dodged it.

"You're cleaning that up."

I closed the door, grabbed a book, and went to the couch to wait. I hoped he would use the towel before he turned back into a dog. He'd make a mess if he shook out in there. After a minute, I actually opened the book and started to read.

Several minutes later, the water turned off. With my attention divided between listening and trying to associate an action to each sound I heard, I couldn't concentrate on my book. A moment of silence. Then running water. It sounded like the sink. Brushing his teeth? Then silence again. It remained quiet until I heard the doorknob turn. Quickly, I held the book higher to block my view, just in case he chose not to wear his fur...or the towel. A chuffing bark, apparently his dog version of a laugh, had me lowering my comically high book.

He strolled over by me and hopped up on the couch. Incredibly, his fur looked even fluffier.

"Don't get too comfortable, I don't know Rachel's rules about pets on the furniture." I curled my legs under me to give him more room.

Forgetting myself, I leaned over to smell him.

"Much better," I said straightening. At his intense look, I went back to reading my book and pretended I hadn't just leaned over and smelled a man. We stayed like that, side by side in companionable silence, until lunch when both our stomachs rumbled.

On the way to the kitchen, I noticed his wet towel on the bathroom floor.

"Next time, fold it over the edge of the tub," I said. The bathroom lacked any other available space to hang a towel, and I didn't want his towel hung in my room, either. That seemed a little too domestic.

I made us both dry ham sandwiches. Dry because I'd refused to pay four dollars for a miniature jar of mayo.

"I'm guessing your bowl of dog food will always be full," I said as I set his plated sandwich on the floor. Sitting at the table, I started to eat my own sandwich. He finished his in two bites.

"So, we have a week before my classes start up. What's your plan?"

He cocked his head at me.

"Did you want to try to enroll in any classes? Study anything?"

He lay down on the floor next to his empty plate, eyeing it sadly.

"Okay...well, if you change your mind, let me know."

I washed our dishes and went back to reading. Eventually, he joined me on the couch.

Later that night, Rachel breezed into the house and tossed

her keys and purse on the table. She had a manly spiked collar in her hand along with a leash.

From my position on the couch, I watched her kneel down next to Clay, who stood near his bowl of water. I wasn't sure, but she appeared to have interrupted his contemplation of drinking from the bowl. The thought made me smile.

Trying to ignore the pair, I focused on my book. Shuffling movements sounded from the kitchen. Rachel mumbled something that was too quiet to hear. When the noises didn't stop, I went to investigate.

"This is a joke," she said. She knelt in front of Clay, face to muzzle, trying to get the collar on him.

I laughed from the doorway as I watched them struggle. She would wrap her arms around his neck to buckle the collar, and he would duck or shift to avoid her but he never got up and walked away. I caught a twinkle of amusement in his canine eyes.

I knew Rachel wouldn't give up getting a real collar on him. He needed proof of license. Yet, he appeared very determined to avoid the collar. It served him right. He was the one who chose to be a dog.

Rachel mumbled again, and I decided to take pity on her. I knew how to reason with him. If Clay ever wanted to leave the house with me, he had to have a collar. I just needed to point that out.

"Here." I held out my hand. "I'll try."

"Good luck," she said with a laugh as she got off her knees and handed me the collar. She took my position in the doorway.

"It was the biggest collar they had. I don't even know if it fits, he won't let me get close enough."

With a half-smile on my face, I knelt in front of Clay. I liked that he had a sense of humor when he interacted with Rachel. It made having him in the house tolerable...almost. I looked him in the eye.

"Clay, if you want to be able to go anywhere with us, you need a collar we can clip a leash on. Not just the twine you have holding your tag around your neck."

He didn't move so I leaned forward and reached for the string that held his current joke of a tag. He held still for me while I removed the twine and replaced it with the real collar.

"At least it's not pink," I said and patted him before I realized what I was doing. I'd forgotten myself again and treated him like a dog.

I quickly stood and avoided Clay's direct gaze.

Rachel laughed. "Hey, I wouldn't do that to him. No pink for our man. I don't know why he sat still for you and not me."

I'd forgotten about Rachel. She moved to pet and praise him for his good behavior. If I wanted a chance of having a friend as a roommate, I knew I needed to deal with Clay as a pet. But, I needed to watch myself. The direction of my thoughts—his assumed permanent residency in the house—troubled me. Making him comfortable and buying him a license wouldn't help me get rid of him.

Rachel gave him a kiss, and he sighed. Maybe, he'd grow tired of her affection and run back to Canada. I held onto that happy thought.

"He's moody," I said, looking into his eyes. Moody and stubborn with a quirky sense of humor. Not a good combination.

CHAPTER EIGHT

As soon as Rachel sufficiently praised Clay for wearing the collar, she went to her room to change. From her room, she asked if I wanted to join her for a girl's night out. She explained she typically didn't stay in too much; when not busy working, her social life called. Still too unsure of our relationship—I didn't want to risk having someone Rachel might be interested in hitting on me—I declined. Thankfully, turning down her invitation didn't seem to bother her.

While Rachel exceeded my expectations as a roommate, adjusting to Clay's presence was something else entirely. When I woke Tuesday, Rachel was already gone. Clay still lingered at the foot of my bed.

"Get out," I said as soon as I opened my eyes. He left without complaint.

I took my time to dress, then went downstairs to check out the basement. Clay followed me. I tried to ignore him as I looked around. There wasn't much to see. The washer and the dryer were right by the steps, and there were a few utility shelves against the walls for storage.

With nothing else to do, I decided to take advantage of my idle time by sunbathing. I walked back upstairs and went to my room to change. After our talk the day before, Clay didn't attempt to follow me.

The second time wearing the suit was a little less nerve-racking. I didn't stare nervously in the mirror and eye all the pale skin glaring back at me. Instead, I appreciated the vivid coloring on the suit. Rachel had good taste.

Intent on finding the beach towels Rachel had used, I opened the door and stopped short at the sight of Clay. His huge dog head moved up, then down, as his eyes traveled the length of my body. I flushed, slammed the door, and changed back into shorts and a tank top. I opted to cut the grass, instead.

Clay sat on the porch and watched me push the mower back and forth. When I moved to the front, he followed. He was never in the way, just always there. After I went back inside to read, he did disappear for a bit. He had apparently taken my complaint about his hygiene seriously and had chosen to shower again. I hoped he would make it a daily routine.

Since he'd bathed and given me privacy as I'd asked, I had no reason to complain when I went to my room that night and saw him lying on the foot of the bed. However, when I woke Wednesday morning with him lying next to me, I did complain. Lividly.

"Now, just hold on," I whispered with a scowl. "You're a dog. Act like one. Fur stays at the foot of the bed."

He grudgingly moved to his place at the foot of the bed, watching me the whole time.

"Don't give me your doleful eyes. This is your choice, not mine." As soon as I said that, I recalled his talent for misinterpretation which had caused this co-ed housing in the first place. "Not that you'd get to sleep next to me in your skin either. So, don't even think about it. If you don't like the end of the bed, you can always sleep on the floor."

AFTER GETTING THE PAPER, I scoured the classifieds for a beater car and found two promising ads. Both required a long walk. I fetched my bag, tucked the folded newspaper inside, and grabbed the house keys.

Clay beat me to the door. I scowled down at him. He stared back at me. After a moment, he shook his neck, jangling his tags. Defeated, I clipped on his leash. He negotiated well without using a single word.

I used my cell to call the number for the first ad. The man sounded a bit brusque as if my planned visit inconvenienced him. Shrugging it off, I led Clay to the address. A rusty car parked on the front lawn with a "for sale" sign affirmed I had the right place. Clay and I walked toward the car.

A man called hello from the open garage and made his way toward us. As he neared, his demeanor changed, and I inwardly groaned. He introduced himself as Howard and looked me over with interest. Clay moved to stand between us, his stoic presence a good deterrent.

Howard talked about the car for a bit, going through the laundry list of its deficiencies. Then he popped the hood so I could look at the engine. In the middle of Howard's attempt to impress me with his vast mechanical knowledge, Clay sprang up between us. Howard yelped at Clay's sudden move and edged away as Clay placed his paws on the front of the car to get a good look at the engine, too. I fought not to smile at the man's stunned expression. At Clay's discreet nod, I bought the car, not bothering with the second ad.

No matter what errand I wanted to run during the week before classes started, Clay insisted on tagging along. On Friday, when I drove to the bookstore, Clay rode a very cramped shotgun and waited in the car while I made my purchases. Later, he sat in the hot car again while I bought some basic school supplies.

However, Monday, when I tried leaving for my first class, I put my foot down. He bristled and growled and tried to follow me.

"Your license only wins you so much freedom. Dogs aren't allowed on campus and definitely not in the classroom."

Thankfully, Rachel had left first and didn't hear me scold him.

I tried to leave again, but he stubbornly persisted. Finally, exasperated, I reminded him that he slept on my bed because of my good grace. He resentfully stepped away from the door.

AFTER THE FIRST week of classes, I didn't have time to mind Clay's constant attention. Maxing out at eighteen credits, desperate to get the general requirements out of the way so I could delve into clinicals sooner, I spent much of my day on campus in a classroom or in the library. When I actually found myself at home, I spent my time studying. I'd known when signing up for the courses that they would occupy all of my time and prevent me from having much of a life. Other than the fact I couldn't get a part-time job while taking the overload, I hadn't minded the commitment.

Even though I ignored him, Clay still stayed close to me. I realized how bored he'd grown when I came home and found one of my books on the couch, the bookmark on the wrong page. The next day, I took pity on him and brought back some books I thought might interest him. The one I thought particularly clever, about flora and fauna of North America, I included to remind him of home. He eyed the titles dispassionately. The day after, a bookmark nestled between the pages of two of the books.

I woke up one morning with a single-word note on my dresser. It simply said "mechanics." The first stack of books lay next to the note.

I turned to glare at Clay, who still lounged on the end of the bed.

"So you can write words to me, just not speak them?"

He blinked at me.

"Whatever. You're going to get caught creeping around the house at night."

Later that day, I returned the books on forestry and wildlife and checked out several books on mechanics. For fun, I threw in a do-it-yourself book for home repairs.

THE SECOND FRIDAY after school began, I sat on my bed with the door to my room closed. Clay lay in his usual spot beside me, his eyes devouring the words of his current book. He'd spent enough time reading next to me that I'd grown used to our system, a nudge when he needed a page turned. Trying to turn the page with his nose hadn't worked out well for him or the first book.

When he nudged me, I turned his page without looking up from my own book. When he did it again, I lifted my head. He read fast, but not that fast. He briefly met my eyes then turned toward the door. Just then, I heard the front door open, and I froze at the sound of Rachel's voice.

"...and this is where I live. Please have a seat, and I'll change quickly. My roommate and our dog should be around here somewhere."

"No rush," a man answered. "Our reservations aren't until six."

I turned wide eyes to Clay. Rachel had brought a man home? I didn't have time to think about it further because she knocked on my door. I wanted to ignore it, but instead, quickly closed the book in front of Clay.

"Come in."

Rachel walked in still wearing her scrubs. Her smile and flushed cheeks spoke volumes, as did the way she tactfully closed the door behind her.

"There you are. Come meet Peter." She walked close and leaned in so she could whisper more. "Don't kill me, but he has a friend without a date tonight, and I said I had a friend without a date tonight...please come with."

I groaned quietly. "Don't do this to me, Rachel. This won't end well, and you'll probably never forgive me."

"Come on...please?" she said, sitting on the bed next to me. "I really like this one."

"That's the problem. Remember what I said? It's always a guy that ruins a friendship. I don't want to go out tonight." I looked at Clay from the corner of my eye. He glared at Rachel. Not good. Too human. I nudged him with my foot while keeping my focus on Rachel.

"I like having a friend," I said.

She smiled at me. "If he hits on you, then it wasn't meant to be. Don't worry so much." She pulled me off the bed, and I reluctantly followed her out the door. Clay was close behind.

Peter, a pleasant looking man with light blonde hair and blue eyes, stood when we walked into the living room. He was an inch shorter than Rachel and, with his coloring, seemed her polar opposite. He immediately smiled at Rachel, and I could tell he had eyes only for her. I sagged with relief. His kind were rare.

"Peter, this is Gabby. Gabby, this is Peter. He's going to med school. I bumped into him at the library last week. Peter, why don't you tell her about Scott while I go get dressed?"

Rachel left the room in a rush, probably so I couldn't retreat. I smothered a grin as I watched Peter's gaze follow her. It took him a moment to collect himself.

"Nice to meet you, Gabby."

"You too. Want to sit?" I motioned him back to the couch and took the chair for myself. Clay settled on the floor between us. "This is Clay."

"He's huge," Peter said, appearing to notice Clay for the first time.

A huge pain in the butt, I thought without any malice.

"Yeah," I said instead. "So, who's Scott?"

"Oh, a friend of mine," he said looking up from Clay. "He's

also in med school. We had plans to go to O'Donell's tonight for dinner and a drink or two. Then, I ran into Rachel and invited her to join us. We thought it'd be more fun if you could come, too."

Rachel waltzed back into the room at that moment. Amazingly, she had already changed into a skirt and complementing silky top. She'd heard Peter's last comment.

"Of course you will, won't you, Gabby?"

Two love-struck fools, who wouldn't even consider my presence if it weren't for Scott, had me cornered. Rachel really didn't know what she was asking of me. A public restaurant wouldn't be enjoyable. Yet, as she watched me hopefully, I knew my answer.

"Okay...but I need to be home early enough to let Clay out." A lame excuse, but I needed to prep the idea now so I would have an out later.

"I'm sure he'll be fine for that little while." Rachel waved her hand dismissively at Clay. Clay huffed, but she didn't notice. Instead, she shooed me toward my room.

"Go get dressed."

I stood to go to my room, but Clay leapt to his feet in front of me. I stepped to the right to go around him but he mirrored my move, blocking me.

Rachel laughed. "Come here, Clay. Come here and let Gabby get ready." She squatted down and patted her leg.

I'd seen her do this a few times before. Usually, Clay grudgingly responded. Not this time though. He kept his gaze focused on me and copied my feinted attempts to get around him.

"I've never seen him act like this," Rachel said to Peter.

I kept my narrowed gaze on Clay.

"I'm surprised you have such a wild looking dog. It seems too big compared to the house...and the two of you." Peter eyed Clay, too.

Giving up, I dropped to my knees and wrapped my arms around his thick neck, pretending to hug him so I could whisper in his ear.

"I'm not crazy about the idea either, but you have to let me go and stop acting weird." I pulled back. "Ready to be good, Clay?" I said as I stood and scratched him behind the ear just as a pet owner would do.

He turned and trotted into my room. Nope, not ready to be good.

Rachel laughed again. She knew I usually kicked him out when I wanted to change and had already teased me about it. I'd pointed out she wouldn't know how awkward it felt because he never tried to watch her change.

Resolutely, I followed Clay into my room and closed the door. I could just barely hear Peter and Rachel talking as they waited for me. Clay sat on my bed, watching me.

I folded my arms and kept my voice low. "I am not changing in front of you."

My words evoked an eerie canine smile from him, and he settled down onto my comforter and continued to watch me.

"Fine. I'll change in the bathroom."

I went to my closet and started looking at my clothes already knowing very few things in there compared to the style Rachel wore. The skirt I'd bought a few weeks ago would look nice but added to my pull, it would scream "hit on me." Biting my lip, I reached for the skirt. Clay began to growl fiercely.

"Zip it," I mumbled and grabbed one of the dressier tops I owned, a fitted cowl neck top with three-quarter sleeves.

Clay started barking, a deep menacing sound that raised the little hairs on the back of my neck. I spun toward him.

"What the hell, Clay? Cut it out." I knew he didn't like that because he got louder.

Rachel burst in without knocking, and Peter followed right behind her. Clay, who had been sitting at the end of my bed, sprang to his feet as soon as they entered.

"What's wrong?" Rachel looked at Clay, who continued to bark at me.

If possible, his volume increased, and I had to yell over him.

"Nothing. Just give me a few minutes to calm him down, okay?" I walked to Clay with the clothes still under one arm, and he growled at me. I faltered and eyed him with a hint of fear.

"Uh, I'm not so sure you should do that right now," Peter said.

Clay turned and started barking at Peter.

"Enough." My voice echoed in the small room. It apparently took Clay by surprise because the noise stopped. However, his attitude hadn't changed. Teeth still exposed in a fierce snarl, he glared at all of us. At least he'd finished barking and growling. For the moment. I turned toward Peter and Rachel.

"I'm fine. Thank you. Just give me a few minutes to change."

They shared a glance then left the room and shut the door behind them.

Closing my eyes, I took a deep breath. Without trying, I could "see" Clay in a painful burst of light. A first. My other vision usually required an amount of focus.

With a sigh, I opened my eyes and turned to him. He looked seriously pissed. My stomach churned. Sam had promised he could control himself.

"Will you bite me if I sit next to you, Clay?"

He snorted, and I watched the silent snarl ease from his muzzle. His hackles slowly laid flat. When he settled onto his haunches, I knew he'd calmed down and sat next to him.

"You know I don't understand dog, right? It'd be so much easier if you just told me what was wrong."

I turned my head to meet his gaze. Our faces were close together. Because of his height, he was looking down at me. He let out a gusty sigh and bent his head to nudge the clothes I still held.

"You don't like the clothes or that I'm going out?" I watched his face, trying to figure out what he was getting at. He actually bobbed his head yes.

"You don't like both?"

He lowered himself down onto the mattress and watched me with his sad puppy eyes, not trying to communicate further.

"You're really frustrating me, Clay." I moved to get up, and he growled again.

"Now, hold on..." I did get up, but spun with my hands on my hips to look him in the eye. Aware that only a door separated us from the suspiciously silent couple in the living room, I kept quiet despite my anger.

"I'm trying here, Clay, and you're not. So stop growling at me. Got it? And so what if I go out? Do you trust me so little? Have you not been paying attention? I'm not comfortable around guys. It's not as if I'm going to go out tonight and come back with a boyfriend or something. So, just chill out about your Claim, all right?"

He continued to growl at me and gave me a dog-eyed glare. In his mind, he and I shared a tie. I knew that. I also knew from a werewolf standpoint, in a strongly tied pair, the male often acted in an extremely possessive manner. If other unMated males came near before the Claim was completed, a fight typically broke out. Sometimes to the death.

"But we're not talking unMated males," I whispered to him, thinking aloud. "They're just men."

He chuffed out his canine laugh and hopped from the bed to walk toward me. I couldn't help it, after all that barking and growling, I stepped back from him. His sides heaved as he sighed and stopped advancing. I knew my fear disappointed him.

"Sorry," I mumbled automatically. Although, he'd done nothing but try to communicate why he didn't want me to go out tonight, I didn't appreciate his chosen methods of communication. They could use improvement.

"Let me think, Clay." I sat on the edge of the bed while he stood on the floor, and watched me. I still didn't understand what continued to bother him. The date wasn't with a werewolf. I had no interest in Scott. I only wanted to go as a favor to Rachel. And the clothes were the only going out clothes I had.

"Can we compromise? I don't want to spend the entire year sitting at home with a possessive dog who won't talk to me." Yeah, that sounded weird. "What if we went somewhere dog friendly? There's a bar with cute little bistro tables on the sidewalk. If you're on your leash, you could come."

He stood, turned around so he faced away from me, and sat again.

"Is that a yes?" I leaned to the side in an attempt to see his face. He didn't move.

"I'm taking that as a yes. If you turn around while I'm changing, I'm going to have you neutered."

He just laughed again, so I hurried into my skirt and switched my t-shirt for the fitted top. As my head cleared the neckline, I met his eyes in the mirror. Thank the stars I hadn't changed any underthings.

"Hope it was worth it," I said. "You're on the couch tonight."

Rachel and Peter sat talking on the couch when I walked out of my room.

"All set, but can we change our plans? I think Clay was freaking out because he knows we're leaving. He's been left alone so much this week..."

Predictably, Rachel made soothing noises and went to cuddle Clay. He tolerated it with as much dignity as a man in fur and a collar could muster.

"What if we went to that bar with the bistro tables that you were telling me about?" I said to Rachel.

Rachel leapt at the idea. "That'd be perfect. It's still nice enough out. Besides, I think this is the last week they do the outdoor dining. We should go before it's closed for the season."

Peter stalled. "Are you sure he will be okay? He looked pretty aggressive in there."

Rachel stopped petting Clay to look back at Peter. "He's never done that before. I think Gabby might be right. We've been leaving him alone a lot. I even forgot to let him out this morning before I left."

Peter looked adoringly at Rachel, and I knew we'd be going to the bistro bar.

"Let me grab my shoes. I'll follow you guys in my car just in case I need to leave early."

"I'll let Scott know about the change in plans." Peter pulled out his cell and started tapping the screen.

"I'll let Clay out." Rachel got up, walked to the back door, and called to Clay. Clay looked at me imploringly but, after what he'd just pulled, I had no pity.

"You know the drill. Go do dog business."

He left the room without a backward look. I went to the hall closet to search for my black flip-flops, the best footwear I had to offer the outfit, and grabbed a light jacket.

"You talk to him like he's a person," Peter said.

"I tease her for it all the time," Rachel said with a smile as she rejoined us. "You should hear her scolding him at night for taking up too much room on the bed."

Annoyingly, I started to blush. "Well, he's huge. Most of the time I have to sleep curled up. But, I'm sure I'll appreciate him more in winter." I slipped my feet into the plain flip-flops and made my way into the kitchen where I grabbed my keys.

I locked the back door while Rachel and Peter left via the front.

Clay already sat in the passenger seat when I turned toward the car. It meant he'd switched into his skin to open the door. I shook my head, got in, and started to buckle up.

"You're going to be seen doing stuff a dog shouldn't do. That or someone's going to call the cops because a naked man keeps popping up in my backyard." He didn't laugh this time. I turned to look at him while I started the car.

"You okay?"

Clay met my eyes, but I couldn't tell what bothered him now. I wished I could read him better.

"Fine. No growling, no biting, no barking. Pretty much no anything but acting like a passive, well-behaved dog," I said, laying down the rules as I backed out of the driveway.

I followed Peter's red compact through traffic with ease.

"I'm really nervous about this and don't want to worry about you, too." I sighed and started to doubt my decision. Although Clay had witnessed how the man who'd sold me the car had acted, he didn't know how guys acted around me in general. Maybe this wasn't a good idea. He would flip out when someone started to hit on me.

"Clay, you should know...men make me uncomfortable because of the way they act around me. They usually start flirting or ask me on a date. Most girls would be flattered, but if you really pay attention, there's something unnatural about it. It's like they can't help themselves. And sometimes, after I tell them no enough, they walk away with..."

I groped for the right word, but came up blank.

"I don't know...a look. Like they've been caught doing something they're ashamed of. I just want to try for normal tonight, okay? It'll be hard enough being in a public place. You'll see. I just need to know you're not going to make it any harder on me."

Out of the corner of my eye, I saw him turn to look out the window and reached over to ruffle his fur gently.

With increasing frequency, I caught myself touching him as if he were a dog. If I didn't think about him as a guy, petting him comforted me.

"Does it bother you when I pet you?" I asked, keeping my eyes on the road. I knew his answer when he contorted his large body to lay down with his head against my leg so I could reach him better. I laughed, feeling lighter than I had in a long while.

"Okay. If I start annoying you with it, just move away. I promise I won't pester you."

Peter considerately picked a parking spot with a free space next to it for me. Clay unwedged himself as I parked. I grabbed the leash and snapped it on. He watched me exit, hopped out after me, and stayed close to my side as we walked.

Rachel and Peter politely included me in their conversation. It helped distract me from my nervousness about meeting Peter's friend. I knew what to expect even if neither Rachel nor Clay fully understood. Peter's lack of reaction had pleasantly surprised me. But, his response wasn't the norm. I just hoped Clay would behave.

Scott waited for us at one of the outside tables. He stood and flashed a welcoming smile when he saw Peter. From a distance, I saw several female patrons at nearby tables cast speculative glances Scott's way. Fit and tall, with light brown hair and a carefree smile, no doubt his good looks warranted it. But, something about the way he held himself bothered me. It sent off an insincere vibe as if he'd practiced his pose.

His smile turned secretive and cunning as his pale blue eyes fixated on me. The subtle change probably escaped everyone else's notice, but not mine. Depressed, but hiding it well, I rested a hand on Clay's back. Whether in comfort or restraint, I couldn't be sure.

"Scott, this is Gabby," Peter said when we stood next to the table.

I smiled a tentative greeting but didn't offer my hand.

"A pretty name you don't hear often," Scott murmured, pulling out a chair for me.

Taking the chair he offered would put me across from Rachel and force me to sit between the two guys. Clay wouldn't like that. He didn't like the comment about my name either, but other than a twitch I'd felt with my hand on his back, he behaved.

"Would you mind if we switched spots, Scott? That way our dog won't be so close to people walking by. He's very friendly, but big. I don't want anyone to be intimidated by him."

"No problem." He gave me a reassuring smile and pulled out his own chair for me.

Loosely holding Clay's leash, I moved to the chair next to Rachel. Scott politely pushed the chair back in as I sat. Then he leaned close to move his drink. Clay quickly went to lie between my chair and Scott's. He nudged Scott's chair further away before Scott could sit. I pretended not to notice.

We made small talk while we perused the menus. I felt Scott's gaze continually return to me but refused to look up.

After we ordered, each of the more experienced students shared their knowledge of the university. Scott offered—twice —to take me on an official tour when I admitted I didn't know many of the campus locations they mentioned. As soon as I declined the second time, he looked less like the nice guy I'd met and more like a guy who would give me problems. I looked down at Clay. He still lay next to me, head on his paws. Only the twitch of his ears indicated his attention to the conversation.

"Why not have a drink with us, Gabby?" Scott asked, pointing at my water.

He hadn't worried about what I drank until I'd turned down his invitations for a tour.

"I'm a bit younger than the rest of you." I glanced at Rachel and saw her studying me. Crap! Was she noticing? Was she getting mad? I should have stayed home. Folding my hands in my lap, I tried to play it cool.

"Really? How old are you?"

"Eighteen. I'm not much of a soda drinker either, so water works." I tried to turn the conversation off myself. "How much longer until you graduate?"

"It depends on how far I want to go," Scott said, his intense smile relaxing a little. He nodded toward Peter. "Peter told me he declared his major freshman year and has never changed. I, on the other hand, have changed twice. I like what I'm learning now, so I hope I won't change it again, but you never know. What about you?"

"I'm going for massage therapy. So, I won't be here as long as the rest of you."

"Massage therapy? I hear they ask for volunteers to come in for those classes." He leaned closer with a fascinated smile on his face. "If you ever need someone to practice on, let me know. I'd be happy to come in." He reached over to pat my hand. The timely arrival of our food saved me from having to avoid his touch.

Clay nudged my leg with his surprisingly warm and dry nose, and I glanced down. He stared at me a moment then shifted his gaze to Scott, who was moving his drink for the waitress. Clay returned his glance to me and pulled his lips back in a silent snarl. Without the growl, it looked more like a scary, crazy wolf smile, but I got his meaning. Scott was getting on Clay's nerves, and Clay wouldn't put up with too much more.

Peter spoke up while Scott was distracted. "I think you'll both be in some of the anatomy classes next semester, Gabby. If you want a study group, you should let Rachel and I know. I've already been through them." He gazed admiringly at Rachel. "And since you're graduating in spring, I know you have, too."

"Thank you, Peter, but I really do study best on my—"

"That's a great idea," Scott said. "We should start now so the class won't be so hard later. What do you think about Tuesday nights?"

"It's a good idea to get a head start," I said ignoring Clay's insistent bump against my leg. "But I'm so swamped with classes and homework now that I don't even have time to take poor Clay for walks."

I reached over to pat Clay reassuringly, but stopped when I noticed Scott's gaze drop to my chest. The cowl neck had dipped away and revealed a little glimpse of the shadows within. Scott's eyes went from glassy fixation to glazed obsession. This was getting ridiculous.

Turning back to my dinner, I stuffed a few bites in my mouth to prevent me from needing to converse. Unfortunately, Scott took the opportunity to try to slide his chair a little closer. Thankfully, Clay didn't give an inch.

"What's your dog's name?" Scott asked, looking down at Clay.

"Clay," Rachel answered after seeing my mouth full.

Clay, I noticed, didn't look up at the sound of his name. Instead, he tensed and laid his ears back. Time to go.

"Nice name," Scott said, but I could tell he didn't care. "Let's bring him home after this and go out to a new club that opened downtown."

"Rachel?" I looked at her pleadingly, hoping she'd know that I wasn't begging to go out dancing. Her perceptive gaze locked on Scott.

"I see it," she said with a serious expression.

"See what?" Peter said. His gaze bounced between the three of us.

"Exhaustion. She's been studying like crazy." She waved over the waitress and asked for boxes and the check for the two of us.

"And she needs rest, not a night out. Although, I am really glad we came." She looked at Peter with a smile.

My weak smile didn't cover my gratitude at her diplomacy.

I reached for my purse which I'd hung on the back of the chair. Desperate, Scott moved to grab my hand. Clay stood abruptly. He successfully knocked Scott's hand out of the way but also bumped the table in the process. Peter reached out to steady his and Rachel's drinks, and I hurried to pull a twenty from my purse.

The waitress returned with the bill and the wrapped up leftovers. Since Rachel was still digging in her purse, I just handed the waitress the twenty after a quick glance at the bill. I was willing to pay for Rachel if it helped us leave faster.

"I better drive her home," Rachel said to Peter. "You have my number. Give me a call if you want to do something next weekend."

I stood, and Rachel shadowed me, ready to go. Clay bumped into me, knocking me off balance so I had to grab Rachel for support. I looked down at him and noticed Scott stand and hand the waitress his portion of the bill.

"Rachel, you can stay with Peter. I don't mind taking Gabby home," Scott said. Oily enthusiasm dripped with each word, and I didn't even need to look at Rachel for her to decline.

"No, Scott, I think we're done for tonight." She waved to Peter and grabbed my hand.

Poor Peter looked at us all, bewildered. His night out with Rachel had fallen apart fast, and I truly felt bad about it.

I went with Rachel, relieved to escape before Scott's recklessness grew. An "oof" sounded behind us, and I panicked, realizing I'd forgotten Clay. I spun around in time to see Scott hit the ground. He'd tripped over Clay in his hurry to catch me. I suspected Clay had done it purposely to slow Scott down.

Clay wasted no time. He ran to me and bumped his head against my back to get me moving before Scott could pick himself up again. There wasn't yet enough distance between the table and us to mute Peter's next words.

"What the hell is wrong with you, man? You come on too..." What he still had to say faded as we quickly walked away.

"I'm sorry," Rachel said. "You told me, but I didn't really get it. Even the men sitting around us were eyeing you."

I'd been too busy keeping an eye on Scott and Clay to notice. We continued to speed walk to the car.

"No big deal. You should see me in some of my classes. 'No' is the most common word in my vocabulary. Scott's reaction was worse than most because he already considered me his date. If you say 'no', consistently and to everyone, it doesn't get so bad." I handed Rachel the keys when we reached the car. "You really can drive."

She nodded, and we got in. Clay climbed into the back and stretched out so his head lay on the console between the two front seats. Rachel wasted no time backing out and leaving.

Halfway home, she pulled into a gas station. "Tonight's an ice cream night. Be right back." She jumped out and strode into the convenience station with the determination of a girl on a shopping spree.

Laying my head back, I sighed, and my hand found its way to Clay's soft fur. I pet his head and ears. He exhaled loudly, but stayed still so I figured he didn't mind. I was just glad he wasn't rubbing in that it'd been a disaster of a night out.

I looked out the window, watched traffic zip past, and allowed myself just a small amount of self-pity. I'd wanted normal so badly. No werewolves. No second sight. No weird pull on men. Yet, I *knew* I would never be normal. I would never have a normal date. I kept trying to mold myself into something I could never be. Why?

Clay lifted his head under my hand, and I reigned in my emotions, knowing he could sense my melancholy.

"I'm fine," I said as I met his gaze. "How are you doing?" He scooted forward to lay his head on my lap in response. Yeah, that was pretty much how I felt.

The door opened, startling us both.

"I got double fudge brownie for each of us," Rachel said as she slid in behind the wheel and handed me the bag. "Sorry, Clay. Chocolate's poison for dogs. None for you."

She made me smile.

When we got home, I went straight to my room to change. Clay stayed with Rachel as she praised his good behavior and good sense to trip Scott when he'd started to follow us. No doubt, he'd get the other half of her burger before I finished. Tossing the shirt into the closet, I vowed never to wear it again and pulled on the comfortable clothes I slept in.

Shaking off my mood, I walked into the kitchen.

"Where's my chocolate?"

Clay moved to my side, and I patted him again. I'd asked a lot of him tonight, and he deserved a real reward. He'd been surviving on sandwiches and leftovers from Rachel. Tomorrow, we'd go to the store, and I'd buy him a big steak.

Rachel handed me my pint with a spoon standing in it. She'd already dug into hers. After eating another spoonful with a blissful groan, she set her container of ice cream on the table.

"I'm going to go change. Want to watch a movie or something?" Rachel stripped out of her shirt on her way to her bedroom.

I looked at the wall clock and savored another spoonful of ice cream. It was only seven, but I was tired. I put the lid back on and tucked my container in the near empty freezer.

"What do you think?" I asked Clay, noting he watched me and not the striptease Rachel had unknowingly put on or the chocolate ice cream she'd left unguarded. "Stay up and watch a movie, or go to bed early? Lead the way." I waved him forward, and he trotted through the living room to my room.

"Rach, we're just going to go to bed early. 'K?" I leaned against the wall in the living room, waiting for her answer.

"It's okay. Go ahead," she said, appearing again. She wore short shorts and a tank top for bed. "I won't keep you up with a movie, will I?" She glided past me and flopped on the couch.

"I'm so tired I doubt anything will keep me from sleeping."

"'K. Night, Hun. Thanks for going with me even if it did suck," she said, giving me a smile.

"Don't worry about it. Night." I walked into my room and closed the door behind me as she turned on the TV.

Clay lay on the foot of the bed, his usual spot. His head rested on his paws. He still had his eyes open.

"Thanks, Clay." As I passed him, I stopped to kiss the top of his furry head. He made a funny grunt noise that made me smile. Probably his wolf version of "no problem." I crawled under the covers and wiggled my feet under his body to the spot he'd already warmed.

I felt Clay relax a moment before he let out a gusty breath. He started to breathe deeply, and I tried to unwind as well. Going on a double date hadn't turned out as badly as it could have.

CHAPTER NINE

It was still dark when I woke. Not only dark, but also colder. The mild weather we'd enjoyed last night while eating outside had apparently fled with the sun. I nestled under the covers, trying to avoid the chill in the air. When I stretched my legs searching for Clay's weighted warmth, I felt nothing. His spot was cool.

"Clay?"

My bedroom door creaked open, and he jumped up on the mattress, causing it to bounce. He settled on my feet, and his heat immediately warmed me.

"Thanks."

Laying my head back down on the pillow, I burrowed deeper. The warm nights of summer, of sleeping with the window open, had retired for the year. Soon, going outside during the day would require a jacket. The thought was a little depressing. I didn't really care for the cold.

I wanted to sleep a little longer and tried to close my eyes again but they popped back open on their own. Clearly awake, I knew I should really get out of bed and do something. Yet, the thought made me cringe...until I remembered I owed Clay for last night. This early, there'd be no one around outside, especially with this first cold snap. We needed to take advantage of the still above freezing weather and do something together. He'd like that.

"Hey, Clay. Wanna go get breakfast with me?"

With a sigh, he jumped back down off the bed.

"You could have said no," I said with a soft laugh as I rolled out from under the covers.

Grabbing my clothes, I tiptoed to the bathroom. When I reemerged, Clay sat next to the back door, waiting patiently. I glanced at the car keys. Drive or walk? Walking would save money, and I enjoyed it.

"You up for a walk?" I kept my voice low since I didn't want to wake Rachel.

The idea of walking outside with Clay before dawn made me smile. He looked like a beast. Any sane man would keep his distance. It would be vastly different from the heckling first walk I had taken to campus.

When he didn't move away, I took that as affirmation and clipped on his leash, loosely looping it around his collar so I wouldn't need to hold it. He turned to me with a questioning look.

"What? I'm following the law...you're on a leash. Let's go."

I opened the door, and we soundlessly slipped outside. As expected, crisp air engulfed us, but the lack of wind made it tolerable. After pulling the hood up over my loose hair, I tucked my hands into the pockets of my hoodie and stepped off the porch, suspiciously testing the air to see if my breath clouded. Clay trudged next to me, still looking a little tired.

We walked in the direction of the campus, toward a small

diner that was open all day, six days a week, closed Sundays. Well-known on campus, Ma's Kitchen served good, cheap food for the perpetually broke college kid. With ten dollars in my pocket, I figured we could stuff ourselves before walking back home.

The sidewalks remained empty. Streetlights buzzed overhead. The soft scrape of Clay's nails on the pavement comforted me, and I filled my lungs, relaxing. Very few cars passed us as we made our way from one pool of light to the next.

The walk to campus offered an eclectic array of buildings. Businesses jumbled in with residences. Some so close together their shadows merged, creating perfect places for hiding. But Clay's calm presence allowed me to enjoy the walk without using my sight.

We strolled in companionable silence for a few minutes before I spoke up.

"So what do you like for breakfast? Oatmeal?" He laughed, and I smiled back. "Yeah, I was thinking you're more a steak and eggs kinda guy."

"Who you talking to dar'lin?" a man called as he stepped out from the shadows across the narrow street. His sudden appearance made my heart race.

"My dog." Even though I considered this area safe, it paid to be smart. So I whispered to Clay, asking him to bark. He obliged with a deep "woof" that almost scared me. The sound bounced off the surrounding buildings. I hoped it wouldn't wake anyone.

"Damn," the man called back, keeping pace with us on the opposite sidewalk. "That thing on a leash?"

"Yep, but there's no holding him back. I'm safer letting him go or he'd just drag me along."

The man laughed. "I bet. Have a good morning," he called before turning at the next corner to walk around the block.

"You trust that?" I asked Clay, watching the man's retreating form. Clay harrumphed.

"Me neither. And thanks for warning me there was someone close by," I said. He made a noise I interpreted between a snort and a laugh.

"Brat." I smiled down at him.

Night sounds began to fade, and I heard the occasional bird call out, though dawn was still an hour away. Clay continued to pace alertly by my side until we reached the diner. Judging from the empty parking lot, they didn't get much business this early. Still, the air outside smelled like frying breakfast sausage. Delicious. Beside me, Clay's stomach rumbled.

"Since they don't allow dogs, I'll go in and get our food for carryout," I said, pulling open the door. He obediently sat just outside, the position enabling him to watch me through the glass.

When I entered, the waitress set down the basket of jellies she'd been using to refill the jelly holders on the tables and moved to the register.

"Good morning," she said with a chipper smile. "How are you this morning?"

Wow. A people-person and a morning-person. I weakly smiled back and ordered.

As soon as I had our breakfast, I brought it out to Clay. We sat together on one of the cement parking blocks in front of the building. The early-morning traffic crept along quietly, keeping the illusion of solitude.

I opened his container and started to cut up his steak. He laughed at me again, and I shushed him. He could laugh all he wanted. He usually ate so fast I worried he'd choke. I set his container on the ground for him when I finished. He dug in, making it hard to think of him as a man.

"I hope you're a slower eater when you're in your skin," I commented.

He stopped eating and looked at me. Too late, I realized how critical my comment had sounded. I tried to soften it.

"It's just that you eat faster than me. That's all." It sounded lame.

I felt worse when he made an effort to eat slower. He still finished first. In an attempt to make up for my thoughtless comment, I offered him the rest of my breakfast, too. When he finished, I threw our containers away in the parking lot trash can.

We began the long walk back, with each of us lost in our own thoughts. Well, I was lost in mine, anyway. I didn't know what to say to take away the sting from my words. Why didn't I think before I spoke to him? I sometimes forgot about the man beneath the fur and tended just to talk, letting anything flow from my mouth without much thought. Sure, I may have meant what I said, but I could have found a better, nicer, way to say it. Maybe.

Distracted and dwelling on my own thoughts, I paid no attention to my surroundings until Clay began to growl. My head snapped up in surprise at the soft, menacing sound. Clay stopped walking. His head turned so he watched the space between two houses on our left. Dawn still hadn't lightened the sky, so I saw nothing but shadows.

I closed my eyes and focused, depending on my other sight

—something I'd mostly ignored since coming to school—to see what my eyes couldn't. The yellow-green sparks of the people in the houses around us glowed softly. To the left, closing in fast, a blue-grey light surged. Stunned, I blinked at it and glanced at Clay's spark. Blue-grey compared to his blue-green. Another color variation?

"What is it, Clay?" I whispered, taking a cautious step back. The colors I saw classified into werewolves, humans, and anomalies like Charlene and I. This new color moved too fast for a human.

Clay remained alert to the other werewolf's advance.

"What should I do, Clay?" I tried not to panic, but I could think of only one reason a werewolf would run at us like that. It wanted to challenge Clay.

If I walked away, it would think I was rejecting Clay's Claim. As much as I didn't want to Claim Clay, I didn't want a tie to anyone else.

Clay's growl increased in volume. I looked at the darkened houses around us. Perhaps I could use them to our advantage.

Clay tensed in front of me. I retreated a few more paces until I stepped into the road, no more than five feet from Clay. The faint, rapid thud of the werewolf's paws hitting the ground resonated from the darkness ahead. I tracked its spark. It sped forward. Suddenly, the rhythmic sound of its approach stopped even though its spark continued toward us.

Clay braced himself. In that moment, an enormous object soared at us from the darkness. I scrambled back. Its large body rivaled Clay for size. But, it was the newcomer's dark grey fur and bright blue eyes that forever burned into my memory.

The flying mass hit Clay hard. Clay let loose an aggressive snarl as he twisted, and worked to keep his back legs under him. His claws dug into the asphalt, scraping and scrabbling to slow the skid toward me. The two werewolves grappled, swiping claws and snapping jaws.

Eyes wide, I continued to maintain my view of the human sparks while watching the fight before me. Focused on each other, neither looked my way.

The challenger scuttled out of Clay's reach and regained his own footing. Clay lunged forward and snapped down on the other's muzzle. His sharp teeth ripped into tender flesh. I wanted to cheer when the other werewolf yelped in pain. They broke apart. Clay continued to growl. The low rumble made my heart beat even faster. The challenger responded with his own snarl but didn't attempt another attack. Instead, he sidestepped, looking for an opening.

I moved with them and maintained a small distance from both.

The noise escalated as they stalked each other. The challenger feinted toward Clay, lips drawn back and teeth parted. My heart beat harder with fear. Clay gave no ground, carefully keeping himself between the newcomer and me, while I tried to stay out of the way. The dogs in the neighborhood started to bark. The continued use of my sight began to strain me, but I saw a spark moving in a nearby house.

Time to take the offensive.

"Hey!" I yelled loudly.

Clay didn't jump, but the other werewolf did. His bright blue gaze flicked to me. A light turned on in the house.

"Whose dog is this? Someone help me get him off my dog!" Another light went on in the house.

Clay took advantage of his opponent's momentary distraction and went for its throat. The other wolf dodged the attack, but just barely. Bleeding freely from Clay's first strike, red began to color its muzzle.

With a deep-throated bark, it lunged again at Clay, refocusing its efforts. The lunge caught Clay in the shoulders and almost knocked him off balance. I forgot to breathe for a moment. Clay exposed his neck in an attempt to bite his opponent's front leg rather than to spin away and leave me unprotected.

The other wolf grunted in pain as Clay's teeth clamped down. Still, he went for the opening. His teeth clicked against the metal that studded Clay's collar. The wolf growled, pulled back, and made to try again. Clay quickly released his hold on the wolf's leg and backed away, as did his limping adversary.

Clay's leash unraveled from its coiled pile under his collar and trailed in his wake. The other werewolf noticed it, moved forward, and attempted to step on it. Brown fur ruffled as Clay twisted sharply to flip the leash out of the way.

I looked around, trying to figure out how to stop this. In the houses closest to the fight, more lights burst on. In the house across the street, someone pushed back a curtain to peer out.

Behind me, I heard a shrill whistle. "Duke! Come here, Duke."

The neighborhood was waking.

This time, the sudden interruption didn't distract either of them. Both maintained focus on their opponent. This had to stop now before Clay got hurt.

"The noise has everyone waking up, whoever you are," I said. "You don't have enough time to finish this. It'd be better to leave now when Clay won't be able to chase you. Someone's going to call the police, and when they get here, they'll see a dog that's neither licensed nor leashed. You'll either have to change and expose yourself, or let them take you away thinking you're a dog."

The challenger continued his circling attack as if I hadn't spoken.

The front door of the house closest to us opened and a man shined a flashlight at the fighting dogs, then at me.

"Can you help me?" I called, my voice purposely coming out high-pitched and fearful. "Do you know whose dog this is? It came running at my dog from the direction of your backyard."

"It's not ours. Want me to call the police?" he yelled over the snarls and growls.

I didn't get a chance to answer. The grey werewolf broke away from the fight and bolted back into the darkness from where he'd come. Apparently, he had heard my warning.

Clay, panting heavily, stayed close to me and watched the other wolf retreat. The challenger conceded with his withdrawal. For now.

"Did you see what kind of dog it was?" the man called as he left the safety of his house to look at his side yard where the wolf had disappeared. He cautiously shined his flashlight to search for it.

I let out a shaky, thankful laugh, knelt beside Clay, and wrapped my arms around his neck. My hands shook, the strain and fear taking their toll, as I ran my hands over the area around his collar. I didn't find any injuries. Relieved, I leaned against him. He really was growing on me.

"Ma'am? You okay?"

The man pointed his flashlight at us but stayed near his house. Any closer and he'd feel the pull. I didn't need to deal with any more problems. Across the street, a door opened, distracting the man.

"They okay, Mike?"

I lifted my head from Clay. "You okay?" I whispered.

He turned his head and licked my cheek, reassuring me.

"Next time I'll just carry the leash," I promised. My eyes watered. It had been too close. It would have only been a matter of time before the other wolf would have pinned him because of it.

"We're okay," I said as I stood. I kept a hand on Clay's head. "The dog was as big as Clay here but had dark grey fur."

"Doesn't sound like any dog from this neighborhood, but I know there are some big dogs a few blocks away. Do you want me to call the cops?" The man started toward us.

I picked up Clay's loose leash and nudged him to get him moving.

"Nah. I think we're fine," I said taking a step back. Too late. The man had gotten close enough that the pull had him. I saw the interest in his eyes.

After a few moments reassuring him that neither of us had suffered injuries and that police involvement was no longer necessary, I grudgingly gave him my phone number just in case anyone had called the cops and they showed up. Clay remained quiet and unusually calm throughout the conversation.

Crisis averted, we hurried home. I didn't talk. Instead, I concentrated on scanning with my second sight. I pushed to see further than ever before, and it drained me. My legs grew heavier with each step. I tried not to let it show.

While I scanned, so did Clay. His eyes missed nothing, and he constantly scented the air.

The sun cleared the surrounding rooftops, and its bright

rays lit the sidewalk. My hurried walk degraded to a plodding step somewhere along the way, and it took us much longer to get home. No further sign of that weird light reappeared during the rest of the walk.

Because I watched my shuffling feet as we retraced our steps to the back door, I didn't see Rachel standing on the porch.

"There you are!"

My hand flew to Clay's thick mane at the same time my heart skipped a beat. The scare distracted me from my second sight, and it snapped closed at my loss of focus. I struggled to reopen it but a sudden pain in my head stopped my attempt. I'd done too much.

"Nice morning for a walk," she said, moving toward us to pet Clay.

I unclenched my fingers from his fur, not wanting her to notice my death grip. She fingered one of his ears. He shook off her touch. She laughed and bent to kiss the top of his head. He endured the kiss but rolled his eyes at me. Some of my tension melted at their antics. He appeared more relaxed, too.

"I made a call this morning and can get him into the vet for his shots," she said as she tugged the leash from my loose grasp. "I figured after the way he acted last night, we should have him current...just in case."

It took a moment for what she said to click. My stunned gaze dropped to Clay. He calmly met my eyes, not giving any indication what he thought of her announcement. I looked back at Rachel. I didn't know what to say.

"You okay, Gabby?" She looked at me with concern.

No. Not okay. What had started as a nice thank you breakfast for Clay had turned into a dog fight. And now she wanted to take him to the vet? He didn't deserve that. Besides, after the attack, would he be willing to leave me? Wait. Could a vet figure out he wasn't really a dog? I tried to contain my panic.

"Uh, I didn't budget for it," I blurted, hoping at the very least to put the visit off until I talked to Sam about the risks.

"Don't worry." Rachel untangled his leash. "I can cover it for now, and you can pay me back."

"Let's all go." The words popped out of my mouth before I thought about it. What good would that do? Did I think I could block the vet from touching Clay? Rachel would definitely know something was up, then.

"No offense, Gabby, but you look like hell. I think you'd be better off with some quiet time. Don't worry; we'll be fine." She tried to pull Clay toward the garage again, but he didn't move with her.

Instead, he nudged me toward the back door, almost knocking me off balance. Rachel tugged on his leash and scolded him, but he ignored her and stayed focused on me.

"Would you mind giving him your standard pep talk? I don't know why he only listens to you. I'm the one that feeds him treats." She handed the leash over to me. I rubbed my forehead still unsure what he wanted me to do.

"Is it safe for you?" I breathed in his ear as I bent to give him a hug.

He snorted, which I took as a yes. Did he want me to stay here, then?

"I'm so sorry about this. I'll need to call Sam and let him know what happened."

I straightened, looked him in the eye, and smoothed the fur

on his head. "It's your choice." I dropped the leash and stepped back.

He gave me a long look as Rachel moved to open the car door. He sighed then followed her.

"The control you have over him is weird but cool," Rachel said as he jumped into the back seat.

Control? I didn't have any control over him. He only listened when I threatened to kick him out of my room or leave him behind.

"Yeah. Just don't be gone too long. He'll get upset."

"The vet's just a few minutes from here. We should be back soon." She climbed behind the wheel, closed the door, and rolled down her window.

I couldn't believe we were actually doing this. What did a vet usually check for? Shots...Age...Neuter... Crap, crap, crap! The engine roared to life.

"Just don't have him neutered! Or anything that involves blood or blood work. It's expensive, and I promised him he'd keep his jewels." Oh how I wished those words back when Clay started to make an odd coughing noise. I could only assume it was his version of laughter. I really needed to start filtering what I said.

Rachel swiveled to check on Clay. "Maybe we should have the vet check his lungs."

"He's fine. Think cost," I said from the deck as she backed out of the driveway.

I went inside and immediately called Sam to let him know about the attack. He assured me of my safety, but I wasn't worried about that. Paul and Henry had long ago educated me in regard to challenge etiquette. A challenge questioned Clay's right to me. If present, I needed to stay near him to show my support of his right. Fleeing rejected him. Though rejecting him sounded tempting on the surface, doing so would put me back into the eligible pool. I didn't want that.

Sam said he would let Elder Joshua know about the attack, too. He also felt certain the challenger wouldn't try again anytime soon given the extent of his injuries.

A werewolf's tough hide deflected many things that could damage human skin. What it couldn't deflect, it reduced in severity. A knife could still cut a werewolf, for example, but not lethally like it could me. On top of the nearly impenetrable skin, nature also threw in a phenomenally fast healing process. A shallow cut would knit together in less than an hour, with no scar visible in less than a day. However, injuries from another werewolf tended to take twice as long to heal. Still faster than a human's, however.

Talking to Sam helped settle my nerves. Though the werewolf's odd light still bothered me, I couldn't bring it up. I'd never shared the details of my ability with Sam. However, I did almost bring up the vet visit. Only Clay's willingness to go had me keeping it to myself at the last minute. I felt guilty enough and didn't need to add a lecture to it.

Before I hung up, Sam reminded me that challenges weren't unheard of and that I had no reason to worry, yet. I agreed, and neither of us said what I already knew. Challenges occurred when more than one werewolf became interested in the same potential Mate and the potential in question didn't have a preference. So, the challenge was my fault.

An hour and a half later, I had showered, scrubbed the

kitchen floor, and vacuumed every room in the house in an effort to keep myself awake.

At the sound of Rachel's car in the driveway, I ran through the house and out the back door. Rachel parked the car in front of the garage and smiled at me. I leaned over the porch railing in an effort to see into the back of the car. I spotted Clay lying on the back seat with his head down. He didn't look up at me.

Rachel opened her door.

"How'd it go?" I said, trying to sound indifferent.

"He took it like a champ." She opened the back car door for Clay. He lifted his head and stood with obvious effort. Then he hopped down with care and pathetically climbed the deck steps to my side. I stared at him for a moment.

"What'd they do to him?"

Rachel shook her head and closed the door.

"He wasn't acting like this when we left. I swear. I think he's hamming it up for you." She patted Clay's head with a laugh.

He accepted the pat with a defeated grunt, stopped hobbling, and started to walk with his usual gait. I heaved a relieved sigh. He looked up at me and winked. I quickly checked to see if Rachel had noticed, but she had already walked away from us and into the house. I shook my head at him before we followed Rachel in.

"So what shots did he get?" I poured some orange juice from the refrigerator and took a drink to keep myself busy. Clay's eyes never left me.

"Just rabies. The vet had a hard time determining his age by his teeth, but thought him to be in his prime."

I choked on my juice.

"That's great," I managed to gasp out as I glanced at Clay.

A small smug smile curled his lips. I needed to find a nice way to tell him his wolfie smile looked creepy.

"Hey, while I was waiting for him, Peter called. He said he had a good time last night and hoped Scott hadn't ruined his chance by coming on too strong. He's never seen Scott act in any way but smooth. He naturally thinks Scott's falling hard for you."

Both Clay and I gawked at her. I know my jaw had dropped a little and wondered if Clay's had done the same.

"I'm just repeating." She held up her hands with a laugh at my expression. "Anyway, Peter said Scott's already been bugging him about getting your number to set up another date. Given what you told me, I said no, that last night was just a friendly get together and that you were seeing someone else."

Clay's gusty sigh of relief competed with mine. We'd been through enough today. Okay, fine, he'd had to go through all of it while I just stood by. But still...the stress of it, along with the overuse of my sight, wore me out.

Looking down at him, I realized how much I didn't mind having him there. We'd at least become friends of sorts. But I worried I treated him unfairly by allowing him to hang around. Would that mislead him to think our relationship might grow to more than friendship? I hoped not. If he ever thought I asked too much, he could always walk away.

"You know, sometimes that dog creeps me out with how human he acts," Rachel said, shaking her head. "Anyway, I'm going to meet up with Peter for another try at a date. We're going to see a movie, and this time, I'm not asking you to come with." She had a huge smile on her face as she walked past us toward her room.

"Thank you!" I called to her retreating form.

CHAPTER TEN

THE REST OF THE WEEKEND PASSED IN A BLUR OF STUDYING. Whenever Rachel left to meet Peter, Clay and I would sprawl on the living room floor. I would read my books while he read his, and I turned his pages. We didn't talk much. He seemed content just to lie by me.

Because of Clay's sensitive hearing, we always moved back into my room before Rachel could get from the car to the door.

"I bet I'm looking for a new roommate before the next semester starts," I said to Clay when I heard Rachel come through the door late Sunday night. He didn't have much to say one way or the other.

On Wednesday, I realized I hadn't done my laundry in days. My meager wardrobe lay in a mashed pile in the corner of my closet. With a sigh, I plucked out a semi-clean shirt and the jeans from the day before. After I dressed, I grabbed what I could from the remaining heap and ran downstairs to cram it into the washer. Clay watched me from the top of the stairs. If I didn't leave now, I'd arrive late for class. I threw in the detergent, ran up the stairs, and nearly plowed Clay over on my way out the door.

When I pulled into the driveway that evening, there was a service truck parked in front of the house, and Rachel's car already sat in the garage. Baffled, I watched her hurry out the back door. She wore a wide grin.

"You are brilliant!" she said as soon as I opened my car door.

"What'd I do?" I took my bag loaded with library books out of the front seat and closed the door.

"There's a hot repairman working on the washer in the basement. Thank you for breaking it." She linked her arm through mine and walked me to the house.

"I didn't do anything but throw in a load of laundry before I left," I said quietly as I glanced at the open basement door.

Clay sat in the hallway, staring down the stairs. When he heard me, he turned his head to watch us.

"Hey," Rachel said. "I'm not blaming...I'm just thanking." She continued to grin.

"I thought you were into Peter," I whispered.

"I am. It doesn't mean I don't window-shop. Go down there and flirt with him and see if we can get twenty percent off our bill."

"I will not," I huffed with a laugh. I moved away from her and got myself a drink of water. "It'd be safer to send Clay down there to learn how to fix it than me trying to get us a price break."

"If our dog starts fixing things, we're hitting the road and making some money," said Rachel.

We both heard the heavy tread on the basement stairs at the same time. Rachel's face lit with anticipation while I eyed the door with dread. Was it too late to run past and hide in my room? With Clay so close to the door, I'd probably trip on him, and the repairman would find me lying at his feet.

Then, I saw the guy. Denim hugged his long, lean legs, and a snug shirt displayed his biceps and abs to perfection. I knew better than to stare; he would take my attention as a come-get-me signal for sure. But with a body like that, a girl had to look her fill. When my eyes finally met his, he smiled broadly and flexed.

Well, that just ruined the whole window-shopping experience. A conceited hottie. Their vocabularies didn't include the word no, which made it difficult to fight them off. The situation called for a retreat. I turned to Rachel.

"I have to go pick up my ring before Clay gets here. He'd be heartbroken if he found out I bent a prong on the setting already. Plus, my hand feels naked without it." While I spoke, I held out my left hand dramatically and gave it a wistful look. Maybe it was over doing it, but I wasn't sure he'd get the point otherwise.

"The dog?" the man asked with a puzzled look at Rachel.

A nervous laugh escaped before I could stop it. "We named the dog after my fiancé. He has a good sense of humor and likes the dog, too."

I bolted out the door and got back into my car. Clay hadn't been fast enough for a change, and I had to leave him behind.

Not knowing what else to do, I went grocery shopping and took my time to read the labels of the different orange juices the store offered. Even after the drawn-out shopping trip, I had to drive past the house three times before the truck finally disappeared.

When I staggered in through the back door laden with

groceries, Clay sat waiting for me in the kitchen. I set down the bags and peeked around the corner to look for Rachel. When I didn't see or hear her, I spoke to Clay in a whisper.

"You better keep reading the books I bring home. You can be our repair guy. It gives me the willies that he knows where I live."

Clay nodded his head in agreement...which Rachel saw as she walked into the kitchen. She paused mid-stride, her eyes wide.

"Did he just nod?" she demanded.

I acted natural. "Yep. I've been working on it with him. He caught on really fast. The nodding isn't bad, but his smile can be a little scary."

Rachel stared at us for a moment then shook her head.

"You're weird, Gabby, but in a good way. Anyway, it was one hundred and twenty-five dollars to fix the washer. I covered your half. With the vet bill, you're up to one hundred, minus the burger and drink from disaster night."

Ouch. "Okay. I'll run to the bank after class tomorrow." I chewed my lip for a moment. My pathetic savings couldn't take these kinds of unexpected hits. Life was more expensive than I'd anticipated.

I turned to unpack the rest of my groceries and noticed Clay watching me closely. Not wanting to draw Rachel's attention to him again, I ignored his look and finished up so I could go study.

ON FRIDAY AFTERNOON, Rachel rushed in through the back door while calling my name in a panicked tone.

"In here!" I said as I jumped up from the bed.

We nearly collided as she flew through my bedroom door at the same time I tried to leave it. I caught her by the arms.

"What's going on?"

"Peter broke and told Scott he had plans to go to dinner with me tonight," she panted.

I stared at her. She ran through the house to tell me she had a date? I really didn't see how I qualified as the weird one sometimes.

"So...?"

"Peter's coming here to pick me up, and Scott's coming with. Gabby, I don't think he's going to take no for an answer tonight. Peter can't shake him." Her emphatic expression told me the degree of insistence Scott had used to accompany Peter.

I groaned, flopped back on my bed, and forgetting about Clay, landed on him. He didn't even twitch, but I still reached back to pat him.

"Sorry, Clay." I froze mid-pat then bolted upright. "I've got an idea! Rachel, if you have any clothes that would say I've been dating a guy for a while, can I borrow them?" I didn't want to spend any money unnecessarily.

"Sure, but who are you dating?"

Rachel moved out of the way as I rushed from my room. I heard Clay hop down from the bed to follow me. I grabbed shoes from the closet. My plan could work. I just needed to convince Clay. They both trailed behind me as I struggled to slip on some shoes while I walked to the kitchen. It wasn't easy. I almost tripped twice and covered most of the distance hopping instead of walking. I grabbed my car keys.

"I'll let you know when I bring him home. Come on, Clay," I

called, holding the door open for him. With a baffled glint in his eyes, he followed me.

I rushed to the car and waved for him to hurry. I had the doors slammed closed and the engine rumbling seconds later. Clay studied me as I careened out the driveway and took off in the direction of the shopping district.

"You're here to keep me safe, right?" I took his grunt as a yes. "Then, I need you to be more than my dog." I risked a glance at him. He tilted his head at me clearly confused. "I need you to put on your skin. Be my date tonight. Please?"

I sounded desperate, but I didn't really care. The thought of Scott cornering me gave me shivers. His normal personality probably qualified as nice, but I'd seen how the obsession had worked on others. Scott's fascination with me had obviously advanced. Yet, if Clay were to run interference as my date, it could permanently dissolve.

"You took a shower today, right?" I expected the harrumph he let out. "Do you know what size you wear? Shirt, pants, shoes?" Unhelpful, he continued to stare at me.

Given what he'd worn when I first saw him, he probably didn't know. It made my work a little bit more difficult, but I would manage.

I found an open spot and careened into it, slamming on the brakes at the last second. Only Clay's good balance kept him from falling out of the seat.

"I'll be back in a few minutes," I said as I rushed out the door.

Inside the store, I tried to remember how he'd looked as a man. Hairy. Dirty. Tall. Well, taller than me. Had he seemed thin or chubby? I couldn't remember. His jacket had obscured most of his shape, and I'd been distracted by the whole "hey, I'm your Mate" thing.

Usually, when I shopped on my own, it didn't turn out well. However, my crazed sprints from rack to rack held most of the men I encountered at bay. So, I scoured the clearance racks and guessed at sizes while trying to stick with safe styles.

Panting for breath, I raced to a register. I bought Clay a linen pant and shirt set, the largest brown foam bottomed sandals I could find—I could always cut the foam down to size—and a few other essentials.

Then, I ran out of the store. Clay was standing on the seat. He just stared at me as I opened the car door and tossed the bags at him. They landed at his feet.

I started the engine and tried to think where I could take him to get dressed. Somewhere he could walk in as a dog and out as a man. I couldn't think of a single place that allowed dogs in changing areas. I'd just have to try to pull a fast one on Rachel. I put the car in gear and drove it as if I'd stolen it. I made it to the house in record time.

Rachel was already dressed and standing outside by the back door when we got home. She had a stack of clothes in her arms.

"Where's the date?" she said as her eyes searched the empty car. "They are going to be here in fifteen minutes."

I waved her back into the house. "He'll be here in a few minutes. I hope."

We followed her in, and I paused to toss the bag of new clothes in the bathroom for Clay. I really hoped he'd help me.

"Let's go in my room, and you can help me pick what to wear," I said to Rachel.

"Really?" she said with an excited smile. She'd already noticed I liked my privacy and usually left me alone. But, I expected the opportunity to dress me would distract her from noticing that Clay hadn't followed us from the kitchen or, later, his absence.

"I need something a little tropical, or hippie-ish," I said as I closed the door and started to undress.

Rachel set the clothes on the bed, her expression filled with suspicion.

"Who is this guy? Why do you need to dress like a hippie?"

"He's a good friend, and he didn't have much notice to go home to change. Because I'm cheap, I got him some clean clothes from the summer closeout racks." I spoke a little louder for Clay's benefit. I wanted him to know why I purchased what I had.

Rachel looked up at my sudden surge in volume. Clearly, my weirdness had just increased a level. I motioned to the pile of clothes to distract her. She began to riffle through them, searching for something to fit my requirements.

"He's got longish hair so I think he might look like a hippie in what I bought." At least, I thought he might still have longish hair. It'd been months since I last saw him. "He was just behind me. I told him he could use our bathroom to change."

"How good of a friend is he?" she asked.

I smiled. "Well, we've slept together."

She surprised me by not saying anything. Instead, she held up a few options. I picked a flowing, knee-length, cream skirt with a light yellow, scoop-necked top and hurried to get dressed.

"You do know that the best way to appear like you've been dating a long time would be to look like you don't care how you look, right?" she asked.

I rolled my eyes at her, gave the skirt one last tug to straighten it, and studied myself in the mirror. Dressing up was a gamble. It might send the wrong message to Scott even with Clay present. Maybe I should follow Rachel's advice and dress down. But then Clay would look out of place in his clothes.

"That looks great on you," Rachel complimented as she scooped up the rejects.

Worried Clay might need more time, I stalled by asking her how I should fix my hair. I didn't own any make-up to apply.

"So what's the guy's name?" Rachel watched me closely.

"Clay," I admitted reluctantly. Since I'd asked a huge favor of him, I couldn't lie about his name.

"Shut up," she said with a laugh of disbelief.

"Not lying," I said, holding up my hands in the mirror. "He talks as much as the dog, too. So don't bother trying to make conversation."

I figured I'd pushed our time limit and turned to let Rachel inspect me. She smiled her approval then dashed to her room to ditch the extra clothes. We crossed paths in the living room as she went to look out the picture window, and I went to find Clay.

The door to the bathroom remained firmly closed. I tapped on it.

"Do you need help?" I whispered.

Unfortunately, Rachel overheard and started sniggering behind me. Apparently, there was nothing to see out the window. I tried to shoo her away with a wave, but she shook her head and leaned against the hallway wall to watch.

"Please hurry, Clay," I begged.

The door opened. I took a step back to avoid the cloud of steam that rolled out. Clay stepped out with it. Stunned, I stared at him. I hadn't seen him since the beginning of the summer. Well, excluding that brief look at his backside. I'd been too shocked to notice the rest of him, then.

He still looked scruffy. Between the beard that concealed his cheeks and entire neck, and the full mouth-covering mustache, I still couldn't see much of him. His damp hair hung in limp, wavy strands in front of his eyes and covered the top portion of his face almost down to his nose. Yet, clean and dressed in the clothes I'd forced onto him, he looked amazing.

His shoulders filled the short-sleeved shirt, and although snug on his chest, it fell loosely to his waist. He put his hands in his pockets as he waited for my inspection to finish. Embarrassed, I tore my gaze away, but not before I noted he'd left himself barefoot.

"Brat," I muttered. Then, I cleared my throat and added, "You'll do."

I turned and caught Rachel's smirk. "Quiet from the peanut gallery."

Mercifully, the doorbell rang then so she just laughed and rushed to answer it. Their arrival spared me from having to look at Clay again. In a way, I'd forgotten the man under the fur.

I followed Rachel slowly, feeling curiously lost. Clay walked softly behind me.

"Come on in," Rachel said to Peter. Peter stepped in, and Scott followed inches behind. Peter gave me an apologetic look as he moved aside. Scott's eyes found mine, and he smiled widely. I flashed a politely cool smile in return.

I could see the moment Scott spotted Clay. His face first fell then firmed in tense appraisal.

"Hi, Peter," I said. "Nice to see you again, Scott." His face lit at my statement, and I felt badly that I needed to hurt him in order to end his fixation. "We were going to join you guys, but Clay just got off of work a little while ago and suggested he and I take advantage of the empty house tonight." My heart skipped a beat or two at my bold words, and I struggled to control the blush that wanted to paint my face. Thankfully, Clay stood behind me so I didn't need to witness his reaction to my words.

Scott's face was a different story. I watched it turn red.

"Isn't Clay your dog?" he asked suspiciously.

"We named the dog after my boyfriend. It's a bit of a joke. Clay, meet Peter and Scott, Rachel's friends." My disassociation of Scott broke him. His shoulders slumped, and the familiar look of shame stole over his face. Why did this happen? I hated it. Pity and remorse swamped me.

Clay lightly set his hand at the small of my back. A casual touch. His palm slowly warmed a large area. Even in man form, he could sense some of my anxiety.

Scott noted Clay's hand on my back, glanced between us, then turned to his friend.

"Peter, Rachel, I'm sorry to back out on you, too, but I think I'm going to head home. I've been fighting a cold all week." Without waiting for acknowledgment, he turned and left.

Peter, who'd looked apologetically anxious when he entered, watched his friend leave with a concerned frown. Rachel murmured something to him. He nodded and went to the closet to retrieve her jacket. Rachel looked back at me as Peter held out her jacket to assist her.

"Are you sure you want to stay in?"

Rachel accepted Peter's help with an ease that usually came after being together for years. I doubted they even realized how in tune they were with each other. That often happened when people found their perfect match. Their lives blended in a seamless perfection they simply called love. It was more than that, though. Their deep connection put them in tune with each other's needs and wants. It kept them open to suggestion and reason so they would always listen to each other. Yep, I'd need to look for a new roommate soon.

"We're sure," I said with a smile and waved them out the door. "Don't come home early."

When the door closed behind Peter and Rachel, I exhaled slowly, and turned to Clay, breaking our connection. I smiled at him.

"Home free. Thank you, Clay."

The subtle difference between living with Clay-the-dog and standing in a room alone with Clay-the-man tickled the nerves in my stomach. I refused to show it.

He simply watched me as he placed his now empty hand back into the front pocket of his pants. The air cooled the spot on my back that he'd warmed.

"Um..." I wasn't sure what to do. I hadn't thought past getting rid of Scott.

Clay's calm gaze made the nervous butterflies in my stomach worse. Silly, really, considering he watched me all the time as a dog. I took a breath and tried again.

"Did you want to do something since we're both dressed up?"

He shrugged.

"You can talk to me, Clay," I said with a little hope. I really began to wonder if he could speak. When he didn't respond, I spoke again. "Okay, do you want to go out or stay in?"

He moved to the couch and sat in the middle, his choice clear. Stay in tonight.

I hesitated. The chair, set at an odd angle to the TV, gave you a sore neck if you tried to watch a movie from there. That meant I'd need to sit next to him to watch a movie. But I felt so exposed in a skirt and sleeveless shirt. I wasn't sure if I could sit next to him for a full movie.

While I debated my options, he watched me closely.

"I'm going to go change," I stammered. "I'll be right back."

I turned and made it one step before the back of my shirt snagged on something. Surprised, I looked over my shoulder and found Clay standing right behind me. He held a fold of my shirt between his thumb and forefinger. I could see the glint of his brown eyes behind the still damp strands of his hair. He tilted his head back toward the couch and gave a slight tug on my shirt. My stomach dropped, and I couldn't tell if it was in a good way or a bad one.

When I hesitated, he gave another tug. I surrendered, turned back, and sat on the couch.

He padded over to the movies, made a selection I couldn't see, and crouched to start it. It amazed me that he knew how to do that. Then again, he watched everything Rachel and I did. I wondered if anything escaped his notice.

He pressed play, stood, and walked toward me with fluid strides. I felt graceless in comparison. He settled next to me and watched the previews. I tried to focus on them, too, but couldn't. Instead, I noticed our bare feet, the scratch on the wall next to the TV, his leg lightly pressed against mine, the sound of the water as it slowly dripped from the showerhead in the bathroom, his hands loosely resting on his lap. The long list of unimportant details would not let my mind settle.

It was midway through the movie when my mind calmed enough to notice we watched an action-comedy I'd wanted to see. I'd just mentioned it to Rachel this past week. She must have gotten it after that.

Slowly, I began to relax and enjoy the movie. I even laughed aloud at one point. Clay's echoing chuckle startled me, but in a good way. So, he *could* do more than growl as a dog. His deep laugh sounded pleasant.

When the movie ended, I stood and went to put it away. It was still early, just about six.

"Do you want to watch another one?" I asked as I knelt to look at the movie selection. "I can throw in a pizza for us."

When I heard nothing, which wasn't unusual, I turned and saw a pile of folded clothes on the couch. But no Clay.

"Clay?"

I went in search of him, but he wasn't in the house. In the living room, I glanced at the pile of clothes again. He had been so quiet I hadn't heard a thing.

It took me a moment to think about using my second sight. Because of school and Clay's presence at home, I'd fallen into patterns where I didn't use it often. I felt safe enough that I didn't *need* to use it. Still, I checked. He wasn't anywhere in the immediate area, but I wasn't too worried about it. He did occasionally leave my side, but he never stayed away for very long.

With a smile, I picked up his clothes and headed to my room. Good thing I took forever to pick a movie.

Since I had nothing else to do, I decided to watch the movie I had spotted just before Clay disappeared. I changed into some sweats and a tank top then scrounged around in the kitchen and found what I needed to make a big bowl of buttered popcorn.

Popcorn in hand, I headed for the TV. When I walked into the living room, Clay once again lay on the couch. I smiled at his familiar furry presence.

"There you are. Want some popcorn?"

I didn't wait for an answer but went to the kitchen to get him his own bowl and split the popcorn between the two. In the living room, I set his bowl on the floor within his reach. Then, I curled into my end of the couch and tucked my feet under him. With my bowl balanced at my side, I reached for the remote.

I'd barely started the movie when he sighed gustily, repositioned himself, and laid his head on my curled legs. The heat of him relaxed me, and I settled in comfortably, content not to move him. I ate a piece of popcorn as I watched the intro. His head shifted on my leg, following the piece of popcorn. I absently took another piece and offered it to him. He gently ate it from my fingers. I offered him a few more pieces, not fully paying attention when he licked the back of my hand.

The second movie was more an action-suspense than comedy. Halfway through the movie, I'd abandoned my bowl of popcorn to the floor. One of my hands burrowed in the thick fur at Clay's neck, and the other lightly worried his fuzzy ear. He didn't seem to mind my grip as I stared at the screen. At a particularly suspenseful part, the front door opened. It scared me so badly that a strangled scream tore through the air. My scream. My heart pounded as both Rachel and Clay stared at me.

"And that's why I don't watch suspense movies," I said to both of them once I could breathe again. Clay didn't stop laughing for two minutes. Rachel laughed just as hard and thankfully didn't notice Clay's reaction.

Clay licked my exposed midriff then, finally, settled down.

I gently tugged on his ear. "Cut it out," I scolded softly.

"So when did Clay leave? I thought he'd still be here after you said I shouldn't hurry home." Rachel kicked off her shoes and flopped sideways on the chair.

I turned off the movie to give her my full attention. "Nah, I turned my back, and he took off on me." I patted Clay on the head, and he snorted. "It's okay, though, I have my favorite guy here." And I realized it was true. I liked no man better than I liked Clay in his fur. Sam used to take first place, but I still felt disappointed in him for not warning me about the last Introduction and about the possibility of Clay showing up at the back door.

"He was a little scary looking if you ask me," Rachel said as she reached over to pet Clay. Turned away from her, he took the opportunity to arch a brow at me. I fought to keep my face straight.

"When I first met him, I told him he looked like a crazy man. I still think he's crazy, but he's also nice and dependable." Clay heaved a sigh. It seemed werewolves didn't like to be described as nice either.

"So does he ever act like Scott?"

"No way." It came out so fast I had to pause and rethink it. Nope, I definitely spoke the truth. "Most guys talk about themselves to try to impress me, or they just act scary obsessive. Clay's different. I don't think I affect him like I do other guys."

I looked away from both of them, thinking. At times, he

showed his possessive streak—like when I'd gone on the double date—but he didn't act obsessive. According to my reliable sources of werewolf lore, Clay did feel a strong pull for me, but it was dissimilar to what human men felt. His pull, the werewolf version, should make him territorial and controlling, but he never seemed affected by any of that. Yet, for some reason, he stayed.

"I think he just likes being with me," I said. I noticed Clay looking up at me and met his gaze. Even when he wrecked the truck back at the Compound, he didn't creep on me like most guys had. "And I'm grateful that I get to be normal around him."

Rachel laughed at me. "You sound like you're really serious about him. Why didn't you talk about him before this? And why didn't you say the dog had the same name? We could have changed it."

I decided to ignore the part about being serious. "I wasn't sure if or when he'd make an appearance. And I like the name Clay. Besides, he doesn't mind." I wasn't sure if I was talking about Clay-the-dog or Clay-the-man anymore.

Rachel switched topics. "We should probably talk about overnight visitors. What rules do we want to set?"

"Um...no loud noises?"

"Come on!" Rachel laughed louder. "I meant, weekends only? Maybe guests till midnight on weekdays? Notice needed? You know, that kind of stuff."

She grinned at me, still lounged sideways on the chair. I really didn't want to have this conversation with Clay present. He lay quietly, head on my lap, considerately pretending to sleep.

"I don't know. I trust you and your judgment, and you can

trust my lack of a social life. I really don't think I'll see Clay very often so you don't need to worry."

"Oh, he'll be back. I saw the way he watched you. Are you sure the only rule you can come up with is no loud noises?"

I thought of adding that she should warn me when we had a visitor, but I looked down at Clay and figured we had it covered.

"Yeah, I think we're fine."

"Great!" she said with a huge grin. Then she cupped her hands and yelled, "Peter!"

The front door immediately opened and a sheepish looking Peter entered.

"You were supposed to text me," he muttered uncomfortably.

I laughed. "Come on in, Peter. Clay and I were just going to bed." Clay jumped off the couch first, and I got up to follow him into my room. "Night, guys."

"Another early Friday night for us," I whispered to Clay after I closed the door.

I pulled back the covers and slid between the sheets. Clay settled in his usual spot and began to breathe deeply while I lay awake thinking about the conversation with Rachel.

As she'd pointed out, Clay wasn't like the other guys. At the Compound, when I'd felt the pull Sam had warned me about, I'd panicked. I'd thought Clay would be just like the rest and that I would spend the rest of my life trying to avoid him.

When he'd shown up at the door as a dog, and not as a man, he'd thrown me off guard. Now, I realized he'd been pretty smart about it. Somehow, he'd known I would be more likely to give him a chance as a dog than as a man. Again, I'd underestimated his intelligence.

Rachel was also right about Clay watching me. He followed me everywhere. I assumed his attentiveness was to observe and learn. What if it wasn't? His quiet presence had already lulled me into indifference over his company. I needed to be more careful.

CHAPTER ELEVEN

THE NEXT MORNING, I TIREDLY WENT TO THE KITCHEN AND OPENED the fridge. My deep thoughts had kept me awake longer than I'd intended, and I felt like Sam looked most mornings. Instead of coffee, I wanted my OJ.

I squinted against the harsh light and scanned the sparse contents of my designated shelf for the orange liquid of life. No orange juice. Shuffling the contents around didn't change the answer. Nope, not there. Straightening, I surveyed the kitchen and spotted its remains in the recycling.

The shower turned on in the bathroom, and I remembered Peter had stayed over. I looked down at Clay, who silently accompanied me, as usual.

"Great. Another non-coffee person," I complained to him.

Since I drank the last of the milk yesterday, I went for a glass of water instead. The faucet handle jiggled loosely in my hand, and only a trickle came out.

"Seriously?" I mumbled as Rachel glided into the kitchen.

"Looks like I'll have to call the hottie plumber back."

"No, thanks. And no big guy showing two inches of crack,

either." I settled for a third of a glass of water and turned off the faucet.

Rachel might have thought the plumber hot, but he'd been bigheaded about it. I knew I wouldn't be able to get rid of him so easily a second time. Having narrowly avoided one potential stalker, there was no way I would invite another one in.

"I was going to go pick up Clay later, anyway," I lied. "I'll have him look at it." I smiled at Rachel as Clay's head whipped up at me. I'd beg him again if I had to.

"Really? No-talk, leave-early, Clay?"

"Yeah, that one. Not the dog."

"I believe you said you didn't think he'd be around much." She smirked at me while she measured the coffee. I stuck my tongue out at her, but she just laughed.

"Don't remind me. I'm probably going to need to beg."

"Does he know much about plumbing?" Rachel asked as she moved to the sink to fill the coffee pot.

"Don't know...we don't talk much." I laughed while she groaned.

WITH NOTHING TO DRINK, I dressed to go shopping. Clay waited for me just outside my door.

"Wanna come shopping with me or stay here?" I knew he'd want to go even if he did have to stay in the car. He moved to stand by the back door.

We drove to one of those discount supercenters. I left Clay in the car with the windows cracked—it was more for show than actual airflow. If he got hot, he'd just let himself out.

It worried me a bit that I needed to shop several days sooner than planned. In order to feed Clay and myself, I had already made compromises in my original budget. Yet, at this rate, I would surpass even my revised spending allowance for groceries. That meant I needed to change my shopping habits, not just to save money but to fill the pantry with more food. I didn't mind eating light, but looking back, since Clay didn't eat his dog food—not that I blamed him—he ate light, too. A little too light when I recalled how much Sam could consume.

The orange juice I liked cost more than a five-pound bag of potatoes. I put the potatoes in the cart and walked past the fresh juice. Maybe I could buy a decent concentrate. I went to the freezer section, found some cheap veggies, and ignored the speculative look from a man a few yards away.

Everyone found shopping a pain at some point. I found it a pain all the time.

In the next case, I studied the meat options. The flash-frozen chicken breasts were cheaper than the steaks per pound so I went with those. The man moved from the veggies to the meats as I eyed the cart and tried to envision our meals. Meat, potato, and veggie.

Before the man tried to start a conversation, I moved on to dry goods. A large tub of generic peanut butter and another of grape jelly joined the growing heap in the cart. I used my other vision to check for and skillfully avoid as many men as possible while I wove through the aisles. Not for the first time, I wished I could tell men and women apart.

Always on the lookout for deals, I spotted the day-old bakery rack and found two loaves of bread for a dollar. The cart held more than it usually did when I went shopping. Although, it lacked variety, it had quantity; and I'd managed to keep it under twenty dollars. My smug happiness lasted until I recalled I needed something to drink in the morning. Dang. And cereal. Oh, well. Under thirty still helped the budget.

When I thought back to what Clay had already done for me, like putting on clothes last night, I couldn't regret spending more to feed him. And there was still the faucet that awaited him. I frowned as I realized all he had to wear was the linen getup. Surely, I could spare enough to buy Clay a decent set of clothes.

I turned the cart around and hunted the store for the best bargains. The store had off-brand denims on sale. I guessed at his size and tossed a pair in the cart. Next, I stumbled upon a returned three pack of t-shirts that looked poorly repackaged. I saw nothing wrong with the shirts and figured the low price correlated with the packaging. Whatever dropped the price down by three dollars worked for me.

A flannel shirt, hidden within the mass of other shirts on the clearance rack, caught my eye. I looked it over closely. The shirt lacked most of the middle buttons. An easy enough fix. I put it in the cart. It would get chilly soon, and he'd need it. I paused. Would he stay that long? Probably. He showed no sign of wanting to leave. I went to find some warm socks then looked for shoes. I had to guess the size based on the feet that I'd seen last night.

Waiting in the checkout line proved painfully annoying. I couldn't avoid men while standing still. However, I did manage to find an open lane with a female cashier. Two men lined up behind me and persistently tried to start up a conversation with me before I unloaded the cart. The woman gave me a look. Whatever.

I left the store in a hurry. Usually, if I put enough distance between us, my admirers forgot about me.

The cart clattered over the blacktop as I made my way to the car. Clay watched for me from the back seat. His steady gaze tracked my progress. I looked forward to showing him what I'd managed to purchase and smiled at him.

Unfortunately, the man who'd just pulled into the space beyond my car thought I'd meant the smile for him. I mentally groaned as I kept pushing the cart toward my car. The man climbed down from his truck. Like Clay, he didn't stop watching me as he stepped out from between the vehicles to wait for me. Clay tensed inside the car.

"Hi, there. Need a hand?" the man said.

I stopped near the trunk.

"No, thanks. I got it."

He didn't leave.

"My name's Dale. I own Dale's Auto Body on South Mitchell. You should bring your car by. It looks like it might be due for an oil change."

Did I really look dumb enough to believe he could determine the car needed an oil change just by looking at the exterior? It certainly wasn't leaking oil as a giveaway.

"That's a nice offer, but my boyfriend does the oil changes." I unlocked the trunk and started to load groceries.

Dale didn't take the hint and go away.

"He's a handy guy, then?" He grabbed the potatoes and set them in the trunk for me. Unfortunately, it brought him closer.

"Yes, very." A brief conversation sometimes worked to get rid of a pest.

"I'm sorry, I didn't catch your name," he said.

I could see Clay through the back window. Crouched down, he watched the man though the small gap between the trunk lid and the trunk. I bent forward and set a bag in the trunk so

Dale wouldn't see me as I rolled my eyes at Clay. Clay's gaze briefly flicked to me before returning to Dale with serious intent.

"Gabby," I said as I closed the trunk. "Thanks for helping me with the groceries, but I need to get going. My dog's been in the car for a while already."

Not waiting for his reply, I moved the cart to the empty spot next to my car.

"We have an opening at the shop. If your boyfriend's looking for work, send him by. We'll see how good he is," Dale said, opening the driver-side door for me.

Clay hopped from the back seat to the driver's seat. With bristling fur, he growled at Dale, who backed away a step.

I nodded to Dale and nudged Clay over so I could slide in behind the wheel. Braving Clay's wrath, Dale closed the door for me. I started the car and pulled through the empty spot in front of me.

"Well, that was a challenge if I ever heard one." I reached over to pet Clay's head. "But no challenges until you fix the sink." He looked up at me, and I smiled.

When we got back to the house, both Rachel and Peter were gone. That seemed to make Clay happy. It definitely made me happy. I hadn't been sure how Clay would get dressed with Rachel around.

"You go shower while I unpack. Then you can look at the sink and see if we have to call that bigheaded plumber back."

He willingly trotted to the bathroom. After that first time, I'd learned to let him close the door on his own.

It didn't take long for me to put the groceries away. When I finished unpacking, I picked up the pile of things I'd bought for Clay and went to my room. The stuff from yesterday already hung neatly in my closet except for some underclothes which I'd hidden in my bottom drawer. I grabbed an item from his drawer—it made it less personal if I didn't over think it—then moved to the bathroom. I could hear the shower running and tapped on the door.

"I'm coming in, so please stay behind the curtain." I waited a moment then entered. Steam already filled the room. "I have some clothes for you. Better stuff for looking at a sink than what I bought yesterday." I realized then that I'd never actually asked him if he would help.

"Clay, I'm so sorry," I apologized sincerely. "I'm being rude and making assumptions. Will you look at the sink? Please?" I asked using my syrupy voice.

He splashed me over the top of the curtain...again.

"Ok, ok. I'll just leave the stuff here on the floor. If something doesn't fit or you don't like it, leave the tags on it, and we'll take it back. I guessed on the shoes. Some of the stuff isn't for now, but I figured you could try it on." I realized I was rambling at the same time I remembered the missing buttons on the shirt. I closed my mouth and quickly grabbed the flannel from the pile.

The water turned off just then, and I rushed from the bathroom.

In my room, I pulled out my travel sewing kit and got to work moving buttons around. The two spares on the inside seam remained intact. With those and a close match I found in the sewing kit, I solved the missing button problem.

While I stitched, I listened for Clay to leave the bathroom. By the time I finished, I still hadn't heard anything. I set the repaired shirt aside and went to look for him.

I found him in the kitchen. He already had his head bent

over the faucet. The jeans hung loosely from his hips. The white shirt clung lightly to his back, outlining the curve of each muscle and his broad, firm shoulders. I blinked twice, swallowed hard, and caught myself a moment before I tried clearing my throat to swallow again. The clothes I'd picked out looked good. A little too good. And looking at him in them did funny things to my stomach.

Thankfully, he didn't look up and notice my gawking. I pulled myself together and moved to the refrigerator. Opening it, I studied the contents then grabbed what I needed to make him a big breakfast: eggs, bacon, potatoes, and yes, orange juice...from concentrate. I set everything on the table.

When first staying with Sam, he'd amazed me with the amount of food he'd consumed on a daily basis. He'd explained that the werewolf's metabolism ran a bit higher than the average person's did. So, I planned to make enough breakfast for three and only serve myself one portion, leaving the rest for Clay.

While he ran down to the basement, I washed the potatoes under the pathetic trickle of water. When he came back, I noticed he still had bare feet.

"The shoes didn't fit?" I moved to the table to peel the potatoes and stay out of his way.

He shrugged in response. I tried to guess what that might mean.

"So they fit, but you didn't want to wear them?"

No response. He continued to tinker with the sink. I started to cut the potatoes.

"Did you like them, or should we bring them back? I wasn't sure what style you liked. There were several different colors. They're cheap shoes, but I figured it was better than walking around barefoot in the snow. That's got to be cold even for you."

Halfway through my one-sided conversation, he'd turned to look at me. I knew I'd rambled a little...again. Then I realized I'd just referred to him still living here in winter. I had really grown used to having him around. Kind of. I hoped he wasn't looking at me because of that.

"I just don't want you to think you have to keep them if you don't like them. It won't hurt my feelings if we take them back. Just wear the flip flops for now, and you can come in with me next time and pick out what you like." The plain, grey and blue running shoes were muted enough that I'd thought they'd look okay with whatever he wore in the future. I hadn't given the style more thought than that.

I got up from the table and put some butter in the pan on the stove. When I turned to get the diced potatoes, he was sitting on a chair at the table. He already had his socks on and was bent forward to slide his feet into the shoes.

"No, no, no, Clay." I hurried over, reached out, and almost touched his back before I caught myself and pulled my hand away. "I wasn't saying you *had* to wear them." He continued to tie the shoes. "It's okay to bring them back if you don't like them."

When he finished tying, he stood and looked down at his feet. I could see him wiggle his toes through the canvas and mesh tops. The length seemed to fit well enough. The loose, untied lacing told me they ran a little snug in the width. He moved past me and walked to the sink then back to try out the shoes. What little I could see of his expression appeared relaxed, as did his stride.

"You like shoes but you don't wear them much, do you?"

He answered with his typical passive shrug as he moved back to the sink.

The sizzle of the potatoes called my attention, and I got another pan out to start the bacon. He used the tools he'd brought up from the basement to try to fix the sink while I cooked. The sound of water running at full pressure heralded breakfast.

"Good to have a handyman," I commented setting our plates on the table.

Clay cleaned up the tools and disappeared downstairs. I wondered if he would come back in his fur and eyed the plate I'd set on the table for him. We had eaten together before but always with him in his fur. Before I could stop it, an image of him trying to use a fork for the first time popped into my head. I quickly squashed the picture and sat down to wait for him in whatever form he chose. I would not underestimate him again. Nor would I thoughtlessly remark on his table manners no matter how poor they might be.

The soft tread on the stairs warned me that he remained a man. He sat across from me and dug in. He didn't eat like Clay-the-dog or use his hands. Instead, he had perfectly normal table manners. Though his beard shredded it, he even used his paper napkin in an effort to keep himself neat.

"What are the chances of trimming that beard?"

He used his napkin while he finished chewing and then flashed me a full view of his teeth. His canines remained completely elongated as if he still wore his fur. I froze briefly with my fork suspended midair. Then I gave myself a mental shake. The view scared me, but I reminded myself of Sam's words. I had nothing to fear.

"Do they stay like that all the time?"

He didn't answer but continued to eat, slowly clearing his plate. I waited patiently, hoping he'd give me some type of response. This was the second occasion we'd spent time together without his fur since he'd arrived. I knew so little about him and wondered if this was a sign he was ready to start talking to me.

When he finished, he moved to the sink and ran the water. I wasn't ready to give up. I followed him, leaned against the counter, and studied the little bit of his face I could see.

"Is this something you don't want to talk about?"

He shrugged. Okay, not a closed topic...and apparently he wasn't yet ready to speak.

"Is it something I need to guess or can you explain it to me?" I felt like I was playing twenty questions.

He turned to consider me for a moment then went back to washing his plate and fork. Taking the hint, I cleaned up my place while he moved to wipe the stove. I washed and dried my plate and tried to figure out what to ask next. Obviously only yes and no questions even though he hadn't answered when I asked whether his teeth stayed like that all the time. Perhaps asking about them embarrassed him.

When he returned to the sink, I briefly thought of letting the subject drop, but then he dropped the washcloth into the sink and turned to me. He crossed his arms, leaned against the counter, and watched me. Not just looking at me, but studying me...all of me...as if he weighed a decision. I couldn't help but return his stare.

We stood just a few inches apart. The close proximity brought the corded muscles under his snug t-shirt to my attention. I tried not to notice. He was downright drool worthy. I considered reaching out to touch him, just to see how he felt without fur. But his possible reaction stopped me. Would he take it as a sign of acceptance? Of interest? I'd meant what I'd said to Rachel. Clay didn't act like other guys. I didn't want to push my luck.

With a sigh, he uncrossed his arms and leaned forward. His movement shot a wave of panic straight through me, and I froze. Had he caught me eyeing him? Did he think that meant I wanted him to try to kiss me? I didn't know what to do.

His nostrils flared. He slowly shook his head and pulled back, and I knew he had smelled my fear. He didn't completely move away, just distanced himself enough so that I could breathe and think and not freak out. I caught the glint of his eyes behind his long hair. Calm. Patient. So this wasn't about a kiss. But then what was he trying to do?

"You're trying to explain the teeth, right?" I sounded pathetic, like a child who needed reassurance. I tried not to fidget on top of that.

He gave me the reassurance I needed in one of his rare nods.

Okay. No kissing. Just him moving closer. He slept at the foot of my bed every night. That was pretty close—right on my feet—and no big deal. But he had fur on when he did that. Now he looked...

I eyed him again. My stomach did a funny flip. Maybe my fear wasn't about his reaction, but mine. I was afraid I'd forget myself. I needed his control. I took a deep breath.

"It's okay then. Go ahead, explain. I'll behave," I promised quietly. I saw his mustache twitch with a quick smile. The canines explained some of the facial hair, but the full-bearded, crazy-man look seemed overkill.

After a slight hesitation, he leaned forward again while keeping his hands loose at his sides. I pushed back the fear and held still. He didn't stop his slow approach until his whiskers tickled the side of my neck and collarbone. There he paused and inhaled deeply.

As soon as he inhaled, I knew what he was doing, and although I didn't move, fear blossomed. Heart pounding, eyes wide, I waited for him to finish scenting me as a werewolf would a potential Mate, not a distant inhale, but an up-close sample of my scent, infinitely more potent. His warm exhale sent goose bumps skittering over my arms. I braced myself, anticipating some type of slip in his highly-praised control. He leisurely inhaled once more then lifted his head, exhaling as he went.

With his face only inches from mine, he opened his mouth to display his teeth again. The canines had grown even more pronounced, the surrounding gums swollen from their thickness.

I didn't know what to say. He had canines when in his human form because of me.

"So, when you're around me, they're worse? I guess that means they're like that all the time."

He shrugged and casually took a step back. I was unsure what the shrug meant.

We both heard a car pull into the driveway, and I knew questioning him further would have to wait. I remembered the new clothes still on the bathroom floor and moved away from him.

"I gotta move your clothes. I'll be right back."

When I returned, Rachel was kneeling, petting Clay-the-dog. She asked me why we had a man's clothes on the kitchen chair. Clay impassively met my gaze. Darn him. Why hadn't he just stayed Clay-the-man?

"Clay stopped by and fixed the sink. He figured he would leave a change of clothes because of last night," I lied. Thankfully, Rachel focused on the fixed plumbing rather than the fact I had a man leaving clothes behind at our house.

"The sink's working? And for free?"

I shrugged, feeling very Clayish, and grabbed the clothes. As I walked from the room to put them away, she continued to talk to Clay using her normal nonsense babble. He was such a good boy and so handsome. Did I treat him well while she was gone? Did he want a treat? I sniggered, put the clothes away, then sat on the couch and left Clay to his torture.

Done with her affectionate praise, she released him. He trotted from the kitchen and sat on the floor near me. She went to her room to change, leaving her door open so she could talk.

"I just heard the weather report, and we're going to get a cold snap this week. Frost. With past roommates, we always tried to make it to November first before turning on the heat."

"That's fine by me," I answered.

"Even though the landlord replaced the windows, air still somehow gets in. They're better than they were and seemed to help the AC run less. But if Clay knows anything about weatherproofing, maybe that'll help us save even more on the heating bill."

I looked at Clay. "Know how to weatherproof a house?" I whispered.

"What?" Rachel asked from her room.

"Nothing, just talking to Clay."

THE REST of the weekend passed like the one before, with

studying and turning pages for Clay-the-dog. Although I still wanted to know about his pronounced teeth in man-form, I couldn't come up with any reason to ask him to shift again. When I tried asking him about his teeth while he wore his fur, he just walked away from me. I couldn't tell if he did that because he was moody or just bored with my conversation.

Monday night, I got home and Clay stood in the kitchen cooking dinner for two. I had to suppress the happy-dance I wanted to do and, instead, nonchalantly walked by him. A note on the table from Rachel explained she had gone out with Peter and would be back late. The note stressed alone.

Since Clay's last appearance, I'd thought of several questions to ask him—starting with his teeth—and hoped he wouldn't get annoyed and go fur on me again. I decided to ease him into my agenda.

"Wow, I didn't know you cooked. It smells great." I set my messenger bag on a chair and hovered behind him, watching him work.

He pulled baked potatoes from the oven. To the side, two plates waited with steaming chicken breasts. Seeing dinner almost ready, I grabbed flatware for us and sat down.

"So, other than cooking, how did you keep yourself busy today?"

He set a plate in front of me and sat down. He pointed to the last batch of books I'd brought home that he had piled neatly on the table between us.

"You read them all already?"

He nodded.

"That's a lot to read in just five days. Are you skipping chapters?" I teased.

He glanced up at me then back down at his food. Maybe I

needed to work on my teasing. I supposed smiling would have helped.

"So, about the beard...are your teeth ready to play nice?" That got an actual laugh from him. A short one, but still very nice.

"Does that mean we can trim your beard?" I asked, excited by the prospect. The scissors would also make a beeline for his hair. How could I read his face when he kept it so hidden? Since he didn't actually speak, it hindered our communication even further.

He shook his head, and my face fell. I looked back down at my plate, feeling silly for the stab of disappointment because I wouldn't get to see more of his face tonight. Lost in my own thoughts, it took me a second to realize he'd stopped eating. He leaned back in his chair and studied me.

Pretending not to notice, I gave him a slight smile and, for a change, I kept my thoughts to myself.

"This tastes great. Thank you for cooking. Do you have a favorite food? I can put it on the next shopping list."

He watched me for another minute as I ate. I tucked away my disappointment and annoyance, and tried not to let my face show anything I felt. I knew neither emotion did me any good, and both made it hard to enjoy the food. I pushed a few bites around on my plate before he finally uncrossed his arms and picked his fork back up to start eating again.

"Actually, let's keep a shopping list on my dresser. When you think of something, you can add to it so I know what to get without guessing." Maybe writing fell into the talking category, and I'd be out of luck there, too.

I ate the majority of the food on my plate then brought it to the sink. Not wanting to risk him going back to his fur just yet, I grabbed my messenger bag and sat at the table to work on homework while he finished his meal. I usually did homework the same day and left the bigger projects and in-depth studying for the weekend, if needed.

"If you want, when you're done, we can watch a movie," I said.

He shrugged and moved to clean up his plate. I hopped up to help, but he motioned me back to the table, pointing to the open book. I sat and read while listening to him move about the kitchen.

As soon as he washed the stove, I packed up my homework for the night. He wiped down the table, and I hovered with my bag over my shoulder. I did not want to put it away and give him the opportunity to change again. When he had everything clean and the dishrag rinsed, he walked into the living room. I followed him and sat on the couch.

He bent to the cabinet below the TV and picked the movie for the night. A suspense.

"If I scream again when Rachel comes home, no laughing," I said as I curled on the couch and waited for him to start the movie.

A strong wind blew outside, and the curtains moved slightly. Considering where I lived, it seemed pointless to dread the cold, but I did. Soon I would probably start to consider wearing snow pants just to walk to the car. I gave the fluttering curtain one last glare and turned my attention to the movie as Clay settled next to me.

This time, I didn't feel so nervous and actually concentrated on the movie. Clay never twitched, but I jumped twice within the first ten minutes.

The temperature in the room dropped to the point that I ran

to get a hoodie during a suspenseful scene. Thankfully, Clay didn't pause the movie for me.

By the time the movie ended, the wind really howled outside. I sat on my fingers in an effort to warm them and knew it would be a long wait until the first of November.

"Hey, Clay. Do you like cookies?" I sprang from the couch and moved toward the kitchen. I could bake cookies to heat the house, and Rachel couldn't scold me for turning on the heat.

I rummaged through the cupboard, and I saw we didn't have any of the main ingredients. No sugar of any kind or flour.

"Shoot," I grumbled.

I had splurged and bought Clay clothes, something I considered a necessity. Along with many of the other unplanned expenses, it set me behind in my budget. Keeping the heat off longer would help make some of it up. But that meant no frivolous spending, not even for ingredients to bake cookies to warm the house.

I closed the doors and turned to tell Clay the disappointing news. Instead of staying in the living room as I'd thought, he stood right behind me. All that came out was a strangled "gah." He flashed a smile so wide that I saw teeth and couldn't help but smile back.

"Har-har. I told you no suspense movies. Life is scary enough without them. Oh, and false alarm on the cookies. We're missing some main ingredients."

He picked up my car keys and dangled them in front of me.

"It's tempting, but unless I want to get a part-time job, I can't afford to keep spending the money I've saved. I've got to stick to the budget so it lasts through till spring. If we can manage to keep the heat off until November, I should have cookie money for Christmas. That's when cookies are best, anyhow. I'll just need to start wearing more clothes inside."

I took the keys from him and put them back in the dish on the counter. When I turned, Clay wasn't looking at me, but off to the side. I tried to follow his gaze, but he didn't seem to be looking at anything. Shrugging, I left him to his own thoughts.

"I think I'm going to bed." I almost asked if he would come with, but didn't know how to word it so I would be asking Clay-the-dog not Clay-the-man. As a result, I went to my room alone.

Not long after, I heard him enter; and I wondered what I'd do if he tried to climb into bed with me as a man. I anxiously listened to the rustle of his clothes as he removed them. The quick pounce on the end of the bed told me Clay had once again become my personal foot warmer.

CHAPTER TWELVE

On Tuesdays, my first class started later. It gave me time to catch up on things around the house. After falling behind on laundry once, I made a point to wash at least one load each Tuesday.

Clay padded softly behind me, following me down into the basement as I carried a basket of our combined clothes. I teased him that the discount detergent I'd purchased smelled like babies—not very manly. He chuffed out a laugh and watched me fill the machine. Nothing I did seemed very exciting to me, but he followed me as faithfully as a real dog would.

After I finished, he trailed behind me as I skipped back up the stairs. The closed basement door silenced the whir of the washer.

I moved to the bedroom and pulled the sheets from my bed to start making a pile for the next load. While I worked, I told Clay about what we'd covered in my classes so far. He sat off to the side, out of the way, but I could tell he listened by the tilt of his head. Glancing at the clock, I groaned at the time, called goodbye to Clay with a promise to see him at dinner, and ran out the door.

Not only did I like Tuesdays because of the delayed start, but also because Tuesday nights Rachel spent time with Peter. It gave me the house to myself. Well, and Clay, too, but she didn't know that. I looked forward to dinners with Clay since it meant spending time with him as a man.

I rushed to the car. The door protested loudly when I yanked it open. I tossed my bag in, closed the door, started the engine, and thought of Rachel as I backed out of the driveway.

Rachel and Peter's growing relationship made the increasingly frequent dinners with Clay possible. She hadn't come home last night and probably wouldn't come home tonight as well. It amazed me to see two people so meant for each other. When I focused on them, their lights, the essence of who they were, pulsed in harmony.

Although I'd never stopped wondering why I saw the lights, learning werewolves existed had tempered my need for answers. After all, if a completely different species could evolve unknown to the rest of the world, why couldn't one girl develop a uniquely strange ability? Oh, I still believed my ability to see the sparks served some purpose I hadn't yet identified, but I no longer actively searched for answers.

Before meeting Sam, I'd volunteered at the hospital, thinking I'd learn to use my ability to identify different illnesses. But no matter the patient or their illness, I always saw the same yellow-green color. However, because of my time at the hospital, I'd found what I wanted to do with my life. Massage therapy had benefited some of the elderly patients with whom I really liked working.

With a few minutes to spare, I pulled into the student

parking lot, grabbed my things, and started the walk across campus. Students milled around outside a few of the buildings or purposefully strode the sidewalks, like me, to get to their next class.

Someone called my name. I stopped and saw Scott cutting across the dying grass. He jogged to meet me on the sidewalk.

"I think we should start drawing straws or something," he said when he reached me.

"What do you mean?" I shifted my messenger bag, eager to get to my class. Telling someone no only worked as long as I didn't send any cross-signals, and a long conversation definitely qualified as a cross-signal.

"Peter and Rachel. We should draw straws to see who has to put up with the lovebirds. I didn't get much sleep last night." He rolled his eyes, and I noted the dark circles under them.

"Ah. I didn't know you and Peter were roommates. I usually don't have a problem sleeping when he comes over, so if you want them to stay at our place, just tell Rachel. I certainly don't mind." He opened his mouth to say more but I cut him off. "Sorry, I have to get going. I'm going to be late for class."

He nodded, and I walked away without a goodbye. I hoped that counted as a short conversation. I knew Rachel had been staying at Peter's place because she felt guilty if he stayed at ours more than twice a week. I'd never stopped to consider Peter might have a roommate, too. Maybe I should say something to Rachel. They never kept me up when Peter stayed over. I wondered, belatedly, if they kept Clay up.

Realizing I'd slowed a little, I picked up the pace. I wanted to arrive early enough to talk to Nicole, the shy girl in my basic massage class. Today we would start doing more hands-on practice to try the few techniques already described to us along with muscle identification, and she'd agreed to work with me.

Last week, the instructor had warned us we would work in pairs and would be switching partners over the next few weeks. The announcement had given me a mild panic attack. Although the majority of the students were female, the few men had glanced my way. So, I'd carefully prearranged partners.

On the positive side, the instructor had also stressed we wouldn't need volunteers from outside the classroom this term. It was a relief to know I wouldn't need to fend off Scott as a volunteer.

AN UNUSUALLY QUIET house greeted me. The brisk wind rattled the kitchen window as I set my keys down and searched the house for Clay.

I didn't find him but did see evidence of his busy day. The neatly folded items from the laundry I'd put in, and the load I'd set aside before leaving, filled my dresser drawers. Clean shirts hung in my closet. Clay had even remade the bed with the fresh sheets. The baby powder smell of the detergent permeated the room. I grinned, thinking of him wearing his clean clothes.

A knock sounded at the front door. Still smiling to myself, I turned and answered it.

An older gentleman stood on the stoop. Dressed in a smart grey suit that complemented his dark grey hair, he reminded me of Sam, and I felt a moment of guilt. Sam had called several times to check on me, but I hadn't returned any of his calls.

A smile lined his face, reaching his warm hazel eyes. "Gabby? I'm Joshua."

My polite smile froze in place. This was Elder Joshua? I'd pictured a younger man. Doubt crept in, and I did a quick scan. His bright blue-grey spark glowed before me. That color...my stomach dipped in fear. Joshua had the same color light as the werewolf that had attacked Clay. Coincidence? I doubted it. So far, only Charlene and I had unique sparks. A knot formed in my throat.

In the distance, a child squealed in laughter. The sound snapped me out of my other world. I held myself still, clutching the edge of the door while I fought hard to push back the sudden burst of fear.

His nostrils flared slightly, and I knew my efforts were too late. I wanted to slam the door and run but knew it wouldn't work.

"I apologize for startling you, Gabby. Sam was concerned when he didn't hear back from you after the confrontation. He asked me to stop by and check on you."

"Confrontation?" My voice sounded dry and strained.

"Yes, we heard there'd been a failed challenge. Is everything okay here?"

I swallowed hard. "Yes, thank you."

Think, Gabby! Why would the werewolf launch itself at Clay from out of the darkness only to politely knock on my door? And why the front door? The neighbors could see him.

Staring at his puzzled face, his hazel eyes called my attention. The other wolf's eyes had been blue. What did it mean that he had the same color light as the werewolf that'd challenged Clay? I really wanted to believe it was just a coincidence. I had to call Sam and get a description of Elder Joshua to be sure the man before me was who he said.

"How are things going with Clay? Any other problems? Is he becoming too aggressive?"

"Everything is fine. He's very polite." But missing when I really need him, I thought. Convenient that Elder Joshua just happened to show up when Clay wasn't home.

"We were surprised to hear of a challenge. Usually, strong ties aren't challenged," he commented.

I didn't know how to respond so I remained quiet.

He reached into his pocket and withdrew a business card. "Well, if you need anything give me a call, or call Sam. We're here for you." He handed the card to me.

The card simply had his name and number printed on it, no title or business name. I nodded, hoping he would leave so I could give into the panic attack I barely held back. He smiled, bobbed his head in farewell, and turned to leave.

I closed the door and tucked the card into the front pocket of my jeans. This time I watched through the peephole as he got into the car he'd parked in front of the house. The door muffled the sound of the engine as he started it.

When he drove out of my line of sight, I closed my eyes and leaned my forehead on the cool wood of the door. First, a wolf with a uniquely colored spark challenged Clay. Then, Elder Joshua appeared with the same color. For more than two years...through every visit to the Compound...not once did I ever see a variance in the color of a werewolf spark. Just like humans, they remained consistent.

If not for the challenge, I wouldn't have worried about it. But I knew without a doubt, I'd never met Clay's challenger before. And if I'd never met him, why would he dispute Clay's tie with me? I needed to know who the challenger was and why Elder Joshua had an identically colored spark. Yet, no one knew about my ability to see the sparks. I could ask Sam outright if Joshua was different to their kind in some way. The best I could do was verify Elder Joshua's identity without raising too many unwanted questions. I needed to calm down and call Sam. If I called sounding freaked out, he would probably send Joshua right back over.

I pushed away from the door and turned to go into my room. Someone stood right behind me. I produced a full-throated someone's-sawing-off-my-arm scream before I realized it was Clay dressed in jeans, t-shirt, and running shoes. By his shocked expression, I'd just scared him as bad as he'd scared me.

Heart stuttering, I clapped a hand over my mouth. No way would I call Sam now. I wasn't even sure I could speak. The hand over my mouth shook from the adrenaline rush.

He tilted his head, studied me, then reached into my pocket to pull out the card. He glanced at it, shrugged, and shook his head, clearly puzzled. How did he even know it was in there? Had he been watching me?

I dropped my hand and did another round of deep breaths to try to calm down.

"Did you see who was here?" I asked. My voice wavered so I cleared it.

He shook his head.

"How did you know that was in my pocket?"

He briefly lifted the card to his nose. So, he could smell the other werewolf? That was good.

"Have you ever met Elder Joshua before?"

He shook his head.

"Have you ever smelled him before?"

Again, he shook his head.

I closed my eyes briefly and let out a relieved sigh that sounded a bit like a sob. Joshua wasn't the werewolf Clay had fought. Even though I remembered blue eyes, I'd still worried.

The new color variation bothered me, though, and I wished I had someone to talk to. Now that Clay had confirmed Joshua wasn't the same werewolf from the challenge, I didn't see much point in calling Sam other than to yell at him for sending Joshua over.

Lost in my own thoughts, I jumped when Clay lightly tapped my forehead with his index finger.

I gave him a weak smile. "You want to know what's going on in my head?" I guessed.

He nodded, and I finally recognized that my someone-to-talk-too stood right in front of me.

"I'd like to know what's going on in my head sometimes, too." If only I could figure out those lights. "Let's make dinner while I talk. Let me know if you hear Rachel or anyone else."

He nodded, kicked off his shoes, and put them in my room before joining me in the kitchen. He took the lead on dinner prep and gave me busy work so I could talk. I started to peel a potato while he clanked pans on the stove.

"That was Elder Joshua at the door. He stopped by because I haven't talked to Sam lately, and Sam asked him to check up on me. I guess he was worried after that challenge." I picked up a second potato. "Something was odd about him, Clay."

When I was quiet for too long, Clay nudged my chair on his way to the sink with the potatoes I'd peeled. His way of saying I should keep talking, but I struggled with how to tell him everything.

"I'm different," I said abruptly.

He turned from the sink, looked at me, and shrugged as if to say it didn't matter.

"No. Really different. It's kind of hard to explain. Sam told me I was different when he met me, but he doesn't know all of it. He said that I was rare because I was one of only a few humans compatible with werewolves, just me and Charlene."

I sighed and ran my hands through my hair. Based on my mom's reaction when I'd told her the truth, the idea of telling someone everything scared me.

He picked up two more potatoes and handed them to me. I started peeling again as he went to the stove. I spoke slow, essentially thinking aloud.

"Since as long as I can remember, I've seen lights. Not with my eyes, but in my mind. When I was younger, I had to close my eyes and concentrate to see a relatively small area around me. As I got older, I didn't need to concentrate as hard and could see a much larger area. Now, I can see these lights at will, briefly, with little effort, and over a longer distance. And I don't need to close my eyes.

"These lights are people, Clay. I can see the neighbors moving around in their houses right now. It's not an aura I'm seeing.

"To put it in perspective, I can see a square mile around us, but in my mind, the area looks like an inch. The lights within that area are small pinpricks, but I can see them so clearly, they could be the size of quarters three inches from my face. And all those dots are the same color. Every human around us has the same yellow light with a green halo."

Clay handed me a glass of water, breaking my train of thought. He rescued the potatoes I'd cubed into tiny pieces.

"Thanks." I took a drink and studied the glass for a moment

before continuing. "You and I, in the middle of those dots, stand out. I have the same yellow light as everyone else, but my halo is orange. I'm different from the people around us. Even from you. Werewolves have a blue core with a green halo. At least, that's all I ever saw in the past two years, until the night you were challenged. That werewolf had a blue-grey light. Now, imagine my shock when I opened the door and saw a man, who introduced himself as Elder Joshua, with the same color light. Only the difference in the color of their eyes kept me breathing.

"I've been like this my entire life, and I have more questions than answers about this second sight. Why are all humans green and yellow except Charlene and me? We're human. Why does Charlene have a red halo? Or me an orange halo? The only similarities are the yellow cores. I've been thinking it means human, but don't know what the halos mean.

"And I'm sure that you've caught on to the whole guy situation. I call to them somehow, as if I'm a beacon or something. Do I really send out some kind of signal?" I looked up at him questioningly.

He held a plate in each hand. Both loaded with some kind of chicken skillet dinner. He handed me a plate and studied me for a moment before shrugging and shaking his head.

"So nothing as far as you can tell. There's got to be a reason, a connection to it all." I sighed and played with the food on my plate for a minute, thinking.

"I've never told anyone all of this. People figure out there's something different about me if they're around me long enough. But no one knows about the lights. I'm torn. Do I call Sam and tell him everything? Do I tell him the light of the guy who challenged you is the same light as Joshua? There's nothing concrete I can offer about the coloring or why I'm so worried about it.

"Why would a werewolf I've never met challenge you? And why does he share the same coloring as Joshua? So far, the lights have had a category: humans, werewolves, and compatible Mates. I don't think the challenger and Joshua can be compatible Mates because Charlene and I are uniquely colored from each other." I shook my head to try to clear away my frustration at my inability to solve the puzzle.

Taking my first bite, I struggled to swallow the cold food. I looked up at Clay in surprise and saw his empty plate.

"Bet you're wishing you hadn't asked."

He shook his head slowly still watching me. I started to doubt the wisdom of sharing so much with him. What if he started to treat me differently? I didn't want to lose his friendship. It devastated me to think I could lose the one person with which I might have had a chance to be myself. When he didn't say anything, I forced myself to eat.

He waited until I finished eating, took both our plates, and cleaned up the kitchen while I sat at the table and did my homework. The spatter of running water, the soft clicking of dishes, none of it distracted me as much as my own doubts. Uncertainty over what I'd just shared and his lack of response ate at me. Granted, he hadn't spoken to me at all *before* my announcement, but still.

When he finished, he left the room for a few minutes. His nails clicked on the kitchen floor as he padded back in. I didn't have time to wonder why he'd changed to fur. He nudged my arm with his head and looked toward the living room. The tightness in my chest, which I hadn't even noticed, loosened slightly. He watched me expectantly, and I ran my fingers through the fur at his neck, hoping he wouldn't ever act like a real dog and run away from home.

Deciding I'd done enough, I packed up my homework and followed him. We watched some sitcoms then called it a night.

When he curled up on his usual spot at the foot of my bed, I sighed and closed my eyes. He hadn't seemed to treat me any differently after I'd told him everything. I hoped it would stay that way.

Rachel came home after a very late evening shift at the hospital. I knew she was alone because Clay only shifted on the bed to acknowledge he'd heard something. The nights Peter stayed, Clay grumbled a bit. They probably did keep him awake. Poor Clay.

CHAPTER THIRTEEN

While on campus, I still struggled to fend off a few stragglers who hadn't yet grasped the concept of no. Thankfully, those stragglers didn't include Scott.

At home, Rachel and Peter were inseparable even though they made a big fuss about giving each other their own time. It just meant they only did overnights three times a week. It limited my quiet time with Clay, but we managed.

On Rachel nights, Clay-the-dog usually waited for me by the back door. Occasionally, I came home to an empty house. Those absences explained why he no longer consumed five books a week, but they did make me wonder how he spent his time when we weren't together. When I tried to ask where he went, he never answered.

I began to notice things, though, like he now owned more jeans—I'd only bought him one pair—and had a few new shirts. Despite the extra clothes, he still seemed to favor the ones I'd gotten him, especially the flannel shirt.

On nights we didn't expect Rachel home, Clay-the-man

waited for me. He was never missing for those nights. Tuesdays, still one of the nights Rachel stayed over at Peter's, Clay did laundry for me if I forgot to do it before then and always had dinner ready when I came home.

He still didn't talk when he was in man-form, but I gradually learned more about him through many well-phrased questions. I guessed at his favorite color for over a minute. Pink...naturally. What guy wouldn't have a feminine stereotyped color as a favorite? I gave up trying to guess *why* it was his favorite after twenty minutes.

I also found out he liked to try new foods and made it a point to bring home one unique food item each week. Fruits like pineapple and kiwi disappeared quickly. Vegetables like okra and Brussels sprouts...well, I laughed long and hard when I watched him eat those.

Besides the new clothes that he'd mysteriously acquired, I also came across his wallet on my dresser. Since he'd been crouched right behind me when I spotted it, I'd peeked inside. He could have barked or something to tell me to stop, but he didn't.

The contents of his wallet had been informative. On his driver's license, he looked just as scruffy—except with a clearer view of his eyes. I'd stared at that photo until his laughing penetrated my fascination.

Behind the license, I found a folded copy of his GED transcript. With a few questions, I discovered that his dad, now deceased, had taught him how to read at an early age. The education he'd received essentially comprised of home schooling. When I asked him how he managed to get his GED and a driver's license without speaking, he stopped communicating with me for the night. Moody.

The glimpse at his eyes in the photo started me back on the "off with the beard" kick. His standard response was to bare his teeth. Darn canines. But, in a way, his consistent answer proved to me that telling him about my abilities had no noticeable effect on our relationship, other than to open a floodgate in me. I couldn't seem to stop myself from sharing all the weird or exciting things that happened to me on campus—the only time he couldn't shadow me.

When I talked, he sat and listened, always giving me his full attention. I'd grown so used to his attentiveness that he confused me one day when he abruptly walked away after I told him I'd been invited to a Halloween party.

I'd wanted to tell him more, like it was Nicole from my basic massage class who had asked me. Her reason for the invitation was pretty simple. A guy from our class, who she really liked, planned on attending, and she didn't want to go alone. Everything in me had cringed at the idea of a party so I'd told her I'd never been to one because of the way guys acted around me. She'd admitted to noticing, but that didn't change her insistence that I attend. Her acceptance of me felt good. Yet I had to point out the obvious. Having me along could back fire. The guy she liked could start bugging me again. He'd tried for the first two weeks of class before giving up. She didn't care. She wanted the support.

However, after Clay walked away from me, I didn't mention it again.

THE LAST SATURDAY IN OCTOBER, I found myself getting ready for a party instead of studying.

Clay grumbled, making it pretty clear what he thought of me going. I'd borrowed some of his clothes, the stuff that would fit without falling off, and slicked back my hair under a ball cap. Then, I used some funky hair gel from Rachel to comb a portion of my hair to look like pork chop sideburns. While that dried, I began the process of penciling in some thick, manly eyebrows. Clay stood on the bed behind me so he could watch my progress in the mirror.

"What do you think?" I asked, turning to Clay.

He grumped again then jumped off the bed to leave. Obviously not a fan.

"Rach?" I called to let her know I'd finished. She'd started as my costume consultant until she presented me with a skimpy dress from her closest and suggested that I go as a call girl. I'd kicked her out then. Clay had looked ready to rip apart the dress.

The door flew open, and only Clay's agile reflexes saved him from a concussion.

"What the hell did you do?" she said after she took one look at me. Her shocked expression was priceless.

"I'm going for dude. It's safe, right? What guy is going to want to hit on a guy even if he knows that underneath, it's a girl? Guys get weird about that stuff." I thought I looked pretty authentic. My layered clothes safely hid any curves I had.

"You know what's going to happen?" She sat in the middle of my bed. "All the guys are still going to be attracted to you. Only they're going to freak out because you're going to make them think they're gay, and you're going to get your ass kicked tonight."

Clay let out a yowl that sounded like "that's it" and ran from the room.

Rachel stared after him. "I love that dog, but he creeps me out sometimes."

"Yeah, I guess I shouldn't be trying to teach him to say 'No way'. I thought it'd be cool to train him to say it to guys, but I guess it's encouraging him to make other sounds, too." I hated lying, but Clay had just acted much too human.

"Oh, I didn't know you were doing that. Still...weird." She smiled and got up from the bed.

She'd told me earlier that she planned to stay in. I had a feeling Peter would arrive soon. Like magic, someone knocked on the back door.

"I got it," Rachel said as she bounded out of the room.

Shaking my head, I checked myself one last time. I didn't think I'd get my butt kicked...I hoped not anyway. I looked at the clock, expecting Nicole shortly. Nicole wasn't as close to me as Rachel but she still seemed to genuinely like me despite the attention I usually received.

We'd decided I would drive in case fate smiled upon her, and she managed to hook up with the guy she liked. To make it easier to keep an eye on her, I'd suggested she drive here. That way I could see when she came home like a nosey friend should do.

"It's for you, Gabby!" Rachel called from the kitchen. A hint of laughter laced her voice.

I moved toward the kitchen, wondering why Nicole had gone to the back door. When I saw who stood just outside, I stopped abruptly.

He stood motionless in the yellow glow of the porch light. The blue coveralls he wore had the name Clay sewn on the right pocket. Spattered patterns of grease stained the material, and one arm had a tear, making the getup look far from new.

I'd never seen the coveralls before but didn't give it much thought as I stared at his face. I could actually see it. Well, sort of.

Our eyes met, and I couldn't look away. He'd pulled his hair back into a ponytail, fully exposing a broad forehead, nicely shaped eyebrows, and thickly lashed brown eyes, for the first time. His beard covered most of his cheekbones, but everything above his upper lip, he had trimmed shorter.

Stunned, I said nothing in greeting. I could feel Rachel's curious gaze flicking between the two of us. His eyes crinkled at the corners, and I knew he smiled at my reaction. It warmed my stomach and set my heart fluttering.

Thankfully, Nicole chose that moment to knock on the front door.

"I got it," Rachel said, breaking the spell Clay's sudden appearance had cast. She rushed from the room.

Breaking eye contact, I looked at his uniform. "You have some explaining to do, I think." My heart still fluttered as I turned away from him.

"I love your costume," Rachel gushed from the other room.

I turned the corner then smiled in awe of Nicole who was dressed as a mermaid in all its shimmering beauty. The modified silky green body-hugging evening gown included a tail-like train. I anticipated people would repeatedly step on the end of her dress the whole night. A heart-shaped neckline adorned the sleeveless top. She'd altered it to make it appear as if she wore a bikini top. When she turned to give Rachel the requested full view, I also saw a cute fin strategically placed on the back just above her butt. A tasteful dusting of glitter decorated her sleek, straight hair.

"You're gorgeous Nicole," I said. "Are you going to be

warm enough?" Both she and Rachel laughed at me. "Hey, it's a valid question. It's the end of October for Pete's sake."

"I'll be fine." She looked at Clay and smiled warmly. "Hi, I'm Nicole."

Clay nodded and stuck out a hand. She clasped it.

"Uh, this is Clay," I said for him. "He doesn't talk much. And this is Rachel, my roommate. Are we ready?" I didn't want to give Nicole or Rachel a chance to comment on Clay's quiet presence.

"Sure. I parked on the street."

"Great. Let me grab my keys." I turned in time to see Clay already walking into the kitchen.

Because of his head start and longer stride, the storm door was just closing behind him when I reached the kitchen. The car keys I'd wanted to grab no longer rested on the counter. Outside, an engine started. I peeked out the window and saw him sitting behind the wheel of my idling car.

He stunned me with his sudden appearance, distracted me from a vital question—how did he have coveralls with his name on them?—with the first real look at his face, and now sat in my car ready to play chauffeur.

Slowly retracing my steps, I listened to Nicole explain how she'd made the costume herself.

"Nicole, if it's all right with you, I think Clay wants to come with. The way he's acting, I don't think he's ever been to a Halloween party and is curious."

"It's fine with me," she said with a smile as she moved to follow me to the kitchen. "Are you two dating?"

"Don't you dare say you are," Rachel said from behind her. "He's almost never here and when he is, he doesn't talk and he leaves early. That's not dating."

Since I hadn't told Rachel Clay appeared most Tuesday nights, I kept quiet. Better to just leave her with the impression she had than to try to explain our odd relationship.

"So, he's available then?" Nicole said.

"If you're asking my permission to make a move, go for it. Just don't be disappointed. I don't think it will go far," I said as I walked out the door. Giving her permission to hit on Clay didn't sit well, yet how could I not give it when I wasn't interested in making a move...right?

We hurried to the car. I sat up front with Clay, and Nicole shimmied into the back seat alone. I turned in my seat to look at her as Clay put the car in reverse.

"I don't know where we're going. Just tell Clay where to turn and be sure to give plenty of warning. This is the only car I have for the winter." I was nervous about Clay's driving experience. He had never answered how he'd gotten his license.

Clay expertly backed out of the driveway. Listening to Nicole's directions, he got us to the party in less than fifteen minutes. We couldn't park within a block of the address, therefore Nicole shivered as we walked. Within two blocks, I spotted the obvious party house. Music blared, ghosts hung from every tree in the yard, and I thought I saw a keg on the porch. So this was a college party? It looked interesting. People crowded the front lawn in groups that overflowed into the neighbor's yard.

As we neared, predictably, men turned to stare. Their eyes drifted to me, their expressions turned to confusion, then they looked at Nicole.

I wasn't the only one to notice.

"I knew you would make this fun," Nicole said with a

laugh. "Oh, I see him on the porch. Do you think I should say hi?" Her teeth chattered though she maintained a brilliant smile.

"Let's push our way through the crowd and get inside. We can warm up for a minute. It'll be more attractive if you're not stuttering with cold."

Clay didn't wait, but took my hand and guided me through the crowd. Nicole followed in our wake. People moved for Clay, and it didn't take us long to reach the door where a man stood selling cups for three dollars. We declined and went to find a place inside.

The bass of the music echoed in my ribcage. Good thing Clay wasn't a talker. I would never hear him, even though he could probably hear me. I wondered how his sensitive ears handled the volume.

He kept hold of my hand and pulled us through the crowded entry into an equally crowded living room. He forced his way between people to reach the small couch then paused in front of it to glare at the two male occupants. They uneasily stood and left, making room for us to sit. Nicole and I sat while Clay perched on the arm right next to me.

Nicole warmed as I looked around. From the decimated state of the snack table, the party had started a while ago. That also meant the majority of partygoers were drunk. One guy caught me looking around and made his way over.

The man stopped right in front of me and swayed slightly on his feet. I didn't look at him, but watched Nicole's face as her eyes darted to the man.

The music decreased in volume as a ballad came on.

"Hey...wash shore name?" he asked, his articulation long gone.

"Go away." I spoke clearly and rudely, knowing he wouldn't even remember in the morning. It didn't seem to faze him in the least.

"Wanna go up shtairs? They have a pool table," he said drawing out the L's in pool table just a tad too long.

Nicole coughed discreetly next to me to cover her giggle at the drunk's poor attempts at a pickup.

"No. Go away." This time, I added a glare to go with the words.

He looked beyond me with a startled expression, which quickly relaxed into a smile.

"Oh, god it man. Sheesh yours."

He ambled away, and Nicole and I turned to look at Clay.

"What did you do?" I said. Maybe some secret man-sign for "not interested." Whatever he'd done had worked well. I hoped I could learn it.

Clay flashed his teeth, showing elongated canines.

I heard Nicole's whispered "whoa" and glared at him. If he kept flashing his teeth, people would start panicking.

"If you keep those in all night, you're going to have sore gums tomorrow," I said thinking fast.

"Those are so real looking. You have to tell me where you got those." Nicole looked at him in fascination.

"He won't say," I said then changed the subject. "Warm enough? Are you going solo or do you want backup?"

She hesitated. She looked uncomfortable and nervous. Honestly, I felt nervous, too.

A group of guys across the room had started watching us once the drunk walked away. Their gazes pivoted between Nicole and me. Most of them just looked confused. One focused on me with a frown. Maybe, this was a bad idea after all.

Rachel's prediction of a butt whooping appeared likely. Since Clay had already flashed his teeth once with minor provocation, I didn't want to think what he'd do if the frowny man approached me.

Nicole's bright gaze flitted around the room oblivious to the tension I created. Normally an introvert, she seemed to bask in the attention we received, and I understood why she wanted me to come with. Without me, she would have been a wallflower. With me, she shared some of the notice I pulled in. I didn't feel used but did feel a little sorry for her. I wished I could help her get the man she so obviously wanted.

Deciding to speed things up, I reached out to pat Nicole's shoulder. She needed confidence.

When my hand touched her shoulder, a shock ran from my hand to her skin, the sting of it strong enough that we both yelped. I saw an actual spark.

"I'm so sorry, Nicole. I was just going to tell you that we should say hi now, and I go and scare you, instead." That's what I got for getting all touchy-feely.

"No, I know what that was. It was a jump start." She smiled at me, and I noticed the group of guys across the room completely shift their focus to her. The face of the man who'd frowned at me cleared as he watched Nicole.

"I'm going to go out there, now. If I can't get his attention, we can go." She got up and made her way to the door.

The group started to follow her while others in the room viewed her appreciatively as she passed. Girls who had previously smiled a greeting now frowned or outright glared at Nicole.

Too busy observing, I let Nicole's lead grow. Something was wrong. This was what typically happened to me. Granted, dressed as a man, the attention I normally drew had flagged a bit when we'd arrived, but if I'd worn something like Nicole wore...they would be eyeing me as they were her. Their behavior was so odd for me to see as a bystander and not a participant.

Automatically, I got up to follow at a distance. A sudden, dizzy spell sapped the strength from my legs, and I wilted a bit.

Clay had his arm around me, instantly. I didn't look up at him, but instead tried to keep my eyes on Nicole as I waited for the spell to pass. Maybe I'd gotten up too fast or skipped lunch a few too many days this week. Whatever its cause, it passed, and I did my best to follow Nicole despite the crush of bodies.

Clay had to physically shove a few people out of the way since they were too busy staring after Nicole to pay attention to my attempts to squeeze past. When they did see me, they barely spared me a glance. They just moved out of the way while trying to crane their necks to see Nicole. I didn't like their reactions to Nicole. Not out of jealousy, but out of concern. If all these guys didn't snap out of it soon, Nicole would be in trouble. She was too introverted to deal with all of this attention.

I made it to the porch in time to see Nicole say hi. She shimmered beautifully in the light. Randy, the guy from our class who she spoke to, appeared captivated. He'd dressed as the man from the Old Spice commercial, with a towel wrapped around his waist and nothing else. I figured it a frat house thing because I'd spotted several others dressed similarly. As the only spice-guy willing to brave the temperature outside, I guessed keeping the keg company also kept him warm.

He laughed at something Nicole said and offered her a beer. His own. He didn't seem willing to look away from her long enough to fill a new cup. I couldn't believe this was the same Randy. Since school started, he hadn't noticed Nicole once. What was going on here?

As unobtrusively as possible, I moved so Clay and I stood close to a railing. Better line of sight from there. The crowd continued to shift around us as people moved from group to group to talk.

After ten minutes of watching, I didn't know how she could stand the cold. Shivers shook me so badly my head ached. Naturally, I leaned back against Clay and wrapped my arms around myself. The heat of him penetrated through the back of my borrowed flannel and warmed me fractionally, but not enough to stop the shaking.

Giving up on the attempt to warm myself, I reached back, grabbed both of his arms, and pulled them around me. He willingly wrapped me in his arms and tried to warm me. His chin rested on the top of my head. I could feel his heat, but the tremors continued.

"I don't feel good," I said with chattering teeth.

When he placed a hand briefly against my forehead a few minutes later, I knew he'd heard my complaint.

"Do I feel warm?" I turned my head to look at him.

He met my eyes and shook his head. I lost my train of thought for a moment. I'd forgotten he'd pulled his hair back so I could see more of his face, and I smiled absently. He had nice eyes. Expressive. My brain began to feel foggy, and I knew he could tell when his brows drew down in concern. I didn't like his frown. It detracted from his lovely brown eyes. Chocolate. That'd taste good.

I realized my mind had wandered and reined it in.

"I think I'm ready to go, but I don't want to leave Nicole

here. What are my chances of getting her away from him, you think?"

He shifted his regard to the couple on the other side of the porch. I followed his gaze.

A few of Randy's towel-wearing friends had joined them, and their quiet talk had grown into an animated conversation. Nicole still smiled, but I could read a new tension in her stance. I'd been right. She wasn't ready for all the male attention she was receiving.

"I think now's a good time to s-see." The chatter at the end slipped out despite my Herculean effort to keep it in.

Clay loosened his hold on me and let me lead the way while he kept a hand on the small of my back. Whenever someone moved in my way, an arm snaked out from behind me and jostled them aside. There would be a few hung-over people tomorrow wondering how they bruised their shoulders. But I wasn't going to complain. It felt like a plague had struck me, and I really wanted to get to Nicole so we could leave.

The men in the group saw our approach and bristled. I tried on a rare smile but knew it lacked wattage because I felt like crap.

"Hi, guys. Sorry to interrupt, but we need to pull Nicole away for just a minute."

"I'll be back in just a bit," Nicole said to them. "Can someone get me a soda?"

She took me by the arm and turned me around so fast that Clay had to step aside for us. We didn't look back but walked right off the porch and cut across the yard in the general direction of my car. Her arm linked through mine propelled me along more than she realized.

"Thank you for that. It was really weird the way they were

acting tonight. I guess mermaid sends off the wrong vibes. I hope he remembers talking to me, though. I liked it until his friends showed up."

Her astute observations brought a trembling smile to my lips.

"Yeah," I agreed, "He s-seemed okay. D-don't trust his friends."

"Are you okay?" Concern laced her voice.

Behind us, I could hear Clay's soft footfalls.

"I think I'm getting sick or s-s-something." I felt colder without Clay's borrowed warmth. "Clay felt my head, but s-said I didn't feel warm."

"Is Rachel going to be home tonight? You said she's going to school for nursing, right? She'll probably know if there's something going around on campus. The nursing students doing clinicals always seem to know." Nicole switched position so her arm wrapped around me, chafing me in an attempt to warm me. I thought it funny since I wore flannel and she had a strapless dress on.

"Good idea." The sounds of the party slowly faded to a normal decibel. I tried using my sight to make sure none of the men followed us and felt a sharp pain in my head, instead. I flinched and immediately stopped. Nothing had appeared in my brief peek. No lights at all. That had never happened before.

When I spotted the car down the block, I sighed in relief. All I could think about was getting home, taking a hot shower, and going to bed. Clay surprised me by jogging ahead to the car. I heard the engine start a moment before he was back on the sidewalk, opening the door for me. He looked worried as Nicole helped me into the front.

"Do I look as b-bad as I f-feel?" I tried to joke.

Nicole looked at Clay but he kept his eyes on me so she answered.

"Well, you do look like you're coming down with something. I'm so sorry I begged you to come out tonight."

"Don't w-worry about it. It w-was r-really interesting," I said, forcing the words through my tensed jaw.

Very interesting. The sudden interest of the men...the animosity of the woman...I was certain I'd somehow passed my pull onto Nicole. And broke my mental fish finder in the process, too.

Clay drove fast, dividing his attention between the road and me. I continued to shiver despite the heat pouring from the vents. Minutes later, Clay smoothly pulled into the driveway. The house was dark.

"I hope you feel better," Nicole said. "I'll see you on Tuesday."

I nodded, unable to speak. My clenched jaw ached from shivering so much.

Clay was out as soon as he parked by the porch. He stalked around the hood. His eyes never wavered from me as Nicole slid from the back seat and left. I blinked tiredly and wondered how I'd get into the house.

He opened the door, and his eyes traced my face a moment before he wrapped an arm around my shoulders to help me out. Between the shaking, the headache, and the stiffness I felt from shaking, I had all the symptoms of the common flu. And I wanted it to go away.

With his arm supporting me, we made it around the car and to the porch. My shivers increased to spasmodic and he still easily managed to unlock the door without dropping me. I figured unlocking the door as a dog made this kind of move child's play.

The quiet house told me Peter and Rachel must have gone out after all, and I was glad. I would rather not have an audience to whatever had decided to plague me. I slipped from Clay's helpful embrace and started to tug off the flannel on my way to the shower.

"Clay c-can you get my towel?" I asked, dropping the shirt on the carpet outside the bathroom.

Had I felt better, I might have worried about how that sounded. But, really, I just wanted to stop shivering.

He moved past me and strode to the bedroom. His coveralls caught my eye again. I had to remember to ask him about those later.

I closed the door, struggled out of my t-shirt, and lost my balance as it cleared my head. I bumped into the sink. The chilly porcelain along with the cool air prickled my skin and caused more gooseflesh. Curling the fingers of one hand on the sink for support, I lowered myself to sit on the toilet seat.

Tired and cold, I weakly kicked off my shoes then began to remove my socks. Without meaning too, I started whimpering like a little kid. I needed to warm up. Shivering sucked. The more clothes I took off, the worse it grew. It messed with my finger coordination.

I stood and tried to manipulate the button on my jeans but couldn't get it. I'd just begun to debate if a hot shower was worth the effort when Clay tapped on the door.

"J-just a s-sec," I said in a panic. "I'm not ready, y-yet." I desperately yanked at the button and it sprang free a moment before Clay opened the door.

"Hey!" I crossed my arms over my chest even though I still

wore my bra. Sick and outraged, I glared at him for a moment. It cost too much energy to maintain.

He tossed the towel on the toilet lid and moved past me without a glance. Nudging the shower curtain back slightly, he turned on the water. I wanted to groan and smack my forehead. I hadn't thought to turn it on so it would warm up.

He turned from the shower, bent, and had my pants unzipped and around my feet before I could move. I stared down at him in complete shock.

"Clay, g-get out!" Had I not stuttered, it would have been an impressive shriek. Instead, it came across weak, and he ignored it. Embarrassment flooded me. "Really, I c-can do the rest."

He stayed crouched, kept his eyes averted, and indicated I should step out of the pants. Of course, he wouldn't listen to me when I sounded ready to have a seizure. I looked down at his turned head so close to my belly, and wanted to push him over. But my legs quivered, and I knew I'd just end up falling over, too. Obstinate man.

Sacrificing my pride and my coverage, I placed a hand on his shoulder to steady myself and stepped out of the pants.

"N-now out, Clay," I said, crossing my arms again.

He picked up my pants and stood. Then, still turned away, he shook his head.

"The h-hell you s-say!" Oh, if my grandma had heard that, I would have gotten an earful; and then she would have laughed because I'd learned it from her at a tender age.

Clay reached around me and set the pants on the towel. His sleeve brushed my waist, and his hair tickled my arm. When he straightened, he pulled back the curtain and held out a hand for me. Steam started to fill the air as I stared at him belligerently. Did he really think I'd undress all the way in front of him?

He continued to look at the wall, patiently waiting for me. The shivers grew worse, and I debated my stubbornness. With his hair pulled back, I could clearly see his eyes and knew he wasn't peeking. Yet, I didn't understand why he continued with his own pigheadedness and wouldn't just leave to let me do the rest.

As if he'd read my mind, he nodded his head toward the shower and tapped the tub with his booted foot.

I looked down at the high ledge. The shivers prevented any coordinated movement. If not for Clay's support, I would have fallen when stepping out of my pants. Suddenly, he made sense.

"You're s-staying until I'm in? So I don't fall?" I guessed.

He shrugged, and I knew I'd guessed right.

With a defeated sigh, I uncrossed my arms and clasped his hand. The showerhead angled toward the front of the tub so I could step in without getting my remaining clothes wet. He closed the curtain behind me, and I waited to hear the click of the door.

Once I knew left, I finished undressing. I tossed my things on the bathroom floor and stepped into the hot spray.

It felt so good that I stayed there, just standing under the spray for several long minutes. My only movement was a slight side-to-side rocking motion to keep all of me as warm as possible. The shivers lessened but didn't disappear. I began to worry they weren't really due to the cold. My energy continued to drain , and my headache progressed to a steady thump. When I heard the click of the door again, I knew I'd pushed it.

"Clay?"

I heard a grunt, but peeked around the curtain to be sure.

He held out a towel with his eyes closed. I turned off the water and grabbed the towel.

It took a moment to wrap the towel securely around me. Covered, I peeked out again. Clay faced the door but had a hand extended to help me. Clasping it again, I stepped from the shower. I was warmer but more exhausted than when I'd gotten in.

I hustled as best I could to my room. Clay remained outside the door as I threw on the warmest pajamas I owned and did my best to blot the water that dripped from my hair. My arms quickly grew too tired, and all the heat I'd gained from the shower left me. Giving up, I tossed the towel to the floor, crawled between the covers, and curled into a ball. I couldn't even rub my feet together to try to generate more heat.

Clay walked in and turned off the lights. I listened to the familiar rustle of clothes. Instead of the usual bounce of him jumping up on the end of the bed, he peeled back the covers, and the bed dipped as he slid in next to me.

I didn't bother to pretend I wasn't interested in what he offered. Heat radiated from him, chasing the chill from the sheets.

"I really hope you're wearing shorts or something," I said with a slight slur. I stuck my cold feet right on his legs and shimmied over to his side to huddle against his warmth. Boy, was he warm. It didn't matter, though. The shaking didn't stop, but I was too exhausted to worry about it.

Sighing, I immediately fell asleep.

BRIGHT LIGHT FILLED the room when I peeled my eyes open, still barely conscious. I lay against Clay, basking in his warmth. My headache had faded from a steady thump to an annoying dull ache. I felt drained and very tired.

I tilted my head and met Clay's observant gaze. Worry glazed the chocolate brown depths. I tried to swallow, but the muscles didn't want to work.

"I'm thirsty," I rasped.

He gently moved me and got out of bed. I closed my eyes; I didn't want him to prove me wrong about the shorts. After a few seconds of silence, I forced my eyes back open. He stood next to the bed, holding out a full glass of water.

Shakily, I leveraged myself up on an elbow and grasped the glass. The cool water felt good going down. I drank it all and handed him the empty glass. He watched me curl up with my pillow.

I closed my eyes.

THE NEXT TIME I WOKE, I checked my alarm clock. The red digits showed two in the afternoon. Turning my head on the pillow, I happily noted the absence of weakness and pain. Whatever I'd done to cause my sudden illness, over sixteen hours of sleep appeared to have helped.

Gingerly, so as not to bring my symptoms back, I boosted myself into a sitting position. Clay no longer lay beside me. I glanced at my closed bedroom door. He must have gotten bored watching me sleep. I didn't blame him.

Although I could have slept longer, I pulled myself from bed. I grabbed my books then hopped back into my warm nest of blankets. Pillows stacked up behind me, I spread the work out. I'd lost a night and most of today because of the party. I couldn't afford to lose more time. I still had a few assignments from Friday to finish. In addition, I needed to review the prior week's materials to make sure I didn't miss anything.

After about fifteen minutes, I smelled bacon. My stomach growled loudly. The aroma tempted me to leave my warm bed. As I sat thinking about closing my book, the door opened fractionally, and Clay peered in. When he saw me sitting up, he nudged the door further to show a plate of food and a glass of juice. His appearance ended my internal debate and saved me from exposure to the cold.

"Thank you. I'm starving." I moved the book to the side, and he handed me the plate with a fork and set the orange juice on the dresser. I dug in right away, not realizing the extent of my hunger until the first bite touched my tongue. Eggs, bacon, potatoes, and toast vanished in minutes.

Without a word, Clay handed me the glass of juice.

I drank it slowly, starting to feel the pull of sleep. Resisting it would prove difficult. I patted the bed next to me.

"Want to read by me?" Maybe company would help keep me awake.

He flashed me a smile, collected the dishes, and left the room. I heard him move around in the kitchen. The sound of running water had me wrinkling my nose; I knew I'd need to risk the cool air once again for a quick visit to the bathroom.

When I dashed back into my room eager for the warm bed, I saw Clay already lounging on the covers. He was reading a book.

We spent the rest of the day together in my room. Clay read next to me while I paged through notes and completed assignments. Each of the few times he left my side, he returned with a drink for me.

Near dinner, Clay closed his book with a snap and left the room. I heard Rachel's car pull into the driveway a few moments later. Before I heard her car door close, he returned wearing his fur again. Somewhere in the house, Rachel would see a pile of clothes.

I grinned at him as he jumped up on the end of the bed. He settled with a sigh, and I stretched out to tuck my feet under his warm body.

CHAPTER FOURTEEN

MONDAY MORNING I FELT BETTER AND GOT READY FOR CLASS under Clay's scrutiny. He didn't voice any complaint when I left, but I knew he worried that a full day so soon after recovering would overtax me. And he was right. By the last class of the day, I wanted to go to bed.

Dinner waited when I got home; two steaming bowls sat on the table. I dropped my bag next to the back door and flopped into the closest kitchen chair. Soup. Perfect. Clay picked up my bag and carried it into my room while I started to eat. After the first bite, I eyed the contents. I couldn't remember buying it and guessed he'd somehow managed to go grocery shopping.

He rejoined me and sat across the table. We ate in silence for a few minutes.

"Are you going to tell me about the coveralls or where you got the money for groceries?"

He shrugged in response.

Sighing, I pushed my bowl away. "I know I'm supposed to start asking you a bunch of questions, but I'm still too tired. Just don't be doing anything illegal, 'K? It would be hard to visit you in jail on top of school."

I used a battered plastic container to put the rest of my dinner in the refrigerator and quickly washed the dishes, despite his silent protests. He dried. Skipping homework, I changed and went straight to bed.

AFTER ANOTHER NIGHT'S SLEEP, I felt more energetic and noticed more than I had the day before. The people I encountered during the day treated me indifferently. The continuation of the phenomenon I'd experienced at the party surprised me.

I saw Scott crossing the campus again. He only waved when he saw me and continued on to his destination. A friendly wave from one acquaintance to another. Confused, I made an effort to interact more. I smiled at the people I passed. I'd grown so used to the pull I had on men that it felt odd when they didn't turn to look. Eventually, someone did stop me, another freshman, but he only wanted recommendations for a nice place to take a date. Why he stopped me out of all the other people drifting around on the campus grounds, I had no idea. However, it was the most normal, random conversation I'd had in my life, and I loved it.

Nicole caught up with me after our basic massage class and gave me the details of her weekend. Randy hadn't forgotten her and had called her on Saturday to ask her out on a date Sunday night. She'd excitedly accepted.

"He was nice and everything, just not the way he normally is in class. He seemed a little more intense on the date. I talked to him before class today, and he seemed more like his old self. We're going to go out again tonight."

Then she told me about her walk across campus that morning. She'd turned down no less than eleven date requests and two blunt one-night stands. She giggled as she related the details, but the humor didn't reach her eyes. I gave her a few pointers about keeping her physical distance if she didn't want someone to bother her and to say no bluntly. She nodded her thanks.

I wished her luck and hurried home to tell Clay my suspicions. I felt sure that something had happened to make Nicole the magnet for unwanted male attention instead of me. The shock we'd felt seemed to have been the turning point. I wondered how long the effect would last.

RUSHING through the back door with a smile on my face, I felt a stab of disappointment at the greeting I received from the dark and empty kitchen. I set my bag on the table and dug the leftover soup out of the fridge.

While I leaned against the counter waiting for it to warm, I wondered again about Clay's coveralls. I'd never gotten an answer about them. He probably worked somewhere, which would explain the wallet with the GED and the driver's license. But where? I could drive around and look for him, but I had no idea where to even start.

I sighed and settled at the table to eat and study. That he might have a job didn't bother me. That he bailed on what I considered our dinner night without a note or warning, did.

When he wasn't home by six, I decided to head to the

library to work on my speech. I needed the reference materials for research.

Studying at the library without my pull thoroughly increased my efficiency. Thanks to the uninterrupted work, I finished my speech by eight and headed home.

The windows glowed with light, and I felt a spark of excitement. I really wanted to share my unusual experience at the library. However, when I pulled into the driveway, I saw Rachel's car already in the garage. It meant I couldn't talk to Clay freely, but maybe I could still manage to whisper to him when we went to bed.

Inside, Rachel sat on the couch alone. There was no sign of Clay. She said she'd just gotten home and asked if I wanted to watch a movie with her. She didn't mention Clay-the-dog so I told her I felt a little tired and went to bed early. I had no explanation for his disappearance and didn't want her to worry. I hoped that she thought he was already on my bed.

THE NEXT MORNING I woke snuggled up against Clay, who must have snuck in at some point during the night. Though Rachel had technically turned on the heat, she kept it low. It made Clay's extra warmth nice.

When the sleep cleared enough from my head, I realized he laid next to me on his back...in man-form. I held still, trying to decide how I felt about it. When I'd been sick, he'd done it to help me. There hadn't really been a choice. I wasn't sick now. But he wasn't being weird about it. So, should I really make a big deal out of it? I decided not to. Warm feet felt nice; a warm all of me felt better.

Considerately, he wore a shirt, and although I wasn't going to check, I felt sure he'd included shorts. I shifted my head from against his side to look up at him.

He lay with both arms behind his head. His hair again covered the majority of his face. I thought he'd gotten over that phase. Since the party, he had kept it pulled back whenever he was Clay-the-man.

"It's annoying not being able to see you," I said in place of a good morning. I flipped to my stomach and propped myself up with my elbows to get a better look at him.

"If you don't talk, and I can't see your face, how am I ever supposed to figure out what you're thinking?"

I reached out to move some hair out of the way, but he stopped me in a blurred move, catching my wrist gently in his hand. He didn't let me any closer. First, he ditched me on dinner night then he wouldn't let me touch him? The thought stopped me. I really hadn't touched him before either, at least not as a man. Maybe he was like me, a little standoffish. I could understand that.

"Seriously, Clay, what kind of bribe is it going to take for you to get rid of some of that hair?"

He flashed his elongated canines at me again in explanation.

"Can't we at least trim it back some?" Okay maybe a lot, but I knew to start with baby steps.

He tugged my hand to his chest, laying it flat. So much for my theory about not wanting to be touched. I patiently allowed it because with him, everything was guessing or pantomime. His chest warmed my palm.

Using his free hand, he tapped my mouth. I frowned, perplexed.

"What, you want me to be mute like you?" Was he hinting I talked too much?

He shook his head and reached out again. This time, he cupped my jaw and lightly ran his thumb over my bottom lip. The gentle touch caused the pull in my stomach to intensify. Though I couldn't see his eyes, I read his intent.

"Whoa!" I scrambled out of the bed as if it had caught fire.

He stayed where I left him and turned his head to study me as I stood trembling beside the bed. I nervously rubbed a sweaty palm, the one that had moments before rested on his chest, against my leg. His whiskers twitched down. I couldn't recall him frowning at me before.

I almost asked where that idea suddenly came from, but guessed it was long overdue. According to the Elders, when an unMated male finds his female, he begins a courtship of sorts. The end goal is to Claim his Mate.

But Clay hadn't courted me. He just lived here in his fur. And sometimes cooked for me. And sometimes helped me with chores...and when he wasn't around, I felt disappointed and missed him. My fearful expression slackened to one of stunned amazement. He *had* been courting me these last few months. Clever dog.

Not comfortable with simple contact to begin with, I naturally balked at his request. Then I paused, reconsidering my hesitancy. Yes, I'd held myself back from everyone. Contact meant an emotional connection, either for me or for the other person. But Clay didn't act like the rest. He wasn't compulsively drawn to me.

Maybe I needed to stop treating him like the rest. Hadn't I already started doing that? I'd sat next to him to watch movies, ate dinner with him, and, yes, technically snuggled with him at night. At least, my feet did regularly. And I had to admit, I liked looking at him—the parts I could see. Thinking of that caused a blush. I sent another panicked look his direction, but he remained motionless.

But he didn't ask for just a simple kiss. Our current relationship placed so many strings on it. Strings I'd never before had to deal with. It definitely took us one step closer to Claiming in his book. As I thought of it, I realized my stance on Claiming had subtlety shifted. I wouldn't mind having Clay around indefinitely. We meshed well together. But there still existed aspects of a werewolf relationship I wasn't ready for. Like biting his neck hard enough to break the skin and establish my Claim. My eyes drifted to his throat. That didn't sound like something nice to do to someone you cared about.

Clay waited patiently for me to consider his request. Would it really hurt to give in to just one little kiss? I wiped my hands on my pants again.

The male's drive to Claim his Mate increased with each passing day, building to a compulsive need. There'd never been a courtship that lasted more than six months. Paul and Henry shared that tidbit with me long ago.

I calculated back and cringed. We'd just passed six months. He hadn't pressed for anything from me in that entire time. I'd been so focused on school that I hadn't given any thought to the Claiming stuff I'd learned other than to be glad he wasn't pressing me.

I edged closer to the bed and touched my bottom lip, thinking. Was he struggling to hold back his aggressive side? Could that be why his canines were elongated more often than not? Had I put too much faith in his control? But the toughest question was if I trusted Clay. If I did give him what he asked for would it be enough to satisfy him or would he want more and then become unbearable to live with?

Glancing up at him, I considered my options while he continued to watch me in silence. I really wanted to see his eyes again.

"I have some questions before we talk about my bribe and your price." I crawled back upon the bed and sat on my heels once I reached his side. "Will you try to answer my questions?"

He continued to watch me without answering.

"Are you able to physically speak?"

After a brief hesitation, he nodded.

"Are you ever planning on talking to me?"

He smiled wide and nodded again.

I nervously noted his teeth were bigger than they'd been a minute ago. My stomach did a flip, and I could feel the fading blush rekindle and spread across my face.

"Clay, were you asking for a kiss?" I had to know for sure.

He nodded slowly and reached out to twine his free right hand with mine. His thumb soothed the outside of my hand while he waited for me to decide what to do.

"Clay, I can't even see your mouth to know where to kiss. I hope this bargain includes a shave."

His whiskers twitched, and I guessed he smiled. He appeared laidback, completely calm as if my answer didn't affect him at all. It bolstered my courage.

I let go of his hand and leaned forward, bracing myself on his shoulders. I could see the glint of his eyes as he watched my slow descent. My stomach churned with nerves and anticipation. Despite my teasing comment, I found his lips without any problem and lightly touched mine to them. His warm breath fanned my face, and I pressed closer. Something inside me melted a little.

Closing my eyes, I reached a hand up to gently brush against his face, exploring his brow, ear, and jaw. He changed the kiss by tilting his head slightly. His lips began to nibble at mine, slow and easy. My stomach dipped, and my heart started to flutter with desire.

When I realized how easy it would be to keep kissing him, desire changed to panic. I pulled away then gasped at the sight of the black eye I'd exposed.

"What happened?" I said, forgetting desire and panic. Then, thinking of Rachel I dropped my voice to a whisper. "I thought werewolves weren't supposed to get hurt like this."

Seeing his eyes again gave me a nice advantage. I easily read the frustration in them. Before he could try something else, I bounded off the bed again.

"A deal's a deal. Go shower and shave. After you're done, we can play charades until I have the story behind the black eye." The stubborn look in his eyes had me adding, "That or I call Sam."

I stayed well back while he ran his hand through his hair in agitation. Then he sighed and sat up. The flex of his abdomen under his snug shirt dreamily distracted me. When he swung his feet over the edge of the bed, he turned his back to me. Part of his shirt had ridden up exposing more bruises on his back.

Forgetting to stay away, I rushed around the bed. He heard me and stayed where he was. He didn't fight me when I started tugging his shirt over his head, either. Numerous bruises covered his torso.

"What happened?" I demanded again. I nudged his right

arm away from his side, saw a huge, ugly purple mark, and lightly ran my fingers over it. He held perfectly still for me.

"This is really scaring me, Clay. I thought werewolves were supposed to be this tough, nearly indestructible, race."

I'd lost my mom to a car accident and my grandma to cancer. With no other family, I had endured as an orphan, truly alone in the world. Then, when I'd realized Sam's plan to pair me with one of his kind, a single thought had resonated with me: If I found a werewolf Mate, he would never die on me and leave me alone.

"Is this why you were gone last night when I came home?"

He didn't move at all.

"Fine." I turned to leave him, but he caught my wrist again and gently tugged me to his side. He brought my hand to his mouth, kissed the back of it, then my knuckles. I felt a tug in my stomach. That stupid, annoying, kinda-growing-on-me-a-lot pull which tied us together. My annoyance at him evaporated. Unable to help myself, I brushed my fingers through his hair. I liked the feel of it.

"I've lost everyone that's ever really mattered to me. I thought caring about a werewolf would be safer," I admitted softly.

He raised his head to look at me for a long moment then pulled me into his arms.

Normally, I wouldn't like someone hugging me like that. But with Clay, it felt safe. I hugged him back gently, not wanting to hurt him more, and hoped the safety I felt wasn't because I'd already lost too much of my heart to him. I'd never fully recovered from losing my mom or grandma. I doubted I could lose much more and remain the same person. Losing Clay, even now, might break me.

Eventually, I pulled away first. His stomach began to rumble and mine answered. I tiptoed out of my room and moved my car, knowing Rachel would need to leave soon. Then, while Clay waited in my room, I made him breakfast. I didn't want Rachel to see him when she woke. We ate together on my bed. Before we finished, I heard Rachel leave.

While I washed dishes, he slipped into the bathroom with scissors and a razor.

It would be an understatement to say I was a little curious about what he really looked like under all the fur, er, whiskers. The anticipation built while I put away the dishes.

I walked by the bathroom door but couldn't hear anything. Trying to keep busy, I went back to my room and sorted laundry before deciding what to wear. It didn't take me long to dress. I paced around the house listening to the shower run.

CHAPTER FIFTEEN

THE ANTICIPATION HAD ME SO DISTRACTED THAT I JUMPED WHEN someone knocked at the front door. Of course, the shower turned off at that moment. Bad timing. I scowled, took a breath, then walked to the front door. Smarter this time, I checked the peephole.

Sam stood on the doorstep, and he looked very serious. He must have left in the middle of the night in order to get here first thing in the morning. I frowned. The surprises just kept coming, and it wasn't even eight.

Fixing a welcoming smile on my face, I pulled open the door.

"Morning, Sam. This is a surprise." I wanted to see Clay freshly shaven without an audience, but I motioned Sam in anyway. If he took the time to drive here, I would take the time to listen to whatever he had to say. Maybe it would be a short visit.

He stepped inside.

"Um, don't get me wrong, I like seeing you, but is there a reason you're here?" I said, trying to hurry him along.

"We'll wait for Clay."

His cryptic answer caught me off guard. It'd been more than two months since we'd seen each other. Sure, we had talked, but it wasn't the same as seeing someone face to face. I'd expected him to look at least slightly happy to see me.

Just then, the bathroom door opened. I excitedly turned to look for Clay. Dressed in a t-shirt and jeans, he stepped into the living room. But I didn't waste my time ogling him. My eyes honed in on his face. Only Sam's observant presence kept me from wrinkling my nose.

Clay still sported his beard, but he had trimmed it back. The neat length continued to obscure his teeth while revealing a hint of his lips. At least now, I'd be able to see when he smiled. The whiskers that had covered his neck were gone, leaving the clean-shaven column of his throat exposed. My eyes lingered on that skin for a moment before moving on. He'd also run his fingers through his hair so it lay back out of his face. The deep purple of his black eye had already faded to an ugly green-yellow. Even with his bruising, he looked really good. Just not shaven all the way.

I smiled warmly at Clay, wishing we were alone so I could tell him what I thought.

"You know why I'm here, Clay," Sam said from behind me.

My smile fell as I turned to look at him. What was he talking about?

"I'm told you didn't take the news well."

I turned back to Clay in time to see him shrug and cross his arms.

"What's going on? What news?" I said glancing between the two.

Sam gave Clay a sharp look. "You didn't tell her?"

"He's not talking to me, yet," I said, wondering what bad news Sam had to share.

Sam shook his head at Clay. "You've dug your own hole then, son." He focused on me. "A group of Forlorn have asked Elder Joshua to approach you for an unofficial kind of Introduction. Joshua approved, but he made it clear they were to keep it brief and then leave, unless any of them had a further request of him."

The meaning of Sam's words sunk in deep like a vicious bite. It also explained his less than warm greeting. He stood in my living room as an Elder on pack business, not as family or a friend. I struggled to contain my anger.

"I thought I was done with that. We had a deal." I crossed my arms and coldly regarded Sam. "I know I said I was done."

The carefully, composed expression on Sam's face faltered a bit. "Honey, there are rules we must follow to keep peace in the pack. Clay had six months to convince you of his suit. That time has passed. That means unMated can once again approach you, with permission."

My mouth popped open. Six months. Permission from an Elder. That's why they'd stationed Joshua here. A backup plan because they knew I didn't want to Claim Clay. They failed to understand I didn't want to Claim anyone. I'd never been free. I clenched my fists. My temper boiled.

"That's complete crap," I gritted out. "First of all, I didn't reject anyone. Second, no one ever told me about this stupid rule." My voice rose to a yell, and I took a deep breath and closed my eyes briefly to restrain myself. When I reopened them, I felt more in control and able to speak calmly. "You know what? I don't care what the pack rules are. I gave you my word and my time. Now, I expect you to keep yours. I worked hard to get here, Sam. I won't let anyone take this away from me." My hands shook. That Sam had cared for me in the past and given me a place to call home for two years, kept my tongue marginally civil.

"By not completing the Claim, you've become eligible again. Charlene was granted a special consideration because, at that time, we weren't even sure a Claiming would be possible between a human and a werewolf. Now that we know it is, you fall under the same rules," Sam explained calmly, his face again carefully devoid of emotion.

"No, I don't." I knew I could stand there and argue all day with Sam, and he wouldn't budge. It would always be whatever's best for the pack with him. "Is this why Clay was beat up?"

Clay made a noise—like a snort of disagreement —behind me.

"Feel free to jump in at any time," I said, turning to arch an eyebrow at him. He remained mute, but his eyes softened when he looked at me.

Sam spoke up from behind me, but I didn't turn to look at him.

"Gabby, it's the reason he's been fighting. He's not relinquishing his tie to you. Every time an unMated shows up here, he will challenge that man for his right for an Introduction. Did Clay get beat up? Only as a byproduct of handing out beatings."

Clay steadily met my gaze the entire time. It broke my heart a little to know he was fighting so hard to keep me, and all I'd given him in those six months was a kiss. Not even spontaneously given, but relinquished as part of a bribe. I hadn't rejected him. I just didn't want to be forced into a choice. If I chose to be with Clay, I wanted it to be on our terms.

"Why is two years of school too much to ask for?" I said to Sam, tearing my guilty gaze from Clay.

"And after that? Then you'll want time to establish your career. Let's face it. There will never be a perfect time for this in your life. You just need to make the best with what you have."

As in, suck it up? My temper boiled over. Screw respect. He just crossed a line. I walked right up to him and poked him in the shoulder.

"No, Sam, you do. I'm not your pawn in this game you play with women's lives. I went to your Introductions and fulfilled any obligation I felt I owed you for the roof over my head. You have no say in who I see..." Poke. "...or what I do, unless you intend to drag me back to the Compound and physically force me to bite someone."

Clay growled slightly behind me, obviously sharing my sentiment. I stepped back from Sam and moved closer to Clay.

"It's time for you to leave, Sam. Don't come back." Saying those words hurt just as much as knowing I only mattered to him because of what I meant to the pack, rather than what I meant to him.

"You were never an obligation to me, Gabby." When I looked away, he tried to persuade Clay. "You know it'd be safer for both of you if the Introductions continued at the Compound. If you keep going like this, there might be someone you won't beat. Are you willing to risk leaving her alone, then?"

What did he mean by that? Clay could get hurt even worse? I thought they were nearly invincible. Glancing at Clay, I looked at each bruise and saw the real answer. They were hard to beat but made to break, just like the rest of us.

I walked to the door and opened it for Sam, signaling the end of the conversation.

"All right, then." He walked to the door and turned toward me. "Gabby, call me anytime. I'm here to help you, no matter what you might think right now."

I nodded stiffly and closed the door behind him. His help would only extend as far as it could help the pack. He'd just proven I meant less to him than they did, but I'd always known that. Why, then, did I let it hurt me?

For a few seconds, I just stared at the door's surface and tried to let go of my anger. Sam made his choice. I needed to make my own.

I turned to look at Clay. He'd moved closer to me, probably waiting for my reaction to everything Sam had just said. I didn't want to deal with it, yet. Instead, I reached up and teased my fingers through the whiskers along his jaw.

"Much better, but I'm going to keep at you until it's all shaved off, and maybe a haircut, too."

He briefly bared his teeth, re-explaining the reason for the beard.

I spent a moment studying his face. I ran my fingers over his forehead and traced his black eye. He held still, patiently letting me look my fill. Would things have progressed differently if I'd known about a timeframe? I doubted I'd have even let him in the door if I'd known he only had six months to try to convince me.

With a sigh, I stepped away. "I need to get ready for class. Before I go, would you show me where you got the coveralls from?"

He nodded and his lips curled in a slight, secretive smile. I definitely liked seeing his lips.

My hunch had been right. He pulled into a small auto body shop on South Mitchell. The street name tickled a memory. I couldn't place it until the mechanic currently working looked up at our approach. Cleaning his hands on a rag, he smiled at us.

"Dale from the parking lot?" I whispered, looking at Clay questioningly. He just nodded. It explained his secret smile and his interest in books about auto mechanics.

Clay exited the car and moved to open my door. I'd thought I would get a drive by tour, not a walking one. Wide eyed, I stepped out.

Dale walked toward us. "Hi there, Gabby. Glad Clay finally brought you around." He held out his freshly wiped hand. I clasped it briefly. "I have to tell you that I was surprised when Clay showed up and was as good as you boasted." I didn't recall actually boasting. "Although, it doesn't look like he's been taking care of your car."

Clay said nothing in his defense—of course—leaving the talking to me.

"I'm always running back and forth to my classes. It's hard to give it up for any amount of time." I shrugged away his question. "Speaking of which..." I looked at Clay. "I really need to get going, or I'll be late." I turned back to Dale. "It was nice seeing you again, Dale. I hope stopping in was okay. I really wanted to see where Clay was working."

"Stop by anytime." He waved as we walked out and got back in our car.

"I'm sure there was some type of logic to picking that place," I said to Clay as he drove us home. "Someday you'll have to tell me about it."

By Friday, everything seemed back to normal with my pull. Men once again noticed me. Their eyes followed me around campus. Thankfully, they seemed to remember my repeated rejections from the beginning of the semester and didn't approach me anew.

I did wonder what exactly had happened, though. The suspicions that floated around in my head needed further examination, but I wanted to talk through them while Clay listened.

When I walked through the door just before five, an empty house greeted me. I really needed to find out his work schedule.

Rachel got home a little after five. As soon as she walked in the door, she announced she'd decided to go out to a dance club. She continued to her room without waiting for a response from me. I followed her, needing the company. Life had just been a little too weird for me over the past week.

"Don't suppose you'd like to come with?" she asked, looking at the options in her closet.

I sat in the middle of her bed safely out of the way of any clothing options she tossed behind her.

"You know how it is," I said as I plucked at a string in her quilt. "It's just worse if they're drinking."

"Which one do you like better?" Rachel asked, demanding my attention. She'd pulled two dresses from her closet. "This one?" She held up a red dress with a tuck that crossed the middle to accentuate the wearer's curves. "Or this one?" She indicated a standard black dress with a twist. The real hemline was shorter than the red's, but a secondary hemline comprised of strands of beads hung from the first hemline giving the illusion of another six inches.

"I think the black one would be more fun to dance in."

"I think you're right." She set both on the bed and rummaged in her jewelry box. "I have an idea. Peter can't go out tonight. I think we should make it a girl's night out." She turned with something in her hand and arched a brow at me. "Unless you have plans with Sir Talks-A-Lot?"

"No, but—"

She tossed what she held in my direction. By reflex, I caught it.

"Have you ever tried wearing a ring? Some friends of mine do it when they want to go out to have fun and not be bothered by anyone." She grabbed the black dress, handed it to me, then begged. "Let's just try. It's a club with extremely expensive drinks. The prices discourage an all-out drunk, and it has great music."

I hesitated, thinking of Clay. Did I really want to sit here, waiting? It wouldn't help him get home faster. The niggling concern that his delay related to another challenge reared its head. But, Sam had assured me that the challenger would want to heal between fights. If Clay dished out more than he got, the other guy wouldn't be ready yet, anyway.

She pounced on my hesitation. "You know I'll leave anytime you say you're ready to go. You never seem to let your hair down and just have fun. With that kind of constant tension, you're going to end up with heart disease or something."

Her comment about never having fun hit home. I did tend toward the more serious course. When was the last time I did something just for the fun of it? For myself? The double date with Scott had been for Rachel. The party last weekend had been for Nicole. The Introductions for the last two years had been for Sam.

Pathetically, I hadn't done anything just for fun since before I went to live with Sam. Even going to school and getting an education was more for my grandma than me. Before she died, I'd made her a promise to get an education and find something that made me happy.

But would going out dancing really be something I would find fun? I toyed with the fringe on the dress. Yes, dancing would be fun. The men who I'd rather avoid made it a less than fun idea. I looked at the ring in my palm. The large stone sparkled brightly. It was meant to be noticed, but not gaudy. Would it work?

"We'd leave at the first sign the ring doesn't work? Even if we never make it in the club?" I glanced up at her and caught her hopeful expression.

"I've got your back," she promised. "First sign and we're home, curled on the couch watching a chick flick."

"All right," I sighed and grabbed the black dress. "I've got nothing better to do."

"Gee, thanks," Rachel said with a laugh as I left to change.

Rachel and I had to stand in a long line. It seemed the college crowd favored the downtown club despite the overpriced drinks. We shuffled forward every few seconds while listening to the muted music that thumped from within. Each time the bouncer opened the door it briefly grew louder. The door didn't open frequently enough.

I shivered as we inched forward and tried not to move too much so the cold beads wouldn't touch my legs. Eventually we grew close enough that I could watch the man at the door methodically check everyone's ID. I wasn't worried. I knew I wouldn't have a problem getting in.

"Finally," Rachel said with a smile as she stepped up to the man. She showed her ID.

The bouncer barely looked at her. He eyed me closely, not even glancing at the ID I held out. I withstood his scrutiny, wishing he'd hurry so we could warm up inside. I'd pulled my hair back into a messy knot and added a touch of eyeliner and mascara. It wasn't much of a change, but between the makeup and the dress, he looked at me as if I were a goddess. Maybe this wasn't such a good idea.

Then his eyes settled on the ring I wore.

"You come get me if anyone inside gives you any problems," he said. I nodded. He opened the door for us, and I stepped inside after Rachel.

The music's bass reverberated in the floor and my body. I wouldn't be able to hear anything else but didn't care. The club's warm air enveloped me.

Rachel pointed toward the bar. A long blackboard above the bar, filled with neon colored chalk, listed their specialty drinks and prices. As promised, the drinks were expensive. Good thing we wanted to dance, not drink.

Grabbing my hand, she pulled me to the edge of the

swaying crowd and started to dance. I did a little twist in the dress and smiled to myself as the beaded hemline flared out. The dress was as fun to wear as I'd thought. Then the beads slapped my legs on the back swing. The sting of it made me rethink the fun factor. If anyone got out of line, maybe I could use it as a weapon.

The music freed me from worry about male attention, about Clay, and about Sam and his stupid rules. I danced with Rachel and truly had fun.

Eventually, reality invaded in the form of our own all male crowd, and our dancing became a game of evasion. Rachel arched a brow at me. I shook my head, not yet ready to call it quits. The deafening music made it impossible for them to talk to me, and its fast heavy beat didn't inspire a slow, close dance. As long as I evaded the bump and grind, I could still enjoy myself.

After a few songs, I signaled to Rachel because a persistent member of the group kept rubbing up against my backside. She grabbed my hand, and we both ignored the protests of the men around us as she led the way to the bar. A few of the men followed. One of them managed to pull out his wallet and order drinks for both of us before we could stop him. Rachel took hers, but I shook my head and shouted to the bartender that I just wanted water. The generous buyer sulked a bit, but I ignored him and his shouted attempts at conversation.

Sipping my water, I looked around feeling watched—by someone not in the immediate group of men who surrounded us.

I spotted two women further down the bar. They weren't exactly watching me. They were eyeing the crowd of men around us. Neither looked angry, but both looked a little envious. Dressed very similar to Rachel and me, they stood isolated at the bar. The way they kept glancing at me, they probably wondered what I had that they didn't. I couldn't blame them. I looked a bit frumpier than they did.

I motioned to Rachel, and we moved down the bar so our group would spread out to include the two women, as well. I shouted my name over the music and pointed to myself by way of introduction. The women smiled and seemed friendly. They tried to make conversation with a few of the men.

I didn't notice someone leaning close to me until his breath tickled my neck and his unfamiliar voice spoke smoothly in my ear.

"About time you left your guard dog at home." He was just loud enough so I could hear him over the music.

Curious, I turned. He stood several inches taller than I did. No surprise since just about everyone towered over me. He looked even taller than Clay, but not as wide shouldered. He had copper brown hair and hazel eyes. A humor-filled smile flashed at me as I studied him.

"Excuse me, do I know you?"

He leaned in and spoke in my ear. "No need to shout, love. You know I can hear you just fine." His lips touched the curve of my ear, and I shivered as he inhaled deeply. "Mm, you smell good."

I pulled back, leaned against the bar to make some space between us, and really looked at him. In the background, the bodies on the dance floor moved in rhythm to the steady beat of the music. I opened myself to my other sight and wasn't surprised to see his blue-green spark or several other matching sparks in the crowd behind him. Blue-green I could deal with. The other color I didn't want to face until I knew what it meant.

"What do you want?" I said.

With humans, the "safety in numbers" rule worked. Not necessarily so with werewolves. But they did have their own non-human set of rules they still needed to follow, unless they were Forlorn. I'd be okay, as long as I followed the rules Sam taught me.

He leaned in again. "Just to say hi, love. You're hard to catch by yourself. Did you know your dog follows you to school?"

"Hi, then," I said refusing to respond to his last question. If Clay followed me to school, how did he ever find the time to work? Again, I wished he'd just start talking to me.

The man beside me remained close. I didn't like that his breath continued to tickle my ear. Clay would smell him on me.

Rachel noticed us and sent me a questioning look. I gave her a half-smile to reassure her that I didn't mind—even though I really did.

"I was hoping we'd be able to go somewhere quieter to talk."

"Really? Just us? Or those other guys in the crowd, too?" I took a sip of my water and glanced at him.

His smile stretched wider. "And I thought we were blending in well."

None of their kind could ever blend into a human crowd. At least, not for me.

I decided to be blunt. "Do you have permission to be here?"

"We have permission to approach you and request a second meeting."

"Second?"

"This would count as the first," he clarified helpfully.

"Ah." So talking me into leaving with him would probably be the second meeting that he had permission to request.

However, I bet he didn't have permission to have the second meeting without Elder supervision. Typical Forlorn rule breaking. His eyes never left my face, and the longer I remained silent the more his humor slipped. I didn't think he would accept no to his request. It might even result in my immediate forceful removal from this bar. Could nothing in my life ever go easy?

"I can't go with you tonight. I'm with a friend. But I plan to be at the Compound for an Introduction tomorrow night."

"Really? It's odd that no call's gone out for it." He tilted his head and studied me, probably trying to sense a lie. Didn't matter. He wouldn't sense one as I'd just made up my mind.

"That's because I haven't told my guardian yet. We had a fight, and I'm still pretty pissed at him." Pretty pissed at him, and pretty pissed at you. Why couldn't everyone just leave me alone? "I'm tired of being told what to do and want the Introductions on my terms. I didn't think about the call. Sorry."

He looked at me closely for several moments. "I can understand not wanting to be told what to do. That's why we left our packs."

Forlorn. My stomach dropped, and my hand tightened on my glass. Bad grew worse the moment he smelled my fear. His nostrils flared minutely, and his grin widened.

"Don't worry, little one. We're not going to cause you any trouble tonight. We will see you tomorrow night."

Yep, that sounded like a threat. If I didn't go to the Compound, they would be coming to get me either way.

He nodded to me, turned, and disappeared into the crowd. I used my sight and monitored his progress as he and his group left the club. Once they cleared the building, I grabbed Rachel's hand to distract her from her shouted conversation and motioned for the exit. A true friend, she immediately set her barely touched drink on the bar and moved to follow me.

One of the women noticed and snagged my arm.

"Please stay!" she shouted.

I smiled regretfully at her and her friend. Both pleaded with their eyes as did the men behind them. But the men begged for a different reason—they were only feeling the effects of the pull I had. I felt a moment of pity for the women. At some point in our lives, we all looked for that one being to connect with. These two just wanted a chance to find their special someone.

Though I understood, Rachel and I needed to leave in case the Forlorn changed their minds about waiting until tomorrow. I reached out to the women ready to apologize.

As soon as my fingers made contact with their arms, a large shock took the three of us by surprise. I knew immediately what I'd done. It hadn't stung as bad as it had when I'd zapped Nicole, but the drain of it was worse. Now Rachel and I had even more reason to leave quickly.

The women looked stunned. I just laughed it away and patted their arms.

"Sorry," I shouted over the music and waved goodbye.

This time when I moved to go, no one paid me any attention. One of the men behind the girls had already called the bartender over to order more drinks for the group. I hoped the women would stick together and be smart about the attention soon to be showered on them.

The first wave of dizziness washed over me as Rachel and I pushed our way through the crowd toward the door. The bouncer didn't even give me a second glance as we left. No man did. It confirmed what I had already guessed.

Our heels tapped out a rapid cadence on the sidewalk, but

the clipped sound seemed like it came from under water. I wondered how long it would take my ears to recover from the loud music.

"We need to get home," I said as soon as we were far enough away from the club that I could hear.

"Why? Is someone following us?" She turned to look behind us.

I hadn't thought of that. I hoped the Forlorn would keep their word because I couldn't look for them with my sight. I didn't want to drain myself further.

"No, I'm just really not feeling well."

We reached Rachel's car, and I slid into my seat. By the time Rachel eased into the driveway, I shivered uncontrollably. She had cranked the heat in the car, but it hadn't helped. After all, the shivering wasn't because of a chill or a fever. I didn't argue when she parked and told me to stay sitting. She came to my side of the car to help me out.

"Why didn't you tell me sooner that you weren't feeling well?" Rachel said with one arm wrapped securely around my waist as she helped me into the house. The cold beads of the dress tickled the backs of my legs.

"I d-didn't know. It c-came on f-fast."

Rachel unlocked the door. We'd stayed at the club an hour at least, but the house remained quiet and dark.

"Clay?" I called from the kitchen. No answer. How long did Dale keep him on a Friday night? Rachel helped me to my room and frowned at the empty bed.

"I wonder where he is," she murmured.

Too late, I realized my mistake. When I'd called for Clay, I'd wanted the man, forgetting all about Clay-the-dog. Thankfully, I hadn't said anything more.

She unzipped the back of my dress because I shook too badly to reach it, then left my room to search the rest of the house for Clay. I let the dress fall to the floor and struggled to put on my warm pajamas. Rachel came back a few moments after I'd managed to pull up the pants. She looked even more worried.

"I can't find him anywhere."

"M-maybe he got out. I'm going to bed. I'm sure he'll s-show up tomorrow," I said, crawling under the covers.

Rachel got me a glass of water, set it on the dresser, then felt my forehead.

"Doesn't feel like a fever. Maybe it's low grade."

"I'll be fine. Don't worry about me. I've had this before and just need sleep." I burrowed deeper under the covers and tried to curl up to stop shaking. I wished for Clay again. I needed him. He warmed me, comforted me, and I needed to tell him about my promise to go to another Introduction. That wouldn't go over well.

Rachel continued to watch me—nurse Rachel, not friend Rachel. I needed to distract her before she insisted I go see someone.

"I forgot to tell you. I have plans to leave tomorrow to see Sam. If Clay's back, I want to take him with me."

"You sure you'll be up for it?"

"Yeah, it's not something I have a choice about."

"All right. Wake me up if you need anything." She left the room but kept the door ajar. It made my heart ache as I recalled how, first my mother, and then my grandmother, had done the same for me whenever I'd been ill.

CHAPTER SIXTEEN

I felt Clay hop up on my bed and forced my eyes open. Tremors still shook me, and the mid-morning light sent shafts of pain into my aching head. The last time this had happened, it had taken close to twenty-four hours of sleep before I woke up without a headache. Unfortunately, I didn't have time to sleep this one off. If I didn't show up at the Compound on time, those Forlorn would come looking for me, and Clay would get hurt again.

My mind worked sluggishly as I stared at the time. The clock displayed nine. It would take a little over eight hours to get to the Compound. We'd arrive around dinner.

"C-clay, we need to get to the Compound. Can you drive?" I struggled to sit up. He cocked his fuzzy head at me. "A lot happened last night while you were gone. I'll tell you about it on the way."

I tried to stand, but a wave of dizziness knocked me back onto the bed. Blood rushed to my head and pulsed in my ears. I almost didn't hear Clay move while I sat there panting. I waited a moment, took a deep breath, then tried to stand again.

This time, Clay wrapped an arm around me to help. He'd shifted. I glanced at the door. It stood ajar. Was Rachel still home? He needed to be more careful. My wandering eyes caught our reflection in the mirror.

He stood beside me, looking down at me with concern. No wonder. I had my arm curled around his bare waist in a death grip, just to stay standing. My pale face enhanced the dark circles under my eyes. A frizzy mass of hair haloed my head. I looked like hell.

He, however, looked—I stopped gazing at his naked chest long enough to see his eyes narrow—pissed. He'd just figured out what I'd done again, and for the first time, I experienced a sense of appreciation that he didn't talk. Not wanting to meet his gaze, I decided to go back to enjoying the view. He wore jeans, unbuttoned and low on his hips. One arm wrapped around my shaking shoulders. He started to rub little circles on my skin with his thumb. He reached up with his other hand and lightly touched my forehead. Though he was upset with me, his concern was plain, as was...I squinted in an attempt to see clearly and then scowled.

He once again sported bruises and what looked like a bite mark. How many challengers were there out there? I'd thought just a couple. He came home with bruises too often for it to be the same few. And a bite? I frowned at the mark on his shoulder, but my fuzzy brain distracted itself again. I lost my scowl. Even with his bruises and bite mark, Clay looked incredible. I would have drooled at the view he gave if I weren't so sick.

"I need to use the bathroom then start packing."

He nodded and helped me through the door. My head throbbed with each step. I leaned against him, let my head hang a little, and trusted him to guide me. Because of my position, I saw Rachel's feet as she intercepted us.

"Hi, Clay. How'd you get here?"

I forced myself to look up. Still in her pajamas and sleep rumpled, she looked gorgeous. How she pulled that off, I had no idea. Concern filled her eyes when she took in the sight of me.

"I called him. Sorry, Rachel, I didn't want to bug you."

Her gaze drifted to Clay. "It's okay, I get it." She eyed Clay's bare chest and his face as he continued to support me.

I'd forgotten she hadn't seen him cleaned up like I had. Although bruised and bitten probably wasn't the best first impression, being shirtless kind of made up for it. She certainly wasn't looking at him in a clinically concerned way, and it made me smile. Rachel was a free spirit and loved life. She didn't mean anything when she looked, but I could sense it made Clay a little uncomfortable. I shivered again. Perfect timing.

"Are you sure you should be going?" she asked, managing to look away from Clay.

"Yeah, Clay's going to pack for me, and then we'll go. Oh, and he came by last night, saw the dog out, and took him home. We'll take him with, so don't worry."

I closed the bathroom door on both of them and focused on pulling myself together. I splashed some water on my face, leaned heavily on the sink, and ran my fingers through the snarls. It didn't help much, but I didn't think it would matter anyway with a long drive ahead of us. I took care of business and shuffled out of the bathroom to look for shoes, not concerned about changing.

Clay came in from the back door before I could make it to

the hall closet. He took one look at my chattering teeth and scooped me up in his arms.

My squeal brought Rachel from her room before Clay could make it out the door.

"When you're feeling better, let's talk about rental rates," she called after us with a snicker. "And I'm not talking about the house!"

A blanket waited for me in the front seat of the warmed car. My bulging messenger bag, packed to the point of bursting, sat on the back seat. I twisted, grabbed the cell phone from it while Clay closed my door, then I buckled up. My fuzzy slippers were on the floor, but I curled my legs under me instead and pulled the blanket snuggly around me.

He slid in behind the wheel and took some time to better tuck the blanket around me. His hand smoothed over mine briefly before he pulled away and backed out of the driveway. I struggled to keep my eyes open. Sleep pulled at me.

"I don't want to keep going on like this," I said once we cleared town.

His hands noticeably tightened on the steering wheel, and I could have smacked my forehead if it wasn't already hurting so badly.

"I don't mean being with you. I like that. But I don't like seeing you bruised."

He loosened his tight hold on the wheel and glanced at me. A smile twitched his lips. I scowled at him.

"There's nothing amusing about it. I don't like worrying."

I lifted my cell, dialed Sam's number, and struggled to hold the phone to my ear. My arm trembled from the effort. Sam picked up during the first ring. I didn't wait for his greeting.

"I'm on my way. Put out a call for tonight only." I hung up

before he could speak. I wasn't ready to talk to him. He'd hurt me too much with his last appearance.

I tossed the phone on the back seat and ignored it when it started to vibrate again. My gaze drifted to Clay. He looked outright pissed now. He knew who I'd called and what I intended. I hurried to explain.

"It's not what you think, Clay. I don't want to do another Introduction, but something happened last night. I went out with Rachel to a club downtown, not my best decision, but I think I've figured out what's going on with me." I shivered and pulled the blanket tighter around me. Sleep continued to tug at me.

"Remember the party with Nicole? When I touched her, I gave her a huge shock. That happened again last night. I think I can transfer my gift, that thing with guys, to other people. I didn't know how it happened the first time. But I think I've figured it out.

"Last night, these two women at the club had been on their own until Rachel and I—and the groupies I'd collected—joined them. When we made to leave, the women had been so disappointed. They knew the guys would walk away when we did. I felt so bad for them that I went to...I don't know...pat them, I guess. I'd just meant it as an 'I'm sorry' gesture, but then it happened again just like before. A huge shock." My words started to slur, and I had a hard time keeping my thoughts coherent.

"Both times I was thinking about how I wished I could help find the person they were meant to be with. And I think that's the key." I noticed the speedometer hovered ten miles over what I considered a safe speed, but I didn't comment on it. "I don't understand why I can see the lights, but I know it must be all tied together because when I try to use my sight, it hurts. Really bad." Clay's expression hadn't changed, and I realized I'd skipped the explanation of why I'd agreed to an Introduction.

"Oh, yeah. Before I shocked those two, a Forlorn came up behind me and started a conversation. My fish finder still worked then. There were more of them in the crowd, Clay. The one talking to me said he just wanted a chance to say hi. He was very persistent so I told him I would see them at the Compound for an official Introduction. They left right after but gave me the impression that if I didn't show up, they'd come looking for me. I got the feeling they'd been pushed too far." I watched his face. "Has it been the same werewolves trying to see me or is it always different?"

He didn't answer, but I didn't really expect him to. I sighed and snaked a hand out from under the blanket to touch his leg.

"It hurts to see you like this, Clay. If I have to put up with an Introduction to keep you safe, then that's what I'll do." My lids refused to cooperate any longer and drifted shut.

"I'm sorry, Clay," I mumbled sleepily. "I wish I could just get over my need for freedom and Claim you. We both know you're the one. I just don't want to lose myself." I fell asleep without looking at him to see his reaction.

I WAS SURROUNDED by darkness and in a bed. Clay had carried me around while I slept again.

"Clay?" I whispered, reaching out to feel the mattress beside me. Empty.

Sam's voice came from nearby. "You're safe, Gabby. At the Compound."

"Where's Clay?" I asked, trying to wake fully.

"In the unMated's wing. I was surprised he chose to stay there. After I kicked him out of here, I thought he'd go to the woods."

Sam's words annoyed me. How dare he kick Clay out. He had no right.

Still tired, I could have easily fallen back asleep. Instead, I struggled into a sitting position to keep myself awake.

"You don't know anything about him," I muttered, using Sam's own words. "Can you turn on a light please? I can't see."

The lamp next to the bed clicked on. Sam sat in a chair near the bed. He looked worn, but I didn't feel very sympathetic. I looked around. I wasn't in the same room I usually occupied, but I didn't bother asking why.

"What time is it?"

He glanced at his watch then met my eyes again.

"Just after seven. You look worse than sick. Charlene came in to look at you. You have us all worried. You going to tell me what's happened to you?"

Of course, they were worried. They'd promised their horde an Introduction.

"Nope, I won't. Did you put out the call? Did anyone respond?"

He didn't care for my answer, but let it go. "Yes, there's about fifty or so. There were more, but we explained that you were ill and wouldn't be able to—"

"Put the call out again." Why did he choose now to care about my wellbeing? "They have an hour to get here. Get Clay for me, please." I swung my legs out from the blankets and started to get up.

Sam moved in a blur of speed and pushed me back down, his hand on my collarbone. He didn't have to use much force. I flopped back into the pillow and glared at him. He kept his hand on me for a moment, probably waiting for me to try again. As if I could move a werewolf.

"I get it, Gabby. I disappointed you and lost your trust, but you're sick. This isn't what I asked for when I said you'd be better off doing Introductions at the Compound." His voice turned gruff. "Please, don't push yourself like this. You'll get worse."

His expression and pleading tone swayed me enough to take pity on him. I patted his cheek sadly and half-smiled.

"Not everything is about you, Sam. Yes, I'm still mad at you, but this is about Clay and me. I don't want to see him hurt because he's trying to fight other werewolves away from me. Now, help me up, and go get Clay." I held out my hands, and he reluctantly helped pull me to my feet.

Wobbling a bit, I made my way to my bag that lay at the foot of the bed. Sam shook his head as he watched my determined, but slow, progress. I sat on the mattress and pulled the bag toward me. With a sigh, he left to go get Clay while I rummaged through my messenger bag.

I still dug in the bag when Clay walked in without knocking. He didn't walk past the threshold, though. Concern filled his expression when I looked up. I lifted my hand from the bag and let the bikini I'd found dangle from one finger.

"Really, Clay? You're killing me. Where are my jeans?"

His lips twitched with a smile as he leaned against the frame, content to watch me dig through the bag some more.

Despite my playful greeting, I felt winded and dizzy again. Shocking both of those girls took more out of me than I'd anticipated. I'd expected to feel much better by now, like I had the last time. The shocks hadn't seemed as strong as Nicole's had, but perhaps, because it had split between the two of them, it drained me more.

At least my head didn't hurt. I took a break from my search to look up at the fading bruises on Clay's face. He still wore his hair back. I loved seeing his face.

He must have seen something in my gaze because he pushed away from the door and moved closer. He stopped in front of me, and without breaking eye contact, reached into my bag and pulled out a pair of jeans. He held them out to me and tapped his lips.

I smiled widely. "A kiss for the jeans?"

He nodded. I grabbed the jeans from his loose grasp and tossed them on the bed.

He watched me, curious, as I stood and placed my hands on his chest for balance.

"I don't need bribes to kiss you, Clay. Come here."

His lips covered mine in a move so fast, my head spun even more. I clutched his shirt in my fists, not sure if it was his kiss or my condition that caused the current wave of dizziness. His arms circled around me. I felt safe. And so desired. I pressed myself closer, and he increased the pressure on my lips. His warm breath fanned my face. One of his hands roamed up to curve around the back of my neck.

My heart skipped a beat, and my breathing became more erratic. I knew he'd hear but I didn't care. Standing on my tiptoes, I loosened my hold on his shirt and slid my hands up and around his neck. I didn't want him to let go just yet.

Tentatively, I opened my mouth and ran my tongue across his bottom lip. He growled, and his hold tightened fractionally. A thrill shot through me, heating my limbs and tickling my stomach. I used my tongue again. His mouth opened in response. He took control of the kiss and turned it from tender-sweet to passionately melting. Our tongues touched. I stopped breathing. My world tilted then steadied. He anchored me. How could I doubt this? Us?

My lungs burned for air, and he gently pulled away even though I whined in protest. He kissed my cheek, then my forehead.

It took a minute for the world to right itself again while I caught my breath. Clay placed his chin on my head and held me tight. My head rested on his chest over his thundering heart. The kiss had affected him as much as it had me. It made me smile because now I knew without a doubt; *I* attracted him, not my strange pull.

I heard the apartment door open and figured it was Sam. With regret, I pulled back, and Clay let me go. I looked up at Clay.

"Can you come with me for this, or will that cause more problems?"

"It would be best if he stayed away, Gabby," Sam answered from the doorway behind Clay.

I moved around Clay to look at Sam. "I didn't ask what was best. Best went out the window years ago, Sam, when 'making do' moved in. Is he allowed?"

Sam flinched when I repeated his words then ran his hand over his face. The move muffled his sigh.

"It's allowed. He's unMated, but he's considered rejected.

He'll be challenged by everyone for his place in the Introduction order."

I made a non-committal noise and looked at Clay. "Do you want to be there?"

He nodded sharply.

"All right then. Sam, please head over and get things ready. Clay will walk me there. Clay, I just need to change then I'm ready."

Both men stared at me as if I'd grown horns. I knew I looked like hell. I was probably still pale and definitely had a worse tangled mass of hair than I had that morning. But, it didn't matter. Sam wanted an Introduction, and I wanted peace for Clay. I arched a brow at both of them.

Sam grumbled to himself as he left. Clay followed and closed the door softly behind him, leaving me to dress. I smoothed down my hair, not really caring, and changed into a shirt and jeans. My legs shook by the time I finished, and I had to sit on the bed for a minute.

I took a fortifying breath, stood, and made my way out to the living room. Clay waited for me by the kitchenette. He had a glass of orange juice ready for me. He knew me well. I smiled my thanks and gulped it down. It felt good and gave me a tiny energy boost.

"I need just a minute in the bathroom. Can you find my shoes for me?" I held the wall as I made my way there and leaned on the sink while I brushed my teeth. As I brushed, I dwelled on the fact that Sam had kicked Clay out of my room. If it weren't for the long drive, I'd insist we leave right after the Introduction. But I knew Clay needed sleep soon, too. I wondered what Sam would do when I insisted that Clay sleep next to me later. He was warm and comforting, and I needed both desperately.

Clay stood right outside the door when I opened it. My slippers waited on the floor by his feet.

"Where are my shoes?"

He shrugged and pointed to the slippers. Hey, he'd packed for me and remembered the jeans. He'd even packed underclothes and a toothbrush. If he forgot the shoes, I really had no complaint. I stepped into the slippers then squeaked when my world spun, and I suddenly found myself in his arms.

"I can walk, Clay."

He shook his head and carried me to the door. There, he repositioned me to one arm and opened the door while I clung tightly to his neck. I rather liked the feeling. With an arm wrapped around him, I leaned my head against his shoulder and ran my fingers through his hair.

The few people in the hallways stopped and stared as we passed. At the intersection of halls, which led to the Introduction room, I stopped Clay.

"No, go outside and around back. I won't go in that room ever again." As childish as it might be, I wanted something about the impending Introduction to be on my own terms.

He grunted in acknowledgment. But, instead of turning to go out the nearby back door, he backtracked to the main entrance. He set me on my feet, snagged a spare jacket from one of the hooks, and carefully buttoned me in. I studied his face as he concentrated on each snap. Always thinking of me. When he finished, he scooped me back into his arms. I didn't protest.

Bundled warmly in a thick coat, I didn't cringe when he carried me out into the cold. The sky was dark, and the yard light didn't reach very far. Clay carried me toward the back of the building. I couldn't hear the werewolves as we approached, but saw their sparks briefly before a sharp pain not so gently reminded me not to look. I guessed close to seventy-five waited out there. It meant some of them had returned.

"Put me down, Clay," I said before we rounded the corner of the building. "I'll walk now." I didn't want to give the waiting unMated any reason to believe this wasn't a fair Introduction, even though it really wasn't. I still felt the pull for Clay.

Clay hesitated. It'd be safer for both of us if I stayed in his arms. He wouldn't fight, and I wouldn't fall. Yet, despite my anger over another forced Introduction, I truly felt sorry for the men who waited. The Introduction was just a false hope. One I couldn't take away from them.

"It'll be okay Clay. There are a lot of fast people here. I won't fall on my face." I spoke normally so everyone could hear. I really didn't want to fall on my face.

As soon as he set me on my feet, I walked around the corner with my shoulders back and head held high, determined to look strong. The slippers probably ruined the image, but I pretended otherwise.

The Elders stood by the back door. Only three of them this time.

"I'm Gabby. There will be no Introduction order. I won't have anyone left out, or leaving without a fair chance. So, instead of the stuffy cabin, let's just do this out here." The warmth of the jacket when not supplemented by Clay wasn't adequate, and I started to shiver slightly. "I believe the Elders mentioned I was ill, so if I start to stammer, bear with me."

The men began to line up. So many looking for a Mate, and this was just a fraction of what was really out there. Some were too far away to answer such a short notice call. I wondered how many of their kind I still hadn't met.

I met the eyes of several as I walked slowly down the not yet fully formed, long line. As I'd anticipated, the shivers grew more noticeable. This time the tremors were due to the cold, not my fatigue, and I fought not to duck further into my jacket. They needed to smell me. I kept walking and listened to Clay keep pace with me, just a few steps behind. Several of those I passed glanced at Clay, but no one actually commented on his presence.

Walking helped warm me a little. While the shivering didn't go away, it at least didn't increase.

A few exceptionally young Weres stood mixed in the line. I smiled kindly at each of them. For the most part, I paced in front of the line as if I performed a quiet military inspection. The males scented me as discreetly as possible, so hopeful for some type of connection. Many walked away after I passed.

About halfway down the line, I noticed a man step back and retreat into the woods. No unMated male walked away from an Introduction before being Introduced. It just wasn't done. The possibility of meeting a Mate was too important to them. Suspicious, I used my other sight despite the knowledge it would hurt. I pushed myself to look as far as I was able and gasped. A jolt of pain pierced my temple and forced me to close my other sight. My hand flew to my head, cradling it.

Clay moved so quickly, my hair lifted in his breeze. He stood close enough that I felt his heat at my back. I forced myself to straighten. The werewolf I faced looked confused. His eyes moved to the Elders standing several steps behind us.

"Gabby," Sam began, but I held up a hand.

"A moment, please," I managed to say.

Although it'd been a brief glimpse, I had seen a blue-grey spark moving away from our group. In the distance, three other blue-grey sparks waited. I couldn't say anything to Clay since I held everyone's attention, but I glanced at him. He studied the worry on my face for a moment then looked around. I felt safer because of it but still wished I could reach out to take his hand.

Instead, I turned to the men in front of me.

"I'm sorry. Like I said, I'm not feeling well. The pain in my head just took me by surprise." I took a steadying breath and continued my slow progress. The werewolves I passed watched me with concern. I probably looked even worse than I had just a moment ago.

More than halfway down the line, I came across a face I knew. He studied me, his playful smile from our last meeting absent. I used him as an excuse to stop and rest for a minute. I'd started shaking again, not from the cold.

"A f-face I know. I'm here as p-promised."

His eyes turned slightly remorseful at my words.

"I see that, little one. Although, it looks like you should be in bed instead."

"I would b-be if people would j-just leave me alone." I felt bad for saying it as soon as it left my mouth. How many times had these men stood in line hoping to meet some faceless girl? "B-but it's not meant t-to be. So, you know my name, but I d-don't know yours." I made conversation to make up for my harsh comment.

"Luke Taylor, love." He offered his hand, politely. A human custom, not a werewolf one. With my pull gone, could I safely touch him without causing some type of obsession? I hesitated and studied his face. He'd been desperate at the club, but now he looked resigned. He knew I wasn't the one for him.

Feeling sorry for him, I accepted his hand. A mild shock went through me to him.

Time stopped as my vision tunneled. The world around me disappeared, swallowed by darkness until only a pinprick of light remained. Then the darkness exploded into a spark-filled view of the world in its entirety. The tiny lights dazzled me. The yellow-green of humanity almost consumed the world. However, diversity persisted, though small.

Slowly, the sparks of each human, werewolf, and the yet unexplained blue-grey winked out of existence until a single, faint spark tinted with a violet halo remained on the east coast. My focus changed, honing in on that light. Like reading a map, I saw its exact location. My eyes swam in the yellow-violet light for a moment. Then, with a snap like an elastic band breaking, I returned to myself.

My lungs sucked in a breath with a loud whoosh, and my heart hammered in my chest. I ached all over and felt like vomiting. Only Luke's steady, warm hand, desperately clutched in my own, anchored me and kept me from falling apart.

Clay paced directly behind me. I vaguely imagined he wouldn't like me holding another man's hand for so long. I met Luke's gaze and swallowed down my bile before attempting to speak. He eyed me warily.

"I need to talk to you. Don't leave until I do."

His brow rose in surprise at my heavily slurred words.

"Clay," I whispered. My head lolled to the side as I tried to catch his eye. "Catch me." I let go of Luke's hand, and the world disappeared.

My pounding head woke me. I couldn't tell if I lay in a dark room or just had my eyes closed. It didn't really matter. My skull would certainly shatter if I had to deal with light, too. I tried to whisper for water but only managed a faint croak. When I attempted to clear my throat, the pain in my head brought tears to my eyes. I was dying. I had to be to feel this way.

An arm gently slid under my neck and lifted my head a bit. A cool glass pressed to my lips, and I slowly sipped the contents. I stopped when the darkness began to pull me down again.

I woke several more times, only drinking a bit of water before passing out again. Each time the pain in my head decreased a little until, finally, I woke with more clarity.

"Water," I whispered into the darkness.

Again, an arm snaked under me and lifted me for a cool drink. I drained the cup. The arm lowered me, and I settled back onto the pillow. My ears rang in the silence.

"How long have I been sleeping?" I asked just to hear something.

Instead of an answer, I got a tight hug.

"I really hope you're Clay," I whispered breathlessly.

His gruff laugh wrapped around me, just as comforting as his hug.

"Can we turn on a light?"

He moved away from me, and I took the opportunity to sit up a bit and lean against the headboard. My legs still felt shaky.

The bedside lamp clicked on. I squinted against the light

and regretted my request. My head ached slightly. I rubbed a hand over my face as my eyes watered. A tangle of my hair got in my way. I brushed it aside and felt the knots in it.

Blinking several times, I finally focused on Clay. He was dressed in the same clothes he'd worn outside. Maybe I hadn't been out that long after all. He stood near the bed and watched me with a tender, relieved expression.

"Clay, I think I know what's going on. Can you help me up? I really need a shower." And a toothbrush.

He shook his head.

"Clay, now's not the time to put your foot down. This is really important." I tried to sit all the way up, but couldn't. My head started to throb again. "Okay. Maybe you're right," I mumbled as I rubbed my forehead. "Can you get me something for my head, please? It feels like it going to explode all over the walls."

Clay leaned over me, smoothed back my hair, kissed my forehead, then left the room. The guest apartments didn't have any type of medicine in them because the werewolves typically didn't need it.

I waited until I heard the outside door close, then I struggled up again. My comment about my head was absolutely true. Therefore, I stayed in a sitting position for a minute before attempting to swing my legs off the bed. But headache or not, I needed to speak to Luke.

Reaching for my bag, I smiled again at Clay's packing. Flannel pants and a t-shirt were perfect, after all.

CHAPTER SEVENTEEN

I USED THE PANELED WALL FOR SUPPORT AS I MADE MY WAY TO THE bathroom. Sweat beaded my forehead when I finally stepped onto the cold, tiled floor. I flicked on the light and fan then set my clothes on the toilet tank.

Knowing I had limited time, I immediately turned the shower on to let the water warm. I moved to the sink, caught my reflection in the mirror, and cringed. Sunken eyes, hollow cheeks, and hair that stuck out at varying angles, reflected back at me. Without a doubt, Clay really did care about me. I shook my head then brushed my teeth, giving the water an extra minute to heat.

When I finished, I struggled out of my clothes and further depleted my waning energy. I eyed the high edge of the tub and thought back to when Clay had insisted on helping me. If I fell, I'd never hear the end of it. Bracing myself, I successfully stepped over the edge and tugged the curtain closed.

The hot spray felt great, but I didn't pause to warm up. If I stayed too long, I'd lose what little energy I had or Clay would discover me. I grabbed the all-in-one hair wash and lathered my natty head. My arms grew heavy as I rinsed, and with relief, I turned off the water. Navigating the high edge proved more difficult the second time, and I clutched at the wall after a near fall.

The fan worked to suck the built up heat and steam from the room as I hurried to dry off. My unsteady legs forced me to sit down to finish dressing. The cold helped hurry the process.

I used my towel to bundle my dirty clothes then moved to the door. Though it felt like the process took forever, I knew only a few minutes had passed since Clay left. If I could get to my room and dry my hair, I'd be home free. I pulled open the door and yelped. The steady thump in my head increased its tempo.

Clay stood just outside the door, leaning against the wall. He held a glass of water in one hand and two pills in the other. I tried to read his face, but he kept it perfectly blank. I hoped that meant he wasn't angry with me. Desperate to relieve the pain in my head, I released my death grip on the door and gulped down the pills.

When I tried handing him the empty glass, he shook his head and picked me up again. My feet had been getting cold, anyway. Holding the empty glass, I sighed and rested my head against his chest.

He went toward my room, and I almost complained until I saw what he'd done. He'd changed the sheets and remade the bed. Socks, slippers, and my hairbrush lay on the quilt, waiting. He'd known I would go for the shower and had given me privacy even though he hadn't wanted me to get out of bed. Not only that, but he'd gotten everything ready for when I finished.

I looked at him. He studied me, his arms still securely

around me. I leaned in, kissed his cheek tenderly, and hesitated there. He smelled so good. I just wanted to curl back up with him. But I couldn't. I pulled back and looked at him again.

"You are so sweet, and I truly appreciate this, but I'm not going back to bed, Clay. I need to see Luke."

The muscles in his jaw clenched as he stepped into the room and carefully set me on the bed. He left without a backward glance.

I stared at the empty doorway puzzled until the outer door slammed hard enough that I heard the wood crack. I flinched.

"I shouldn't have said I needed to see Luke."

I hurried to put on my socks and slippers while hoping Clay wouldn't go too far. The movement made my head feel like it would fall off at any moment. The pills needed to kick in soon. I rubbed my brow again, but it didn't relieve the pain at all. This wasn't a normal headache. I just needed to deal with it. With a sigh, I stood.

I'd only made it to the living room when the door burst open again. I stared at Clay as he dragged Luke in by the cuff of one pant leg. Luke didn't appear to mind. Instead, he was laughing. His hands clutched the waistband of his pants to keep Clay from pulling them off entirely. After they cleared the threshold, I saw a crowd watching from the hallway. Not good. News of this would get back to the Elders. No doubt Sam would want to talk to me as soon as he found out I was awake. I moved from the couch to the door and slammed it closed. The poor door would need some repair work.

Clay reached the middle of the room, dropped Luke's leg, and without pause, turned back to the door. I didn't move away from the exit. He reached for the knob without meeting my gaze, but I stopped him with a hand held up.

"Clay, I need you to stay and listen. Please."

He still didn't look at me, and I knew asking to speak with Luke had hurt him. Why wouldn't it? Had I really ever given him much hope we had a future together? Sam showed up at our door just days ago saying I'd rejected Clay and needed to do the Introductions again. Instead of putting my foot down, we went back. Granted I'd told Clay I didn't like to see him hurt and admitted we both knew he was the one for me, but we hadn't talked about what we'd do about it.

"Please," I said again, when he hadn't moved. "Give me a chance." I touched his face and forced him to meet my gaze. "I've asked so much of you already and know it's not fair to ask again, but I am." I chose my words carefully aware of our audience inside the apartment and in the hall.

He sighed, reached up to cup my face, and gently smoothed his thumb over my cheek. A tender look crept into his eyes before he abruptly dropped his hands, turned, and headed toward the still laughing Luke. Clay dragged his feet as he stepped over Luke. Luke grunted when a foot connected with his ribs, and his laughter started to quiet.

As Clay settled on the chair against the wall, Luke sat up.

"Most people wouldn't laugh while being dragged through the Compound like that." I stayed by the door because I didn't want either of them leaving. I knew I couldn't stop them physically even on my best day, but I'd cry if I had to.

Luke stood and turned toward Clay with a grin, ignoring me to taunt Clay.

"I've never seen anyone hold a transformation like that. He was man, but the fangs, ears, fur...it was amazing, and hilarious, mate," he said as he settled himself on the couch.

"Um, isn't that a sign that he's in an extreme emotional state?" I asked Luke. He didn't appear to hear me.

I walked behind Luke and smacked him hard on the back of the head. It really hurt my hand, but it got his attention.

"Meaning, you should stop trying to annoy him."

Since Clay sat across from Luke, I moved to Clay and gingerly perched on one of his knees. He held still for a moment then his hands gripped my hips. He pulled back so I fully sat on his lap and turned me so we could both see Luke. Much better than sitting in my own chair. Warmer, too.

Having successfully gained both their attentions, I decided to get to the point.

"Luke, what happened when I touched you? What did you feel?"

"One hell of a shock. Listen, did you bring me here for a reason, or was it just to rub your relationship with him in my face?" Luke nodded at Clay, and though Luke's usual smile still curved his lips, his words conveyed the agitation he tried to hide.

"It's for a reason." I tried to lean forward, but Clay wrapped his arms loosely around my waist. He didn't give an inch, and I didn't fight it. I'd pushed him enough for the night...or day. I still didn't know how long I'd been out.

"How long have I been sleeping?"

"Two days, love. Everyone's been pretty worried, and the Elders are waiting to talk to you."

"I bet." My eyes drifted to the door. I focused and immediately cradled my throbbing head. My eyes watered as I tried to breathe through the pain. "Crap."

Behind me, Clay grunted in annoyance.

Luke's smile slipped. "Listen, I think you should still be in bed, little one. No disrespect intended, but you don't look well."

My hair hung wet and uncombed around me. I could imagine what I looked like. I pressed my cool fingertips to one temple and wished I hadn't been so stupid. Clay started to rub my back soothingly, working his way up to my neck and then lightly stroking my hair. It helped.

"I know you're right, but I can't go back to sleep yet. I need you to tell me what happened."

Nicole told me that she'd really connected with Randy. Even after my pull wore off, they had continued to date. I couldn't go back to the two women at the club to find out what they'd experienced. I needed to get more information from Luke.

"I don't know what happened, love. You shocked me, told me not to leave, then fainted. After that, Clay picked you up and ran inside with you. He hasn't let anyone near you for two days. We only knew you were still alive because he didn't take off into the woods."

Clay's tight hug when I woke made more sense. He'd been worried about me, taking care of me and keeping the Elders away.

I forced myself to stay focused on Luke.

"And after Clay left, what about you? What did you do?"

Luke began to look uncomfortable. "Uh, I went out for a bit then came back here."

"The constant attention probably went to your head," I muttered. Luke was too sure of himself for any woman to have a chance.

His startled expression told me I was right.

"Did you meet anyone special while I was out?" I asked

glancing at the door again and wishing we didn't have an audience.

I looked back in time to catch Luke shaking his head. Still unMated. I'd thought as much but had to be sure. Normal humans wouldn't tempt him, and there were too few unMated females at the Compound. I had an idea but needed sleep and time to think through everything.

"Luke, there is so much I don't understand, and I really need your help." I nodded toward the door and hoped he'd know I meant with the Elders who probably waited outside. "I need some time to myself to understand what I'm feeling." This is why Clay had to be in the room with me. Anyone standing in the hall would probably think I felt torn between Clay and Luke.

Luke looked from me to Clay then back again. He started to ask a question, hesitated, then gazed at the door once more. Finally, he stood.

"I'll be around," he said.

I hoped he'd understood I wanted his help to get us out of here. The door had barely closed behind him when a knock sounded.

Still sitting on Clay's lap, I turned to him. He met my gaze. I shook my head and wrapped my arms around his neck. His arms cradled me as he stood and carried me to the bedroom. He set me on the bed, covered me, then closed the door. I listened to him answer the apartment door.

I heard Sam's voice but didn't bother trying to hear what Sam had to say. The Elders would come to get me soon enough. My exhaustion didn't wait for them. I fell asleep again.

※

MY STOMACH GROWLED SO LOUDLY it woke me. I listened for a minute before opening my eyes. Clay had left the lamp on so I could see. I turned my head. He lay next to me, on top the covers. Given the steady cadence of his breathing, he still slept. I let my mind drift, content to think and let him get the rest he needed.

Whatever I had in me, I could temporarily pass to people via a shock, but the effect only lasted until I recovered. I could also zap more than one person at a time, and I felt certain now that my emotions, in addition to my touch, triggered the transfer. The drain I experienced afterward varied. It felt like the flu the first time, but when I passed it to the two women, the symptoms intensified.

Shocking Luke had been different. I couldn't say if the drain had been worse since I'd started out drained. However, focusing on a specific person's spark was new.

Based on the yellow-violet coloring, I guessed it belonged to another compatible, like me. Could it mean my ability was to find Mates for the people I touched? But then, why hadn't I zoomed in on a single person when touching the others? Maybe a werewolf amplified my ability, and the view appeared whether I wanted it or not. Or maybe one spark had stood out when I'd touched the rest, but I hadn't focused on my spark-sight to check.

But what about my pull? Where did that play into this? There were still too many possibilities. I needed a test group. Immediately, I thought of Rachel and Peter. When I sensed them without touching Rachel, I knew they were a perfect match. If I tried to pass my pull to Rachel and saw Peter's spark, I'd have my answer. If it didn't work on them, I wouldn't rule out my theory completely. The difference between human and werewolf might be the key to the results. I could experiment on Clay. He knew I was his match.

In addition to figuring out why I had the ability to pass on my gift, I needed to understand why I saw different werewolf colors. The one who'd left the line and the others waiting for him worried me.

Regardless of my anger at Sam, if trouble stalked the pack, he needed to know. But I needed to talk to Clay about it before I could talk to anyone else. He would help me figure out how it all tied together. However, I couldn't talk to Clay here. There were too many ears, and I was still uncertain if I could trust Sam with everything.

I needed to leave before the Elders started pushing me for answers I didn't have. What reason could I give Sam for my sudden faint during the Introduction? He'd know any lie before I told it. And if I gave him the truth, would he then share it with all the Elders? After seeing those werewolves leave the Introduction, I couldn't blindly trust Elder Joshua. Too many werewolves of that same color acted unusually.

Feeling a light caress on my hair, I turned to look at Clay, who watched me again.

"Do I say good morning or is it close to goodnight again?"

He smiled at me, reached down to twine his fingers through mine, and brought my hand to his mouth. Instead of kissing it, he whipped his head toward the door. A silent snarl pulled back his lips. The bedroom door opened, and Luke poked his head in.

"Better hurry. You carry her, and I'll grab her things," he said, speaking directly to Clay.

I let out a relieved breath. Luke had understood and come through. I opened my mouth to thank him, but Clay leapt off the bed and quickly scooped me into his arms, covers and all. With the blankets twisted around me and partially covering my face, I felt a moment of disoriented panic as he lifted me.

I shook my head to dislodge the blanket and sent Clay a quick scowl. His lips twitched.

Over his shoulder, I saw Luke cramming my things into my ragged messenger bag. My bag wouldn't last through another werewolf packing.

Clay left the room. Just in case anyone else roamed the halls, I laid my head on Clay's shoulder. He held me closely and walked quickly. We quietly made it out the main entrance with Luke following us.

The black sky twinkled with stars, and crickets conversed with their night song as the two werewolves stealthily moved over the graveled parking area. It had to be Monday night. I regretted missing a day's worth of classes, but there'd been no way to help it.

The car faced the gate. Luke must have moved it. The door's loud creaking groan made us all cringe. Clay quickly settled me inside, reached across me to secure the seat belt, then silently jogged around the hood to get in behind the wheel.

Luke handed me my bag then moved to close the door. I motioned for him to wait and dug in a side pocket of my bag for a pencil stub and paper. In those few moments after I shocked him and before I passed out, I'd gleaned some information about the person I saw. Whoever she was, Luke needed to find her and help me understand if some of my suspicions were right. Was she like me? Was she his Mate?

I jotted him a hasty note and handed it to him with a wave. He quickly closed the door. I hoped giving him the information was the right thing to do. I barely knew him. Would he even try to find her or just hand the information over to an Elder? Worried, I looked at him through the window. He didn't see me. His eyes scanned my note. He crumpled it in his hand and spun toward a waiting motorcycle.

Clay pulled away from the Compound, spitting gravel with the tires. The motorcycle roared to life and quickly zipped past us. Luke saluted me with a wicked grin then disappeared from sight. I peeked in the side mirror and caught the reason for their loud exit. Sam stood on the porch, his gaze locked on us. He grew smaller as we sped away. I wished I knew whom to trust.

I laid my head back and closed my eyes. What a crappy Introduction weekend. The worst yet. I hoped there were no more in my future.

The drone of the engine and the soothing vibrations of the tires put me right to sleep. I dozed the whole way home, waking when Clay lifted me from the car. With blankets still twisted around me, he carried me to my room and gently set me on the bed.

A few minutes later, he settled next to me. It didn't matter anymore if he wore his fur or stayed as a man. He remained with me. It was enough.

CLAY TRIED to keep me home Tuesday. First, he planted himself, in his fur, in front of my door so I couldn't get out of the bedroom. Then, when I pleaded to use the bathroom, he allowed me out and took the opportunity to hide my keys.

My suspicion rose when he calmly watched me get ready. I discovered the missing keys and resorted to further pleading. I explained my need to talk to Nicole in hopes of piecing together the puzzle of my abilities. The one-sided conversation reminded me of the first time I'd reasoned with him.

Of course, Rachel caught part of my serious chat with our dog and did a double take on her way to the bathroom. I laughed and waved her away, then gave Clay a look. Grudgingly, Clay led me to my keys, and I made it to campus on time.

I parked and took a minute to lean my forehead against the steering wheel, still recovering from sharing my ability with three people in one weekend. Clay had obviously sensed it. If Tuesday hadn't been the only day I saw Nicole, I would have stayed in bed. Steeling myself, I got out of the car and trudged across campus.

For the first time ever, I didn't pay much attention to the instructor. Instead, I sat by Nicole and whispered questions freely, but failed to uncover anything more than what she'd already shared. Men had hit on her quite a bit after the Halloween party. She attributed the attention to the costume, which she planned to reuse. Since it wasn't a bad costume, I didn't dissuade her of the idea. Better to think it was the costume than a freak friend passing some kind of power to her.

I smiled and waved goodbye to her at the end of the class. People pushed past me to leave. I watched them go and dreaded the long walk back to the car. With my pull gone, thanks to Luke and two strangers, I could safely ask someone for a piggyback ride. I'd seen it happen before. Yet, I couldn't picture explaining to Clay why I smelled like another guy.

RACHEL AND CLAY-THE-MAN stood in the kitchen together

making an early dinner. Surprised, I hesitated in the doorway. Rachel typically spent her free time with Peter or at work. And Clay tended to stay in his fur when she was home.

Rachel paused her one-sided conversation to wink at me. I glanced at Clay, stepped further into the room, and slowly closed the door behind me. Clay remained focused on the food he stirred in the pan. Rachel walked past me on her way to get silverware.

"You didn't tell me he could *cook*," Rachel stage whispered.

Giving her a crooked smile, I made my way to a kitchen chair. I was exhausted.

"He cooks, he cleans, he warms up my feet at night, and he keeps the toilet seat down...so hands off. He's mine."

Rachel laughed, and Clay turned to give me an undecipherable look. I had a feeling he liked the "mine" part.

"How you feeling?" Rachel said, coming over to touch my forehead. "I asked Clay, but he didn't say." Rachel gave Clay a pointed look. Clay shrugged and went back to cooking at the stove.

"Not the best, but it's getting better. I think it's mental exhaustion, nothing contagious."

"Mm," she said in a noncommittal way as she eyed me speculatively. "I still think you should go to the doctor. Could it be something you didn't think of yet?" She casually leaned close to me. "Pregnant?" she whispered.

Clay dropped the spoon. It hit the stove and bounced back at him. He caught it tight after a close fumble. Both Rachel and I stared at his back, but with dignity, he stayed facing the stove and kept cooking.

I turned back to Rachel with a wide smile. "No. Now, behave."

We ate dinner companionably. After we finished, they shoved me out of the kitchen with orders to rest while they cleaned up. I went to my room and changed into my lounge clothes while listening to Rachel tell Clay about a cute pair of shoes she'd found. It made me smile. She would never break him. He'd never talk.

Dinner, though delicious and entertaining, had drained my reserves. I lay on top the comforter thinking I'd rest for a bit before I tackled that day's homework. I still needed to talk to Clay about what I'd seen in the woods at the Introduction.

SUNLIGHT PENETRATED the darkness behind my eyelids. I no longer sprawled sideways on the bed on top the comforter but underneath it, snugly tucked in. Clay sat up in the space next to me, pillows stacked behind him as he read a book. His posture didn't fool me. He really sat there to watch over me while I slept. I knew with an unexplainable certainty that he would never leave me again.

"Good morning," I said, pulling the covers up to my chin. Thanks to Rachel-the-heat-miser, the room felt cool, but I enjoyed lower rent.

Clay closed his book as soon as I woke and turned to examine me.

"I want to talk to you but keep falling asleep. If I do it again, wake me up." I smiled at him when he pulled me close to snuggle against him. It was much warmer that way.

"During the Introduction when I said my head hurt, I saw a man step away from the line. I know how your kind view Introductions. It didn't seem right so I peeked at his spark. It hurt like hell, but I saw he had the same color light as Elder Joshua and the wolf that'd attacked us. I thought maybe it could be the same guy, that he needed to leave because you'd recognize his scent. Then I saw three more, further away. Something's going on, but I can't figure out what.

"I know you didn't stay with the pack full-time, but did you ever notice any of them acting different?"

He shook his head, actually giving me a direct answer. It should have made me happy. Instead, I sighed. I still didn't have a clue.

He gently stroked my hair as I thought it through. "If only I could trust Sam. If I could ask him questions about Elder Joshua without him repeating them, I might be able to figure this thing out."

My head started to hurt again. Maybe if I stopped thinking about it so much, the answer would just come to me.

SAM CALLED my cell the following weekend. I'd expected to hear from him much sooner. He surprised me by asking if I'd come back to the Compound over the long holiday weekend. I hedged. Did he want me to return so he could arrange another Introduction?

When I didn't give a definitive answer, he launched into a long speech about how he knew he'd disappointed me and how he really did worry about me, not just the pack. I tried to be understanding but didn't bend much.

Finally, he came right out and asked what had happened to me during the last visit. I answered vaguely, claiming ignorance. Werewolves couldn't recognize lies as well over the phone. A long moment of silence passed. When he spoke, he didn't comment on my answer but again asked that I consider coming home over holiday break. I knew he meant the Compound and told him I'd think about it.

After that, he continued to call me daily just to talk. Most of our brief conversations touched on weather, school, or investments. Anything pack related stayed off limits. I could tell he was concerned, but trust, once lost, took longer to earn back. I wouldn't tell him any of my suspicions until I could confirm some of them.

FOR THE NEXT FEW WEEKS, the challenges stopped, and I pushed the pack, strange colored sparks, and my pull from my head. Instead, I focused on my studies.

Clay worked at Dale's while I stayed on campus. I hadn't given up trying to figure out why he'd picked Dale to be his employer. However, whenever I asked, he responded with a shrug. I never asked him if he followed me to school as Luke had suggested. Some things I preferred to remain a mystery.

I thought Clay's expectations would change after our kiss, but he never pushed for more. He continued to stay in his fur most of the time, except for Tuesday nights when he had dinner waiting for me. I looked forward to our nights together and not just because he cooked exceptionally well.

Rachel knew I was spending more time with him, and on one of our quiet nights together, she asked about Clay-the-man while Clay-the-dog lay curled on the floor next to me.

"You are so weird about him. What is it about the guy that

keeps you coming back?" She sat on the couch, folding her summer clothes and packing them into a tote.

Smiling slightly, I turned the page of the book in my lap before I answered.

"You don't know him like I do."

"How can you know him at all when you two don't talk?"

"You don't need to talk to get to know someone. You just need to listen," I said absently, trying to concentrate on my reading. My words rattled in my head for a moment before what I said clicked into place. I froze and looked at Clay. His brown eyes met mine steadily.

Damn the patient, clever dog. A smile twitched my lips. I never had a chance...and I didn't mind.

"But that's what I'm saying. He doesn't talk. What are you listening to?"

I laughed at her and myself. "Actions speak louder than words," I quoted, finally looking up at Rachel. "He's there when I need him, he's kind and caring, he keeps me safe, and as you've seen, he cooks and cleans. What's not to like, Rachel?"

She grumbled under her breath but didn't have anything else to add.

Clay walked over to her and lay on some of her dresses, ending her mutterings that I should get out and meet other people. She laughed at him then tried to move him. He laid his head on his paws and winked at me. He wasn't mad but enjoyed giving Rachel some grief.

Shaking my head, I went to the fridge and left Rachel to tug her dresses out from under his bulk on her own. In the fridge, I saw a new carton of orange juice along with a double-chocolate cake. Two layers of chocolate frosted goodness. My mouth watered. I usually ignored the food Rachel bought, but that one begged my attention.

"Can I have a piece of your cake?"

"I thought it was yours. It was here when I got home," she called back.

I stood staring at the cake a long time. How could I be so blind? He'd shrugged when I'd asked why he'd gotten his job, but the answer, wrapped in layers of sinful chocolate mousse frosting, sat before my eyes.

Thinking back, I identified several of the little things I'd previously overlooked. Things I'd assumed Rachel had purchased, like movies I'd mentioned I wanted to see. He'd gotten his job for *me* because of my speech the day after we'd met. My heart melted a little as I thought of all the effort he'd put into trying to be what I needed, and I knew I fought a losing battle.

THE AIR GREW COLDER and snow started to fall the week before Thanksgiving. The wind howled outside, still finding a way past the new windows. Despite the low-set thermostat, the heat kicked in often, and I worried about the bill. Even with Clay warming my feet, I'd added another quilt to the bed.

Broke and out of quilts, I lay under the covers, shivering. I wore two pairs of lounge pants, a t-shirt, and a sweatshirt. If I could just fall asleep, I knew I'd warm eventually. During the night, I usually stripped to one layer. But warming the bed took forever...on my own.

"Screw this," I said, sitting up. I started pulling off my sweatshirt. The streetlight filtered through the curtains, so I could make out the shapes in my room. I tossed the sweatshirt toward the closet.

Clay lifted his head, tilting it just so.

I ignored him for the moment and shimmied out of my second layer of pants while trying to stay under the covers. The pants soared through the air and landed next to the shirt.

"Clay, will you keep me warm tonight?" I'd barely whispered the words when he jumped off the bed.

A moment later, he pulled back the covers and joined me. He wrapped his arms around me and pulled me to his chest. Bare chest. I sighed, pressed my face against his skin, warming my cold nose, and wrapped my free arm around his waist. Then, I tucked my feet under his calves. He grunted slightly but didn't loosen his hold.

"No more fur at night. Deal?"

The blankets and his chest muffled my voice, but I knew he heard me. He kissed the top of my head, the only part exposed. I smiled, figuring it meant yes.

The next morning my cell phone rang, waking me. Still wrapped in Clay's warmth, I didn't move right away. He reached over me, plucked it from the bedpost, and handed it to me. Only Sam and Rachel had my number.

I could hear movement in the house and looked at the display, expecting Sam's number. Instead, it was one I didn't recognize.

I answered with a questioning, "Hello?"

"Gabby, I found her, but..."

"Luke?" I hadn't heard from him since we'd left the Compound.

"Yes. I understand you think she's important, but she's not

even eighteen. How am I supposed to get her to come with me?"

I sat up excitedly and knocked back the covers in the process, exposing both Clay and me to the cool air. Clay grunted a complaint.

"I can't believe you actually found her! I need to talk to her. If she's like me, which I think she is, you had better bring her to the Compound. I hate to admit it, but the Elders need to know."

"Fine. You better be there when we get there," he said with an edge. The line went dead.

I pulled the phone from my ear to look at it, puzzled. Luke never had an edge. Slowly, I grinned. Had I been right? Was he now dealing with his potential Mate? Smiling hugely, I hoped she gave Mr. Confident a little hell.

CHAPTER EIGHTEEN

With the freeze came the night Rachel thawed toward Clay-the-man.

A heavy snow started to fall just as Clay and I went to bed. His arm curled around my waist, and my head rested on his shoulder. Asking him to sleep beside me was the best decision I ever made, and it made me finally understand that *I* determined the pace of our relationship. He had waited patiently for me to invite him in and would wait patiently for the next step, whatever I decided that would be.

My phone rang and pulled me from my warm cocoon. I recognized the number and answered.

"Hey. I'm coming home," Rachel said. "It's snowing too badly to go to Peter's." She'd caught on that Clay spent the night often.

"Thanks for the heads up," I said with a laugh. "We'll see you soon."

Clay got out of bed as I ended the call. Puzzled, I watched him dress in warm clothes. He left the room. The back door opened and closed. A minute later, I heard the rasp of a shovel on the driveway. I smiled, moved to his warm spot, and burrowed in.

The sound of the plow scraping past disrupted the silent world and kept me awake. Clay stayed outside, keeping the entrance to the driveway clear until Rachel came home. I heard her thanking Clay as they came in together. He didn't say anything in return, but I imagined he gave her one of his rare nods.

When he returned, I flipped the covers back for him and moved out of his place.

"I was just keeping it warm for you," I lied.

He laughed and pulled me close. Even after being outside so long, he still warmed me.

My lids grew heavy, and he kissed the top of my head.

WITH THE LONG holiday around the corner, I needed to cross a few things off my mental checklist. First, I needed to pin down my next victim for a power swap. After that, I needed to talk to Sam and hope for answers.

I'd planned to test my ability on Rachel before I went back to the Compound, but Clay watched me closely. Since he knew something happened when I touched other people, he subtly kept everyone out of reach. I pretended not to notice so he wouldn't become even more protective.

Luck turned in my favor when Rachel texted and asked me to meet her and Peter for lunch. Having just left my morning class, the timing couldn't have worked better. She suggested a small ma and pa diner close to the campus; the same one Clay and I had walked to so long ago for our sunrise breakfast. I quickly agreed, told her what to order for me, and rushed over the scraped sidewalks to my car.

I cautiously drove the few blocks to the diner. The salt on the roads made everything slushy, and my worn tires liked to slide when I least expected. I eased into the crowded parking lot and snagged a spot near the door.

Through the windows, I spied Rachel and Peter already snuggled in a booth. The waitress had just delivered our food, and they didn't notice me park or get out of the car. They stared at each other. I saw their lips moving in quiet conversation. Rachel kept stopping to grin at Peter.

I opened the door, briefly blasting the patrons with the frigid air. It caught Rachel and Peter's attention. They wore secret smiles as they watched me approach. I slid in across from them, the vinyl seat squeaking, and peeled off my hat and gloves. The warmth of the room heated my cheeks and turned them red in seconds.

"Hi, guys. This is a nice surprise. What's the occasion?" As soon as I said it, I noticed the glint on Rachel's ring finger. "Oh, wow..." It came out sounding as stunned as I felt. The rational side of me said it was too soon, but the part of me that saw them together and saw their synchronized pulses, knew it was perfect.

"Peter proposed last night, and I said yes." Rachel's happiness bubbled from her.

I stood and reached across the table to hug her. She bounced up from her seat and excitedly hugged me back. I grabbed hold of the opportunity. Focusing, I repeated what I'd thought and felt the other times I'd shocked someone. Was she doing the right thing? Was Peter the right one for her? What if I was wrong? I dredged up all my concerns and hope for her, held it tight within me and then let it flow through to her.

The shock jolted us apart immediately. The intensity of it burned my fingertips. Rachel settled next to Peter with a surprised laugh. I sat too, smiled, and opened my sight wide, forcing the full view of the world as I'd seen when I'd shocked Luke. It strained me a bit, but I didn't let go. This time I really looked. The tiny sparks of all living beings covered the world. I focused the view so I could see the occupants of the diner in detail.

Peter and Rachel pulsed in time as usual. I expected Peter to be different, somehow, to signify his match with Rachel, but I couldn't see anything unusual. They did appear a bit dimmer, like their light had faded. I remembered that happening when I'd touched Luke and quickly pulled back from such a close up view.

While I looked at Rachel's tiny spark, something caught my eye. Faint pulses rippled out from her. Much like the ripples made by a pebble thrown into a pond, they spread outward, passing through all other sparks. One approached Charlene's spark. Instead of passing through, it bounced off and came speeding back.

Startled, I scanned the sparks, zooming in and out as needed until I identified five uniquely colored sparks like me. The ripples didn't pass through them. Instead, they bounced off and came flying back. Right at me, not Rachel.

The return wave of the spark midway between Charlene and me hit. I absorbed it, and a wave of dizziness rushed through me. That was the first indication of the drain I'd felt previously. I watched Charlene's wave approach and knew that when it hit, I'd get worse. It made sense now, how I grew weak and sick shortly after transferring my ability. Each hit of return energy knocked me further on my butt. If I'd paid more attention to it before, I would have noticed it when I shocked Nicole and the other girls. But why had it acted differently when I'd touched Luke? Why had just one of the five become focused? I still had so much to figure out. For now, the clock ticked, counting down the time until I would turn into a shaking mess.

I'd noted all of this in the few short seconds it'd taken for Rachel's surprised expression to clear.

"I'm so happy for both of you," I said before she could say anything about my momentary pause.

I smiled while I braced myself for Charlene's energy wave, just minutes away.

"Gabby, after Peter proposed, we both decided we'd tortured you and Scott enough and should get our own place. So as soon as we find something, I plan on moving out. I wanted to give you as much time as possible to find a roommate before I actually left."

I nodded and smiled at her as if I understood. Would another roommate really put up with Clay-the-moody-dog, or Clay-the-mute-man? I couldn't blame them for wanting to find their own place. I knew she missed Peter when they were apart.

She picked up her fork and started eating her salad. Peter took another bite of his BLT sandwich. My burger and fries sat before me, still untouched.

Her announcement and the continued strain of staying focused on the vast scale of lights for so long took their toll. My head started to pound. I saw the second wave rush toward me and couldn't help the slight wince when the pounding in my head increased to full force. I clenched my teeth to keep them from chattering.

Thankfully, Rachel still wore her love-goggles and didn't notice.

"Don't worry about me. Clay will be there enough that I'll make him pay the other half of the rent. So, did you set a date?"

The conversation turned to wedding plans until Peter glanced at his watch and reminded Rachel of their next class. She pouted playfully. I smiled, barely holding back a shiver, and assured her we'd make time to talk wedding stuff soon. The third wave hit, stunning me. Two to go, and they weren't far off.

"You feeling all right?" Peter asked as they stood. "You look very pale."

"I'm fine. I skipped breakfast, and I think my blood sugar is getting revenge. It will pass." I picked up a fry and ate it. My stomach rebelled.

"You should have that tested," Peter warned, helping Rachel into her jacket.

I nodded and reached for the ketchup while they walked out the door. Squirting a big pile on my plate, I looked up in time to wave to Rachel as they backed out of their spot. I pretended to nibble on a fry as I watched their car. Once they left, I dug out my cell with shaking hands and dialed Dale's Auto Body. It looked like I would need to miss a few more classes.

Dale answered after the third ring.

"Hi, Dale, it's Gabby...Clay's girlfriend." It felt weird giving myself that title, but I pushed it aside. Bigger issues to deal with. "If he's there, can I talk to him?"

Dale chuckled. "Sure, but I don't imagine it'd be much of a

conversation."

I heard him call out to Clay. A moment later, a husky voice said, "Hello?"

After not talking to me for so long, hearing his voice startled and annoyed me slightly. He would talk to a perfect stranger, but not me? I opened my mouth to say something about it, but the pain in my head insistently prodded me to get on with the important news.

"Clay, I did it again. I'm at the diner where we had breakfast. I need you to come get me before it gets worse."

He didn't say anything for so long that I looked at the phone to see if I still had a signal. The screen said disconnected. Would it have killed him to say "Okay" or maybe even "Bye" before hanging up? His hello had been too shocking to recall the sound of his voice.

I sighed and put my cell away. With Sam's frequent calls and Rachel's occasional texts, my remaining minutes dipped into the double digits. I needed to adjust my budget to buy more airtime. Did life really need to throw me this many curveballs? And all at once?

I forced myself to eat more of my mostly untouched meal so the waitress wouldn't bother me as I waited.

The last of the waves hit me. Only determination and a hand over my mouth kept me from whimpering. After about ten minutes, I settled the bill and watched out the window for Clay, barely checking the need to curl into a ball and lie down on the padded bench. The waitress kept a close eye on me, probably thinking she would need to clean up barf soon. She might.

Dale's huge tow truck pulled into the parking lot. Clay opened his door and leapt out while it still rolled to a stop.

Through the window, he spotted me. His eyes never left me as he strode in and Dale pulled away.

Clay still wore his greasy coveralls, and with his hair pulled back, he looked like an angel—a grimy one—coming to save me. Again.

"Hi," I whispered, tilting my head to meet his gaze.

His eyes softened as he looked me over.

My legs trembled just sitting there but with so many students from campus, I wouldn't leave by any means other than my own two feet. I handed him the keys to my car, slid out of the booth, and reached for him. Standing, I wrapped my arms around his waist. I hoped it looked like I wanted to snuggle instead of holding myself up. He maneuvered us out the door and to my car with no trouble.

Minutes later, he carried me through the back door. He knew the drill and gave me a drink before he tucked me into bed.

Close to dawn, I woke feeling much better. The shivers had faded while I slept, and the lingering headache was manageable. The full bladder wasn't.

I snuck to the bathroom, hoping not to wake Clay. But when I got back, the light was on and he lay awake waiting for me. With his hair still back, I easily read his expression. I hated when he looked at me like that. All disappointed and hurt.

I stalled saying anything until I slid back under the covers. Warmer, I met his gaze.

"I'm sorry. I didn't plan it..." Technically. "...but I think I've figured out what I am, Clay. I'm like a GPS for werewolves. I can find people. Not just people, but compatible Mates like me." My feet refused to warm so I tucked them under his legs. He didn't even flinch. Probably because I did it all the time.

"When I touched Rachel yesterday, I really paid attention. I saw the energy I release when I shock a person. It goes into them and pulses outward, passing through almost everyone else. And everyone this energy passes through fades in my mind, almost dimming to the point of non-existence. Five people didn't fade, Clay. In the whole world, there are only five. Six if you include me. And when the energy I release touches them, it bounces off to come crashing back on me. That's what's been knocking me on my butt."

Unsure if I should bring up the rest, I played with the quilt for a second. He nudged me, and I smiled at him. I should know better. Even when he didn't like what I had to say, he listened. He always listened.

"It was different when I touched Luke. With him, I zoomed in on one specific spark, a yellow-violet one on the east coast. The paper I gave Luke? That was directions to find her. I think she belongs with him. I think I found his Mate just by touching him." I grinned when I recalled the phone call from Luke. "I don't think he appreciates my help, though."

Through my entire monolog, Clay lay on his side, up on an elbow, and watched me intently. His serious expression conveyed his concentration.

When I finished, instead of shrugging as I expected, his head snapped toward my bedroom window. He snarled softly as he threw off the covers and crouched on the bed, head moving to track something I couldn't see.

I scrambled to my knees, staring at him. Fangs exploded from his mouth, and his ears changed. Now I knew why Luke had laughed at Clay's partial transformation but didn't find it a bit funny as I watched.

Clay remained frozen in a crouch, listening. I held my breath and strained to hear what he heard. The beating of my own heart filled my ears.

Both our heads turned toward a chuffing laugh near the window. A taunt to draw Clay out.

I opened my mouth to point it out but never made a sound. Clay's hand darted out and nudged me backward. I lost my balance. As I tumbled over the edge of the mattress, he leapt toward the bedroom door. He cleared it and switched off the light before I landed on the floor.

The front door slammed against the wall. The explosive sound echoed through the house as did the chilly breeze that gusted along the floor. I shivered, hidden in the semi-darkness beside the bed. The door closed itself on the backswing, cutting off the cold.

I righted myself as I caught my breath. Luckily, I'd landed on a pillow which I'd knocked off with me. Any recovery I'd experienced while I slept had vanished as soon as I hit the floor. My head pounded with renewed vigor, but I thought clearly enough to wonder if Rachel had spent the night here or with Peter. The sudden noise outside distracted me from my thoughts.

Loud snarls and low growls filled the air.

Despite Clay's obvious wish that I stay down, I risked a look over the mattress as my eyes adjusted to the gloom. The window gave a soft glow from the streetlights. The sound of my frightened breathing echoed in the room. I quieted it, pulled myself up, and crawled over the bed toward the window. Cautiously, I inched the curtain aside to peek out.

Clay and another man fought in the snow on the front yard. I cringed at the sight of Clay's bare feet and chest. The challenger at least had shoes and a shirt.

Clay swiped at the man, ripping a good portion of his shirt away. Good. Clay wouldn't be the only cold one.

They skirted the direct glow of the streetlight, but didn't stick to the shadows closest to the house. The neighbors would not only be able to hear them but see them as well. Hadn't the idiot challenging Clay thought of that before he approached our house from the front? Pack law forbade public shifting.

The snow crunched under the challenger's feet as he rushed Clay. Clay spun and avoided the charge. He used the man's momentum to trip him and knock him into the snow. As the man fell, he shifted noticeably.

Clay shifted further as well. His mouth extended to enable the use of his fangs. I cringed at the thought of the neighbors spotting him. There would be no way to explain away the disconcerting appearance of his ears and fangs.

The other man rolled and rose to his feet. His head had almost completely contorted to wolf form. My eyes rounded. He snapped at Clay, narrowly missing Clay's chest. His attempt distracted Clay from blocking a well-placed punch to his gut. I cringed, then silently cheered when Clay gave back as good as he got.

The sky began to lighten, and down the road, a few of the streetlights blinked off. They needed to end this soon, but the fight didn't seem to be winding down.

Their movements increased in speed until they mostly blurred. I heard each time one of them connected—the solid thunk of it reverberated through the house—but didn't see anything. I hoped Clay gave more than he received.

Twice the other wolf feinted away from the house, but Clay refused to follow, forcing the challenger to come back to him. Clay would not distance himself any further from the house and leave me unprotected. The other wolf's attempt had me wondering.

Knowing I'd regret it, I stretched my sight. I saw another blue-grey light nearby and began to doubt this fight was just another Mating challenge. As quickly as I opened my spark-filled view of the world, I closed it. It hurt, and I couldn't afford to distract Clay with my pain.

I studied the man fighting Clay. He didn't look like the same werewolf who'd attacked us on our way back from breakfast. The sprinkling of fur starting to cover his skin appeared lighter than the original challenger's dark grey fur.

Despite their noise, I heard the back door open. So did Clay.

In a fierce move, he hit the other werewolf in the head with a sickening crack. The man dropped to the ground. Clay didn't wait to see him land. He turned and ran for the house before I could even think to scramble under the bed and hide.

The front door slammed again. I thought of the damage and winced. The temperature in the room dropped further.

Clay and the new werewolf met in the living room with a thud. I didn't think, just sprang from my crouched position near the window to scramble over the bed. It might have been safer to stay hidden, but I worried more when I couldn't see what was happening.

I eased off the end of the mattress and edged closer to the door, trying to make them out in the dim light of the living room. I stared at the fight raging in front of me.

Two shapes struggled in the center of the brown rug. I identified Clay by his long hair. His back was to me. The other man had his arms wrapped around Clay, attempting to squeeze him. Clay fisted his hands together and hammered them down on his attacker's face. They broke apart, the attacker almost bumping into the TV.

Cold air wrapped around my legs. I glanced at the front door, which stood ajar, but didn't move to close it.

When I looked back at the men, I had a clear view of the attacker. I stopped breathing and stared at the man, stunned.

I'd grown accustomed to the stomach acrobatics I suffered every time I looked at Clay. Feeling them when I looked at this new wolf devastated me. I gasped in a ragged breath, hurt by fate's cruelty. The sound distracted the newcomer, who met my eyes with recognition then calculation. Clay took advantage and brought the man down like he had the one outside. The sickening thud made me cringe.

Without thought, I moved out into the living room and stared down at the unconscious man. His short, sandy blonde hair contrasted with the brown of the rug. It moved in the breeze that swept the floor. I didn't feel the cold as I studied his tall, lean frame. He had no facial hair. Except for the tall part, he looked like Clay's opposite.

How could I feel that pull for two men? Sam assured me that I would know when I met the right one because there would be a pull, a burning curiosity like no other. This didn't make any sense.

The man's hand lay on the carpet close to me. Some of his fingernails had shifted to glossy black claws before Clay had knocked him out. Looking closer, I saw his ears had shifted, too.

"What do we do, Clay?"

I looked up at him and found him watching me closely. I

shivered and didn't look back at the man on the floor. Having all the doors open made the heat kick in, but it did little to warm me.

"He's part changed. With all the noise, I think the police will be here soon. Can we leave him here like this?"

Clay nodded and motioned me back into the bedroom. His knuckles bled, and he had the start of another black eye. I wanted to walk to him and hug him, but felt too confused. Instead, I turned away to hide my watering eyes.

In the distance, I heard sirens.

Clay put me back into bed then left, closing the door behind him. Moments later, I heard the back door close and then nothing as the sirens got closer.

Fate or not, I belonged with Clay. I wasn't sure anymore if I was his prize or punishment, though. Regardless, he'd earned my loyalty. Reacting to someone other than Clay felt like cheating, and it bothered me a lot. I didn't know what to do about it or how to stop it. It wasn't something I could talk to Clay about. I had hurt him enough already. If I could trust Sam, I could maybe ask him.

The sirens quieted with a chirp before they reached the house. Muted red and blue lights danced on my bedroom wall by my head. I wondered what Clay planned to tell the police. No matter what I'd just felt for the man passed out on the living room floor, I trusted Clay completely. He had a plan, and I just needed to wait.

But Clay didn't come back in. Instead, I heard a knock on the front door and the murmur of several voices. Exhaustion and pain, from pushing myself too soon, shivered through my body.

CHAPTER NINETEEN

AN HOUR LATER, THE FULL LIGHT OF A NEW DAY—WEDNESDAY
morning, the beginning of Thanksgiving break—lit my room.

Clay, still bloody from the fight, stood with the officers to
show them out. They had his written statement and my phone
number, since I didn't plan to stay in the house for a few nights.
I'd decided we'd go to the Compound a day early. I'd waited
long enough. I had too many questions to answer on my own,
and a certain Elder waited for me there. I needed to talk to him.

The police believed we'd experienced a simple break in.
Their deduction suited me fine. I could just imagine the line of
questioning I would have endured if I'd mentioned the men
had broken in to kidnap me. After seeing the second man, I had
no doubt that had been their intent.

The front door closed, and I listened to Clay walk through
the house and close himself in the bathroom. He needed to
wash the dried blood from his face. It had served its purpose
and hidden his noticeably advanced healing from the police.

Flipping back the covers, I got out of bed and started to

dress. The dizziness and headache that had returned when I fell off the bed had faded while they questioned me.

I finished dressing, grabbed my messenger bag, and began to cram clothes in it. My mind wasn't on packing so I didn't treat it anymore gently than Clay or Luke had when they had packed it. How had I felt anything for that man on the floor? It shouldn't have been possible. Agitation burrowed deep. When I turned toward the door and saw Clay watching me, I dropped my gaze to the floor unable to meet his calm regard. He sighed, stepped aside, and motioned for me to lead.

In the kitchen, Clay had my jacket and shoes waiting. I slipped them on, remembering at the last minute to call Rachel to let her know what had happened. Thankfully, she hadn't been home. She promised only to come back home with Peter, just to be safe.

Clay didn't say anything as we got into the car, which was normal, but I sensed his extreme tension. My stomach churned with guilt. However, I didn't know what to say, so I closed my eyes and tried to nap. Still needing to regain my strength, sleep wasn't too hard to come by.

Several times, I woke to the sound of him tapping his grey nails against the steering wheel. When I opened my eyes to look at him, I could see his elongated canines. At those times, I wanted to reach over and pat his leg, but I held myself back.

When I woke to see his ears pointed too, I quietly studied him for a few minutes. I knew I was the cause of his agitation. He'd sensed my withdrawal. I hadn't wanted him to see my confusion. I wanted to talk to Sam first, before saying anything to Clay. But my approach obviously wasn't the right one. Clay had stuck by me through everything. I needed to trust that he wouldn't turn away from me after I revealed what had happened.

"Clay..."

He paused his tapping.

"Could you pull over for a minute?"

He glanced at me, lifted a concerned brow, but did as I asked. The tires crunched on the snowy shoulder. He stopped the car then turned toward me.

A sad smile lifted my lips. I hated to see him like this. I tapped my lips. I needed affirmation that we still had our connection, and he needed assurance I was fine.

His tight grip on the steering wheel loosened, and he shook his head in amusement. I held my breath as he leaned toward me.

Clay cradled my face in his hands and kissed me tenderly. I clutched his shirt, dragging him closer. When he opened his mouth to nip my bottom lip, I groaned and willingly let him in. We steamed the windows. My lungs burned for air. Finally, I had to pull away to catch my breath. He wrapped his arms around me and placed small gentle kisses on the top of my head.

His neck hovered in my line of sight. I could give him what he wanted. A quick bite and I wouldn't need to worry about other potential Mates. I could Claim him as my own. But I didn't want to hurt him anymore. Physically or emotionally. I pulled back from our make-out session.

Clay gave me one last kiss on the lips then put the car in drive. The smooth, tan skin of his very human ears called my attention, as did his clean, pink nails. He looked content, no longer tapping his fingers while he stared ahead at the snow-covered roads.

I turned away and pretended to sleep, condemning myself for my lie. My hesitation to Claim Clay didn't stem from a concern that I would hurt him. No, just like Sam said, I selfishly didn't want to give up my plans.

Deep down, I was unwilling to bend and try to make it work.

WE ARRIVED at the Compound just as the sun's last rays sank below the tree-topped horizon. Vehicles crowded the parking area. I didn't worry though. Holidays always drew a crowd.

Clay grabbed my bag then walked around to open my door for me. Staying close, we walked inside the Compound. Jackets and shoes filled the entry. It meant cramped quarters for the holiday, but I'd done it before.

We went to the apartment I usually stayed in with Sam, but another family with small cubs had commandeered it. After several minutes of knocking on doors, we gave up trying to find an apartment in the main Compound. We turned down a hall I typically didn't travel—the unMated wing—and found the majority of the dorm quarters also occupied. Several men passed us as we searched. They gave us curious looks as they scented the air. I stayed close to Clay.

Clay and I grabbed the first open dorm room and put our stuff on the twin bed. We would figure out our sleeping arrangements later.

"I need to talk to Sam," I said once we were back in the hall. Clay nodded and led the way to the main hall.

Charlene and her crew had done a wonderful job decorating the large room. Cornucopias with harvest produce sat on each of the long tables. Several turkeys with feathers made of construction paper hands hung on the walls. The cubs had obviously partaken in crafts while visiting. It amused me that Charlene insisted on celebrating the US holiday while living in Canada. Her extended adopted family didn't seem to mind. I could hear women laughing in the attached kitchen. Fresh pumpkin pie perfumed the air.

In the midst of all the decorations, I spotted Sam. He sat with his back to me, conversing with several other men at one of the many sitting areas in the main hall. I noticed the weary slope of his shoulders. Part of me—the part that lived with him for so long and thought of him as "grandpa"—wanted to run over and hug him. I ignored that part.

Before he noticed me, I strode over and interrupted their conversation.

"It's time we talked," I said, tersely.

He turned toward me with a hesitant smile then quickly nodded to the others, who got up to move to another group.

"Gabby, I didn't think you'd be up until tomorrow."

Clay and I shared a glance. The main hall didn't afford privacy since all the werewolves present would hear me. Then again, very few places in the Compound qualified as private to that degree. Normally, I wouldn't care who heard me, but I had the mystery of the blue-grey werewolves to solve. I did a quick scan of the room and managed to hold back a wince of pain.

Clay gave an annoyed grunt but gently rubbed my back. He'd become adept at knowing when I used my gift.

In the brief glimpse, I'd noted the sparks all appeared normal. Well, for a werewolf anyway. But it only assured me to a degree. Although I didn't think Sam responsible for what had happened, I still wondered if he might know something about it.

"We came early because two werewolves tried breaking into my house." I watched Sam closely as I said it.

"What?" Sam said, giving Clay a sharp look. Sam appeared genuinely upset and concerned.

"He's still not talking," I said. I slumped into the chair across from Sam. "I believe their intentions were to kidnap me."

Clay lowered himself into the chair next to me. He always stayed close, and I couldn't imagine it any other way. If it hadn't been for Clay, the men probably would have taken me. What would have happened then? I thought about the blonde man who'd been lying on the floor, and my stomach clenched with worry. My troubled gaze swung to Clay.

Clay met my look with calm, brown eyes. Staring into their depths, a tense breath eased out of me. Sure, I had questions, but I wouldn't let the answers to any of them affect the tie Clay and I had.

I gave Clay a small worried smile then turned my attention back to Sam. Different colored lights...a pull to another man when it should only happen once...I could come up with the only possible explanation.

"Is there more than one kind of werewolf?" I asked bluntly. Maybe I'd stir up trouble with my public questioning, but I was tired of waiting.

Sam frowned and leaned forward. "Not sure what you mean, exactly."

Sam watched me closely. I nibbled on my lip and thought back to the original challenger. Physically, he'd looked like any other werewolf. So if Sam didn't already know about another kind of werewolf, I didn't think there would be a way for him to differentiate. Then I thought of the last one I saw on the floor.

"When you go fur, what color variations are possible? Different shades of fur, eyes...what about nose, or nails?"

The door to the commons opened, and a few more werewolves drifted in, slowly walking toward other groups. While they progressed across the room, they kept their heads tilted, listening as if already aware of the important conversation occurring in our small group.

"What does this have to do with—"

I held up a hand. "Bear with me, Sam. I need answers to give answers."

Sam turned his attention to Clay.

"I already told you, he still isn't talking. Look, is there another Elder I can talk to? One willing to answer my questions?"

I wanted to take my harsh words back when Sam's face fell.

The expression cleared after a moment, and he slowly answered. "Fur is like hair and varies just like a human's. Same with the eyes. We are more like dogs when it comes to our noses. Mostly dark, but we sometimes have unusual markings. Did you see an identifying mark, Gabby?"

I ignored his question. "What about the nails?"

He shrugged. "Shades of grey. Mostly a dark grey."

"Black?"

"Well, like I said, a dark grey is possible."

"No. I mean black. A very glossy black you could see your reflection in."

Sam remained introspectively quiet for a full minute. The intense silence claimed my attention. Looking around, I caught the eyes of a few others in the room before they quickly looked away.

"I don't think I've ever paid that much attention to our claws before. But, no, I don't believe so."

I slumped back in my chair, thinking. Everyone in the room watched me, waiting for what I'd say next.

Could there really be another species of werewolf? The sparks I saw indicated the possibility. But if I followed that line of reasoning, did that then mean I was another species of human? Maybe these werewolves just had different abilities. I chewed on my lip for a minute. What about the nail color? Could that small difference carry enough significance to classify two separate species? I was grasping. I needed to grasp. If there were two kinds, it could explain why I had two potential Mates.

Frustrated and still tired from my stunt with Rachel, I scowled and got to the heart of my angst. Sure, I wanted to know what the color differences meant, but I needed to know why I felt what I did when I saw that man unconscious on the floor.

Sam cleared his throat, and I ignored him. Someone spoke softly further back in the room. Others moved restlessly.

So what if I felt the same pull for another guy? It just meant I had a choice. Wasn't that what I'd wanted all along? Yet, now that I had options, I couldn't see myself walking away from Clay...not for school, not for a career, and not for some creep who snuck into my house.

I peeked at Clay, unable to hide my turmoil. He reached out, offering his hand. His hair hid his eyes again, making it hard to read him. I looked down at his hand, calloused and so real.

Realization dawned. Clay and I held the answers. I kept my

eyes trained on his hand to hide my thoughts. When I'd focused on Luke, I saw the yellow-violet spark. When I'd focused on Rachel, I'd expected to see Peter, but I hadn't. Human vs. werewolf testing. If I was right about different species and tried the same test with Clay, I foresaw two possibilities. I would see myself as Clay's Mate or I would see two potential Mates for myself, thus supporting my theory of another werewolf species.

Doubt crept in. What if I didn't see myself? What if it didn't work that way, and I saw the werewolf that Clay had knocked out?

I needed to know.

Lacing my fingers through his, I closed my eyes and focused. I held onto my need to find the perfect Mate for Clay and my hope I'd see myself.

The shock jumped from my hand to his, and my vision of the real world narrowed. I held my breath, terrified of the answer. My second sight exploded into existence. Not the great void filled with billions of sparks, but with the vibrant intensity and color of the sun. The white yellow core pulsed, its energy radiating outward, cooling to a molten orange. Hope flooded me as I realized my own spark filled my vision.

The vision closed, and my eyes once again focused on the real world. My hand still rested within Clay's, but I caught the change in his expression. Clay glared at me. He knew what I'd done, but I couldn't feel bad about it. Joy filled me. I'd been right. It didn't answer my question about the variances in sparks, but I didn't care. It had given me the answer I needed.

I smiled sweetly and leaned over to kiss him lightly on the lips. When our lips touched, something tangible changed. The joy I felt remained, but something else crept in. I pulled back, eyes wide. My heart hammered and my stomach clenched as I stared at him, unable to look away. Mesmerized.

In shock, I realized what I'd done. I'd transferred my pull to him. Only he wasn't pulling in men. He pulled me in, and the force of it consumed me. He represented a hot fudge sundae to a diet-starved girl. Even knowing that what I felt was a result of my power, I couldn't ignore it. He was so handsome, so perfect, and so clueless as he continued to scowl at me.

His fingers still twined through mine, but I needed more from him. I needed an affirmation of us as a pair. I wanted to touch his face and smell his skin. I wanted to hold him tight and never let go.

With speed I never imagined I possessed, I moved from my seat to his, straddled his lap, and leaned my forehead against his. He grunted in surprise, but otherwise didn't move.

Breathing in deeply, I smelled the soap he'd used and closed my eyes. His hair tickled my nose. I pressed my lips to the tip of his nose. My heart twisted painfully. His hand came up, lightly resting on my side. It heated my ribs. The contact of each finger branded me. Better, but not enough. My mind kept chanting "more." I opened my eyes and smiled.

Forgetting our audience, I ran my hands through his hair and pulled back to kiss his exposed forehead. His cautious brown eyes met mine. I lost myself in their depths for several moments as I recalled the first time I saw them. On his driver's license. I needed more from him. No more hiding from each other.

I tilted my head and kissed his cheek. The whiskers abraded my lips, but I didn't mind. I moved lower, finding his lips. He didn't resist me, but didn't join in as he had in the car. I frowned slightly. A stab of doubt pierced my heart. This didn't feel right, yet. He still hid from me.

Nudging his jaw with my nose, I made room to nuzzle his neck. My lips skimmed his smooth skin. His pulse jumped under my mouth. Finally, he reacted. Both his hands came up, holding my sides, kneading me, encouraging. My breath quickened, and my heart hammered. Yes! This was right.

Something took possession of me. With one hand, I gripped his hair and tugged it. He tilted his head to the side and exposed his neck, giving in willingly. My eyes traced his neck where his pulse skipped erratically. The beat matched my own. I couldn't look away from that clean-shaven spot. I recalled when he had started shaving it. He'd known I would need to see it. For this. I kissed it lightly and felt him shudder. Before the shudder ended, I bit him hard on the same spot. Hard enough to draw blood.

The taste of his blood on my tongue broke the hold he had on me and created a new one somewhere deep inside. I pulled back slightly to look at the small marks I'd left. They had already begun to heal.

The pull he had on me and the euphoria of the moment faded as the horror of what I'd just done washed over me.

Clay stared at me in stunned silence...versus his everyday silence. Behind me, someone moved and called attention to the fact that we still had an audience. A Claiming typically occurred in private.

A deep blush seized my cheeks, and embarrassed tears began to gather. I wiped the blood from my mouth with a shaky hand. I didn't regret Claiming him, but wished we could have talked first. I needed reassurance. Would this mean I'd have to quit school? Would he want me to live in the woods with him? If he did, I owed it to him to try after everything he'd done for me.

Then, a really ugly question floated to the surface. Had I just forced him?

Panic bloomed in my chest. Before I could scramble off his lap, he reached up and gently stroked my hair. I froze, hands braced on his chest for stability, ready to flee.

"I've been waiting for that since the moment I saw you," he said in a deep and husky voice. He sounded like a midnight radio DJ.

Hearing his perfect voice ignited my temper. *Now*, he could talk? I scowled at him. The man had the audacity to laugh then scoop me up in his arms.

The room around us erupted in cheers, and I hid my blazing face in his chest, my thoughts a confused jumble. I felt him walk, but didn't have the courage to look up to meet the faces of the people who'd witnessed our Claiming. The sounds of cheering faded as he moved out of the commons. My tears of embarrassment dried before they spilled over.

Part of me couldn't wait to get him alone and yell at him for not talking to me for so long. Another part of me wanted to skip talking altogether and get back to the kissing part. And yet another part of me wanted to ask his thoughts about my gifts and the lights I saw.

When he carried me into our little room and set me on my feet after closing the door, I did none of those things. I stood mere inches from him still too stunned, and very unsure, to do anything but stare. Where would we live? How would we support ourselves? What about my education? His job? Was he upset I bit him under the influence? Should I tell him about the other wolf? Did he have ideas about the weird colored lights?

I trembled. He no longer smiled, but his eyes still twinkled.

"Why?" My high, strained voice made me sound like a child. I cleared my throat and tried again. "Why wait until now to talk?" Apparently, my curiosity had won.

He quietly studied me for a moment then opened his arms. I didn't hesitate, but stepped right into them. I needed his comfort. He tucked me against his chest and gave me his explanation in a simple, heart-melting way.

"If I'd spoken, even just one word, I would have never been able to hold back what I feel for you. You would have run."

I remembered the day he'd plopped down on the towel next to Rachel. Had he arrived any other way, I would have tried to kick him out. If that wouldn't have worked, I would have...run. Even then, he'd known me. I hadn't been ready for any monumental life changes then and wasn't sure if I was now.

I pulled back and met his gaze.

"Can I finally get answers from you now? You'll keep talking?"

He smiled at me and nodded. Well, he'd never be a chatterbox.

"Do you think I'm right about the—"

With sudden seriousness, he interrupted me. "Now's not the time. We'll talk later."

"No way, we're talking now. If not about that, then something else. I've waited over six months to hear your voice."

He didn't look too motivated to talk, yet.

"You owe me. I bit you." It sounded a little backwards, but he smiled for a moment before the look turned puzzled.

"How are you feeling?"

His question gave me pause. Where were the waves of backlash? Shouldn't I feel sick or something by now?

"Good, actually." I'd felt great since I bit him.

Curious, I stretched my awareness. Two of the waves had already hit me, but I hadn't felt a thing.

"It's weird, but I don't feel sick." No backlash. Did that mean I would no longer have a pull on men? The idea excited me. I tried pushing my sight further, and it worked.

In Clay's arms, I focused easily, seeing things I'd missed before. The humans dominated the majority of the space while the werewolves claimed an insignificant portion. Far to the east, a large gathering of blue-grey werewolves hid among the humans. I stayed focused on their group, concerned. If they congregated together, they understood their difference.

"I think we need a safe place to talk." Although werewolves tried to respect each other's privacy, I didn't want to chance anyone overhearing what we needed to discuss.

Clay nodded, but glanced at the door without moving. I followed his gaze and my shoulders slumped as I looked at the wood panel. I had a good idea who hovered outside. He'd given me my answers and now wanted his own.

I slipped from Clay's arms and yanked the door open. As I expected Sam leaned against the wall opposite the door. Waiting. Probably listening, too.

"Sam, since we don't have any privacy, we'd like to use the conference room. There are a few things we need to discuss."

"I couldn't agree more," Sam said, motioning for me to lead.

"Clay and I, Sam," I clarified as I stepped from the room. "I don't have any answers for you."

"Gabby—"

"No. Now it's your turn to be bossed around and told what

to do. I did what you wanted and Claimed one of you. Lay off." My stomach churned, and a little fear crept in. Talking to Sam like that was like poking a bear with a stick. Though he'd never given me reason to fear him, he could rip my head off in a blink. I never forgot that.

Sam didn't say anything behind me, but continued to follow me. I didn't turn around to look but knew Clay followed Sam. I needed to stop baiting Sam and smelling like fear. It didn't help any of us.

I opened the door to the soundproofed conference room and turned to face Sam. He'd schooled his features to appear perfectly calm and blank, but his spark glowed like a fanned ember.

"Sam, I'm trying to do what's best for me, Clay, and the pack. There's a lot I haven't told you, things I haven't told Clay. Give me some time to sort everything out. I need to make sure your goals mesh with mine before I can fully confide in you." He looked hurt by my words, but I didn't regret them. I was trying to be honest and give him what information I could to help explain my behavior.

He studied my face for a long moment then stood back and let Clay join me in the room. "I'll be here."

I nodded and gently closed the door. I'd figured he would wait.

When I turned to Clay, I found him watching me. He looked puzzled. Probably trying to figure out what I hadn't told him. He knew so much already. But what would he think about my reaction to the man who'd broken into our house?

I rubbed my hand through my hair. "I'm not sure where to start."

He pulled me into his arms. "Anywhere. I'll listen."

He always did. I smiled and started with the easiest thing. "I can see everything, Clay. Without pain." I pulled out of his arms and continued to look. "Even without touching you, there's no pain. I can see so much more than before. Why?"

"It's our link."

"Wait. I thought the link happened when..." I didn't really want to bring that up. We'd moved a little fast with the Claiming, and I didn't want to seem overly eager about the Mating. No mixed signals.

He read my hesitation and quirked a smile. "The full link happens after the Mating is completed. With the Claiming we have a more limited version of that connection." His smile faded, and he looked at me sincerely. "It can still be broken. If there's another potential Mate out there...by biting him, you can break our bond and create one with him."

My jaw dropped. I couldn't believe he'd said all those words. I hoped he didn't say that potential Mate part because he thought I still doubted us.

"Don't use up your word quota for the day." He grinned, and I stuck out my tongue before getting serious again.

"Clay, I won't be biting anyone else. Ever. But I do have something to tell you. When those wolves attacked...the second one..." I trailed off, trying to find the right words. I didn't want to hurt him. This should qualify as the best day for us. Would telling him turn it into the worst? He nudged me as he often did when in his fur. It made me smile sadly as I admitted the truth.

"I felt the same pull with him as I do with you. I don't understand why that would happen. Sam said just one. Experiencing that with someone else confused me and made me feel horrible, like I cheated on you."

He sighed and shook his head, smiling softly at me. "I saw what happened. It worried me, but the kiss in the car helped me understand how you feel. Don't worry about it."

He'd known all along? His impatient finger tapping made more sense now.

I met his eyes and smiled back. His easy acceptance of everything that'd happened finished melting my heart.

"I love you." My admission took me by surprise.

I didn't see him move. He embraced me again, crushing me in a spinning hug. The room twirled around us at a dizzying speed, and I didn't attempt to focus on it. Instead, I looked down at Clay's face. He wore a huge smile. I grinned back and noted his canines were normal for the first time ever.

"Oh!" I squirmed to get down, excited at the size of his teeth. He grudgingly released me. "Please can we get rid of the beard?" Yes, I hopped from foot to foot like a kid begging for cotton candy. I wanted to see him just once without facial hair. If he wanted to grow it back, I wouldn't mind. I'd fallen in love with him as he was, after all.

He nodded, laughing at me.

"And I still want to get my degree. Can we stay where we are until then?"

Before he could say anything, his eyes shifted to the door. My joy-filled smile faded. I still needed to figure out what made Elder Joshua different from other werewolves. No doubt, it related to me in some way. Why else would I be able to see the colors? For a moment, I thought about my mom and all the questions I would ask her if she still lived.

I stepped closer to Clay and laid my head against his chest, wrapping my arms around his waist. "Everyone I've ever loved this way I've lost," I said, recalling my earliest memories of my mom and grandma. I hugged him close. "Don't let me down."

"I won't. You're stuck with me forever," he whispered as he held me close.

I pulled back enough to meet his eyes and knew without a doubt I'd found the perfect man. He *would* stand by me. Always.

I kissed his lips, wishing we had time to be just Gabby and Clay, the newly engaged couple. Then, I smiled. We would have time. Eventually. Like he said, he wasn't going anywhere, and neither was I.

Something chirped behind me. It took a second chirp for me to recognize the sound of my own phone. I groaned at the interruption, but pulled back from Clay's warm embrace, not quite leaving it, to pluck the phone from my back pocket. Luke's number flashed on the screen.

As soon as I hit "talk," Luke spoke in a rush without waiting for my greeting.

"Gabby, I have a problem," he shouted over the roar of an engine. Something popped loudly in the background. Luke swore. The phone went dead.

The three-second conversation left me speechless. I pulled the phone away from my ear to look at it. What the hell was going on? Safe in Clay's arms, I stretched my senses and searched for Luke. I found a yellow-violet spark and a lone blue-green spark—Luke...and the other spark like me— swarmed by blue-grey sparks.

"Clay, I don't think I have a choice anymore. Something's happening to Luke. The other werewolves are all around him. We need to get Sam." I turned to look at the door. "I don't know who to trust."

Clay nodded and leaned his forehead against mine. "I'll stand with you, always."

Thank you for reading *Hope(less)*, the first book in the *Judgement of the Six* series! Clay and Gabby are the first of six couples in this interconnecting series. That means, even though you're going to meet some new people in the next book, we aren't done with Clay and Gabby yet!

The series continues with *(Mis)fortune*. Brace yourself!

I hope you enjoyed the first book in the *Judgement of the Six* series and that you fell in love with Clay and Gabby as much as I have. There's something about that strong and silent type. ;)

And if you have a few lingering questions about their story, don't worry...this isn't the last you'll hear from them. Or from Luke. *crowd starts chanting, "We want Luke!"* I know, I know. I'm dying to share what sexy pants is up to. But, before I can, I have to introduce Michelle. Trust me. She's important like Gabby. And her story also ties into Luke's story.

Keep reading for a sneak peek of Michelle's story, *(Mis)fortune*, the second book in the Judgement Series. You won't be disappointed!

For more information regarding other titles, to sign up for my newsletter, or to read exclusive content, please visit my website at melissahaag.com.

I'd love to hear from you!

Melissa

SNEAK PEEK

(Mis)fortune

Judgment of the Six: Book 2

Now Available!

Clotted potatoes stuck in my throat when I tried to swallow. I tried again, and they went down. The overladen plate of food mocked me. I didn't want to eat. I wanted to go hide in my room, away from our dinner guests. I almost blanched just thinking the word guest. It didn't at all describe the men sitting at the table with us.

Blake asked my stepfather, Richard, a question about their latest stock investment, and I looked up dutifully. Just as quickly, I looked back down at my plate like the meek, little mouse Blake wanted me to be. I didn't mind playing a meek part when sitting with these men. Blake didn't give me trouble, but the other ten men with him often did. Dinners went smoother if I kept my eyes on my plate.

Blake sat at one end of the table, with my stepfather at the opposite end. I, unfortunately, always took the middle seat on the side with five chairs. It gave me more room than if I sat on the other side. If given a real choice, I would have rather sat next to Richard.

The six men stared at me through the entire meal. At every dinner different men stared at me. How many business associates did Blake really have? These dinners had been happening since my mother died four years ago. Once a month, every month. I hated them. I felt like a freak on display. *Hey, come on in! Have dinner with the freaky girl who predicts the market and makes us all rich. Don't worry, she doesn't bite. She'll do exactly as I say.*

I thought of my brothers, who slept in their beds, and forked another bite of potatoes into my mouth. Yep, I would do as Blake said. He'd made it painfully clear who he would punish if I didn't.

One of the men across from me nudged my foot under the table. I didn't look up. It would just play into whatever he planned. Probably some lewd gesture. For business associates, as Blake usually introduced them, they dressed more like mill workers, wearing torn, stained jeans and ragged shirts. They were sometimes unwashed, too. I didn't judge them by their appearances, though. Their actions told me what I needed to know about them.

The man kicked me again, harder. I tucked my feet under my chair in an effort to avoid his long reach as Blake asked me a direct question.

"Are you trying to withhold your latest premonition, dear?" He sipped his wine and watched me.

"You know I haven't," I said in a quiet, biddable voice as I met his gaze. If I tried keeping a premonition to myself, I got sick. First it was just a niggling headache. However, the longer I held the information inside, the worse the ache grew until, finally, I broke down and started babbling the information with pain-filled tears.

"Sorry, Blake," Richard said from down the table. "She gave me the information yesterday. When I went in today, I just invested what we discussed last night. I didn't think you wanted me to bother you with it."

I lowered my gaze to my plate again. A puppet, that's all I was. Just then, the man across the table kicked me again. I looked up, eyes blazing with hate and whispered two words— they rhymed with "pluck you"—that sealed my fate.

In a blur, Blake shot from his chair, sailing toward me over the table. His hand curled around my throat and the momentum of his move carried me backward, lifting me up. My long skirt tore when it caught briefly on my tipping chair. Before I could blink, Blake slammed me against the wall, pinning me by my throat. My feet no longer touched the ground.

My stunned mind couldn't comprehend what just happened. *No one should be able to move that fast.*

Barely breathing, I panicked, and fought to pry away his hands, forgetting to be meek. He laughed and squeezed a little harder. Behind him, Richard stood, but said nothing.

The calculated look in Blake's eyes reminded me of his expectation. Swearing at his "associate" hadn't been a bright move. Still trying to wheeze in air, I stopped clawing at his hands and instead wrapped my hands around his forearm for support. His hold loosened, and I gasped. The air burned, but I didn't stop pulling it in.

All the men at the dinner table watched us, and the one who had kicked me, smirked.

"The time for niceties is at an end. We've amassed our fortune. It's time for the next step. You will choose one of us and evolve your abilities as you were born to do."

I barely heard his words. His teeth claimed my attention. As he spoke, they grew. Elongating. Already panicked because of the hand at my throat, my racing heart kicked into overdrive at the sight of his canines. His face changed slightly as his jaws expanded to accommodate his teeth.

He can't be human. What is he?

His grip tightened with his next words.

"You will allow each male here, and every male I bring from this night forward, to scent you. If we decide you are his Mate, you *will* bite him and establish your Claim."

His hold loosened. Still gasping for air, I didn't immediately register that my feet again touched the ground. *Bite one of them?* He dropped his hand and moved away from me but his piercing gaze held me in place.

"Frank, since she offended you, you can go first."

Frank quickly leapt over the table, his teeth also abnormally long and pointy. Swaggering toward me, he leaned in close and licked my neck. A shiver of revulsion ran through me.

"You're mine," he whispered before he moved to allow the next man close to me.

I turned my face from them and pressed myself against the wall. Despairing, I closed my eyes. Tears fell from the scrunched corners. I couldn't escape.

After the last man leaned in close to my neck and inhaled

deeply, Blake commanded me to leave. I fled to my room and locked the door behind me.

When I woke, I found a manila envelope shoved under my bedroom door. A Post-it decorated the front of it. I easily read Richard's scrawl.

Run as fast as you can. Everything is in your name.

I gazed at those words with a sinking feeling of dread. Somewhere in the house, a phone rang. Without looking at the contents, I quickly stashed the envelope in my pillowcase and made my bed. Before I finished, a key rattled outside my room and the door swung open. David eyed me as I stood next to the bed, tugging the quilt into place. I still wore my pajamas.

Since Blake needed Richard in the office and didn't trust me home alone, he'd brought in David as my keeper. Well paid, David did as Blake said. I wondered if David knew about Blake's teeth.

"You're not supposed to be in here until I knock," I said, repeating Blake's rule.

"Today is an exception. Blake's on the phone." David held out a cell phone.

I stared at him a moment before I approached him to take it. What game did they play now?

"Yes?" I said, putting the phone up to my ear.

"Richard's dead. This changes nothing. We'll be back tonight." The line went dead. Richard's scrawled message ran through my head.

David walked further into my room, a suspicious look on his face. He moved past me and pulled back the quilt. I looked at my shelf where my softball participation trophy from middle school sat. When he lifted my pillow, I quietly lifted the trophy. I could hear my brothers' muffled voices on the other side of the wall, still locked in their own room.

David never heard the envelope crinkle.

Other Titles

Touch

Moved

Warwolf

Nephilim